STRIKE OF THE
MOUNTAIN MAN

STRIKE OF THE MOUNTAIN MAN

WILLIAM W. JOHNSTONE
with J. A. Johnstone

PINNACLE BOOKS
Kensington Publishing Corp.
www.kensingtonbooks.com

PINNACLE BOOKS are published by

Kensington Publishing Corp.
119 West 40th Street
New York, NY 10018

PUBLISHER'S NOTE
Following the death of William W. Johnstone, the Johnstone family is working with a carefully selected writer to organize and complete Mr. Johnstone's outlines and many unfinished manuscripts to create additional novels in all of his series like The Last Gunfighter, Mountain Man, and Eagles, among others. This novel was inspired by Mr. Johnstone's superb storytelling.

All Kensington titles, imprints, and distributed lines are available at special quantity discounts for bulk purchases for sales promotions, premiums, fund-raising, educational, or institutional use. Special book excerpts or customized printings can also be created to fit specific needs. For details, write or phone the office of the Kensington special sales manager: Kensington Publishing Corp., 119 West 40th Street, New York, NY 10018, attn: Special Sales Department; phone 1-800-221-2647.

ISBN-13: 978-0-7860-2812-2
ISBN-10: 0-7860-2812-2

First printing: December 2012

10 9 8 7 6 5 4 3 2 1

Printed in the United States of America

CHAPTER ONE

Deekus Templeton had once ridden with Frank and Jesse James. It wasn't particularly a matter of pride for him, especially since the James brothers were well known figures . . . even idolized in some places, while few had ever heard of Deekus Templeton.

What bothered Templeton the most was that he was the one who had planned the train robbery in Muncie, Kansas, where they got $30,000. That was the biggest haul from any train robbery the James gang made, and it was Frank and Jesse who were celebrated, not the one who planned it. Shortly after that, Templeton decided to go into business for himself.

He had learned that the Red Cliff Special would be carrying a money transfer of $50,000 from a bank in Pueblo, Colorado to the bank in Big Rock, Colorado, which was more than any job the James brothers had ever pulled. To stop the train, he had piled wood and brush onto the track.

"The train's acomin', Deekus!" one of his men shouted.

"Torch the pile," Templeton called, and a moment later a rather substantial fire flamed up from the pile of brushwood.

Smoke Jensen had gone to Denver with Pearlie and Cal to set up a plant that would ship beef, already butchered and processed, in refrigerated cars to markets in the East. Handling already processed meat was much cheaper than shipping live cattle, and the result was a greater profit to the rancher.

Smoke built the plant, not only for himself, but also for other cattlemen in Colorado as well as in Wyoming. He had left Pearlie and Cal in Denver to see to the final details, and was on the way back home, changing trains in Pueblo so he could take the Red Cliff Special on its overnight run. He would be arriving in Big Rock at six o'clock in the morning.

There were no sleeper cars on the train so Smoke was napping as best he could in the seat. The train had been under way for five hours when it came to a sudden, shuddering, screeching, and banging halt, stopping so abruptly it awakened Smoke with a start. He didn't know what was going on, but he knew it certainly wasn't a normal stop. He looked through the window to see where they were, but the lanterns that lit the inside of the car cast reflections on the windows, making it difficult to see through them, and into the dark outside.

"Why did we stop?" someone asked.

"Did we hit something? I was thrown so, that I nearly broke my neck," a man complained.

Though he couldn't see anything through the windows, Smoke could hear voices outside, rough and guttural, and he had a feeling the train was being robbed. He pulled his pistol and held it down in his lap.

"Everyone stay in their seats!" a man shouted, bursting into the car from the front. He was wearing a hood over his face, and he held a pistol pointed toward the passengers in the car.

"What is the meaning of this?" a man shouted indignantly. He started to get up, but the gunman moved quickly toward him and brought his pistol down sharply over the man's head. The passenger groaned and fell back. A woman who had been sitting with him cried out in alarm.

"Anybody else?" the gunman challenged. "Maybe you folks didn't hear me when I said everyone stay in their seats."

Another gunman came in to join the first. "What happened?"

"Nothing I can't handle. Is everything under control out there?"

"Yeah, ever'thing is fine. Just keep ever'one in here covered." The second gunman left the car.

The remaining train robber took off his hat. "Now folks, this is what I'm goin' to do. I'm goin' to walk down this aisle and hold my hat out." He chuckled. "You know, sort of like what they do in church. But I don't just want a coin or two like you do when you're in church. I want ever'thing you have. And if I see any of you holdin' out on me, why, I'll have to shoot you."

The gunman started down the aisle making his collection, and though the first few people cooperated, when he got to a young woman holding a baby, she protested.

"Please, this is all the money I have. I'm taking it to my husband so we can buy a house."

"I said, don't nobody hold back," the gunman said menacingly. "Now you just empty that bag of your'n into my hat."

"Leave the lady alone," Smoke said.

The train robber looked over at Smoke. "Mister, this here is a train robbery. Maybe you don't understand how train robberies work. You see, I take the money, and people like you give the money. So you might as well get your money out, 'cause soon as I get the money from the little mama here, why I'll be takin' yours."

"If you want to live, put the hat down now so the people can get their money back, and leave this car," Smoke said.

"If I want to live?" The gunman's laugh was a high-pitched cackle. "Mister, I'm the one holdin' the gun here. Or ain't you noticed?"

"Leave this car now, or die," Smoke said calmly.

"I've had about enough of you, mister." Pointing his pistol at Smoke, the train robber pulled the hammer back. That was as far he got before, in a lightning move, Smoke brought his own pistol up from his lap and pulled the trigger. Dropping his gun, the robber clutched his chest, and staggered back a few steps. "What the hell?" he asked in a pained voice.

One of the other train robbers jumped onto the train. Seeing his partner down, and an armed man standing, he fired at Smoke. His shot went wide and the bullet smashed through the window beside Smoke's seat, sending out a stinging spray of glass but doing no other damage. Smoke brought his own pistol around and squeezed off a second shot. The robber staggered back, hit the front wall of the car, then slid down to the floor in a seated position, already dead.

"What's going on in there?" Deekus Templeton shouted from outside the train.

One of the other men looked into the car, then jerked his head back. "Clay and Dooley are both shot dead!" he called. "I'm gettin' out of here!"

"You can't leave, McClain! We ain't got the money yet!" Templeton shouted.

"Get it yourself! There's only the two of us left!"

McClain started to ride away but Templeton raised his pistol and shot him off the horse.

"Now there's only one of us," he said as he rode hard to get away.

When the train reached Big Rock the next morning the bodies of the three would-be train robbers were laid out on the depot platform. Each one had his arms folded across his chest. The hoods had been removed, and all three had their eyes open. A dozen or more citizens of the town were standing there looking down at the bodies.

Sheriff Carson was there as well, and he was talking to Smoke. "You say you only got two of them?"

"Yes, these two," Smoke said, pointing to the two men he shot.

"Yeah, that's Clay Brandon and Dooley Waters," Sheriff Carson said, pointing to the two men Smoke had shot. "The other one is Len McClain. If you didn't shoot him, who did?"

"There were four of them. It was the fourth one who shot this man."

"I don't suppose you heard his name called out," Sheriff Carson said. It was more of a wishful declaration than a question.

"No, I didn't."

"Well, the bank will certainly be thanking you. There was a fifty thousand dollar shipment on that train."

"That's funny," Smoke said. "If there was that much money in the shipment, why were they bothering with trying to steal the few dollars they could get from the passengers?"

One of the men in the crowd of onlookers was Deekus Templeton. He had already learned that Smoke Jensen was the man who had foiled his robbery attempt and stood behind the others, watching Jensen and the sheriff as they were engaged in conversation. He had heard of Smoke Jensen. Who in that part of the country had not heard of him? But it was the first time he had ever seen him, and he wanted to get a good look at the man. He didn't want to ever blunder into some foolish mistake as had Clay and Dooley.

Templeton smiled as he realized he had an advantage. He knew what Smoke Jensen looked like, but Jensen didn't know what he looked like.

Then he heard Jensen ask the same question that had been puzzling him. *Why were they bothering with trying to steal the few dollars they could get from the passengers?*

Phil Clinton, the publisher and editor of the *Big Rock Journal* had heard about the attempted train robbery and came down to the depot with paper and pen to interview the passengers. He also brought a camera with him, set up a tripod, then took a photograph of the three dead men. A good newspaperman, Clinton knew a picture would supplement the story, and he employed a very good woodcut artist who could make that happen.

His article appeared in *the Big Rock Journal.*

Attempted Train Robbery Foiled

THREE OUTLAWS MEET THEIR FATE

The residents of Big Rock, and indeed of Colorado and other Western states and territories, are well acquainted with the many attributes, skills, and talents of Smoke Jensen. To his long list of accomplishments may be added preventing a robbery of the Red Cliff Special on Friday last.

It is to the fatal detriment of Clay Brandon, Dooley Waters, and Len McClain that they were unaware they were about to encounter Mr. Jensen and, as their final lesson in life, learn of his artistry with a pistol. Mr. Jensen, who owns Sugarloaf Ranch, located some seven miles west of Big Rock, was a passenger on the Red Cliff Special last Friday night, when the ill-fated robbery attempt was made. It was Mr. Jensen's presence, and especially his quick response, that saved the passengers' money, and perhaps even their lives.

That an attempt was made to rob the train is not surprising when one considers that locked in the safe of the express car, and being watched over by a bonded special agent, were fifty thousand dollars in negotiable United States currency. What is surprising is that, despite the large prize available to them, the robbers chose to augment that bounty with the meager collection of money they could glean from the passengers.

It was that particular ill-advised venture that caused two of the robbers to step onto the cars and there encounter Smoke Jensen. The result of that encounter was that Mr. Jensen has added further luster to his already illustrious carrier. It is said that the fourth would-be robber left the scene empty-handed. The identity of the fourth robber is not known.

CHAPTER TWO

Dijon, France

Pierre Mouchette was a French Army Officer and an 1869 graduate from St. Cyr, the leading military academy of France. After St. Cyr, he'd entered Saumur, France's premier cavalry school, and after leaving Saumur, he'd taken part in the Franco-Prussian War. It was there that he encountered the American general Phil Sheridan who was in France to observe the war. Sheridan had told him of the American West, and though it had no immediate bearing on Mouchette's military career, he remembered it later when, after his third duel, he was told he had gone as high as he was going to go in the French military.

In January of 1879, orders were cut appointing Capitaine Pierre Mouchette as disbursement officer. These orders called for him to transfer two and one half million francs from Paris to the army finance office in Dijon. Mouchette made very careful plans, selecting as his assistant a sergeant who was approximately his same build. They picked up the money in Paris, then went by train to Dijon.

In Dijon, they mounted horses and started toward the division headquarters. When they were but a mile out of town, Mouchette turned off the road.

"Capitaine Mouchette, where are you going?" Sergeant Dubois asked. "The headquarters is this way." He pointed down the road.

"This is a shorter way," Mouchette said.

"Shorter? How can it be shorter? This road goes straight to the headquarters."

"Would you argue with an officer, Sergeant?" Mouchette scolded.

"*Non, mon capitaine.*"

"Then this is the direction we will go."

"*Oui, mon capitaine.*"

The sergeant followed Mouchette dutifully until they were deep into a wooded area. "Capitaine Mouchette, forgive me, but we are now some distance from headquarters. I think we should turn back."

Mouchette turned toward the sergeant. "Do you?" he asked with a humorless smile on his face.

It was then Sergeant Dubois saw Mouchette holding a pistol leveled toward him. "Capitaine, what are you doing?" Dubois shouted in fear.

Mouchette pulled the trigger, and the bullet struck Dubois between the eyes.

Working quickly, Mouchette removed his uniform and put on the civilian clothes he had previously packed in his saddlebags. Then, stripping Dubois of his uniform, he replaced it with his own. "There now, Sergeant, you have just been promoted to capitaine. I salute you, Capitaine Mouchette."

It was not by chance Mouchette had chosen that particular spot, for earlier he had hidden a can of kerosene in the bushes. He poured kerosene on Dubois' face and set a match to it, keeping the fire going until all the sergeant's features were burned away and only a blackened skull remained. After that, he put his billfold in the pocket of the uniform Sergeant Dubois was now wearing. In it, were Mouchette's identity papers, the orders appointing him as disbursement officer, his membership card to the officers' mess, and a letter he had recently received from a military clothier in Paris, quoting the price of a new dress uniform.

With his deception completed, Mouchette crossed the border into Switzerland and journeyed to Geneva. There, he presented himself to the bank as a French businessman. "I shall be going to North America shortly to invest in a business opportunity in New York and I should like to change some French currency into American dollars. What is the current exchange rate?"

"It is five francs for one dollar," the teller said. "How much do you wish to exchange?"

"Two and one half million francs."

The teller made no reaction to the large sum. He picked up a pencil and began figuring the amount.

"Your amount comes to four hundred eighty-seven

thousand dollars. That sum is, of course, less the twelve thousand five hundred dollar conversion fee."

"Very good."

The teller counted out the American dollars. "Do you care to recount it, Monsieur?"

"No, I'm sure it is all there."

"Then if you would sign this certificate, please?"

Mouchette signed it as Antoine Dubois.

It was as Pierre Mouchette that he devised the plan to steal the payroll. It was as Antoine Dubois that he exchanged the francs for U.S. dollars. And it was as Colonel the Marquis Lucien Garneau that he boarded a ship in Hamburg, Germany, bound for New York. Lucien Garneau was how he would be known.

New York, New York

Garneau got off the ship in New York and immediately bought a local newspaper. He saw an article that caught his interest.

Intelligence From Overseas

KILLER OF CAPTAIN MOUCHETTE STILL AT LARGE
SERGEANT DUBOIS SUSPECTED OF HEINOUS CRIME

Captain Pierre Mouchette was appointed military finance officer with the responsibility of transporting a large sum of money from Paris to Dijon, but was foully murdered by one he trusted most. When Captain Mouchette did not show up at the appointed time, a search was launched, resulting in the gruesome discovery of the

charred remains of the gallant captain and the
discovery that both the money and the
sergeant were missing.

It is believed that the cowardly Sergeant
Dubois, animated by greed and a lack of
personal morals, betrayed the trust so
necessary in the military between the officers
and the ranks, and when least expected,
killed Captain Mouchette. The foul deed
done, the disgraceful sergeant tried to cover
his action by burning the captain's body. The
attempt was unsuccessful as he was
identified by his uniform and personal
papers. The despicable Sergeant Dubois
remains missing.

Garneau smiled as he realized everything had
worked out exactly as he had intended. He went directly from Castle Garden, his point of entry, to
Grand Central depot to continue his plan, recalling
a conversation he'd had with General Sheridan,
when the American general had talked about Colorado. He'd told how beautiful the mountains were,
but what had most interested Garneau about Colorado was Sheridan's off-hand comment. "A person
could go into the Rocky Mountains of Colorado and,
if he wanted to, just drop off the face of the earth."

Finding a map of Colorado, Lucien Garneau put
his finger on the chart with no particular destination
in mind. The closest town to the tip of his finger was
Big Rock, in Eagle County, so he bought a ticket for
that destination and boarded the train.

Dijon, France

Inspector Andre Laurent of the French Military Police was shown into General Moreau's office.

"Colonel Durand said you had information for me," General Moreau said.

"I do, my General," Laurent said. "The body we found was not that of Capitaine Mouchette."

"What? But the body was wearing Mouchette's uniform. His billfold was found with the body."

"Those were plants, to make us believe it was Mouchette's body."

"Who would do that?"

"I believe Mouchette himself did it," Laurent said. "The body was that of Sergeant Antoine Dubois."

"Dubois?"

"I believe Mouchette murdered Dubois, stole the money, then made it appear as if Dubois was the guilty party. He burned Dubois' face so he could not be identified."

"Then how was he identified?"

"The body was missing two toes on its left foot. It is well known by Sergeant Dubois's friends that he lost two toes in the war. Mouchette had no such wound."

"Then Mouchette is guilty of murder and theft of the money."

"Yes, my General."

General Moreau drummed his fingers on his desk. "Inspector Laurent, you have full authorization to go after Mouchette. Find him, wherever he is, and bring him to justice for France."

Inspector Laurent saluted General Moreau. "That will be my pleasure, General."

Big Rock, Colorado

On August first, the day that three years earlier, Colorado had become a state, the entire town of Big Rock was turned out to celebrate Statehood Day. There were food booths, horse and foot races, horseshoe throwing competitions, shooting matches, and of course, music and dancing.

Smoke hadn't entered any of the shooting contests because he had been asked to judge. In the match for rifle marksmanship, Humboldt Puddle and Dwayne Booker had survived all the others and were the last two shooters remaining. Each had just put three shots into the bull's eye, after having moved the targets to the far end of the street.

"What are we going to do now, Smoke?" Sheriff Carson asked. "If we move the targets any farther, they are going to be in another county."

Those close enough to hear the sheriff laughed.

Smoke took out a silver dollar, then set it up on top of the bale of hay being used as a backstop for the target. Standing it on its edge, he pushed enough of the coin into the hay to keep it erect. The result was that just over half the coin was showing. "Let them shoot at this."

Despite the fact that many other things were going on to attract the people of the town and county, word of the intense shooting competition had spread, and hundreds were drawn up to watch the final two shooters. They flipped a coin to see who would shoot first, and Dwayne Booker was selected.

The crowd grew very quiet as Booker raised the Winchester .44-40 to his shoulder, sighted down the barrel, then pulled the trigger. A few stems of hay fluttered up right beside the coin, but the coin wasn't hit.

"It's a miss," Smoke said, looking through a pair of binoculars.

It was Humboldt's turn. He looked down range at the target, which was at least one hundred yards away. After staring at it for a long moment, he raised the rifle and fired, almost in the same fluid motion.

Smoke didn't have to look through the binoculars, nor did he have to make the announcement. The cheers of at least four hundred people made the announcement for him. The coin flew away from the top of the hay bale, the result of a direct hit.

Humboldt's feat of marksmanship was still the talk of the town as everyone gathered for the dance held in the commodious dining room of the Dunn Hotel. Sally dragged Smoke out on the floor to form the first square. Sheriff Carson stood in front of the band, calling the steps through a megaphone he held to his mouth.

> *Chew your tobacco and rub your snuff,*
> *Meet your honey and strut your stuff.*
> *Right foot up and a left foot down,*
> *Make that big foot jar the ground,*
> *Promenade your partner around.*

"It's too bad Pearlie and Cal aren't here," Sally said. "They so enjoy these things."

"No doubt Denver is also celebrating Statehood Day," Smoke said. "And I expect they are doing just fine."

CHAPTER THREE

Denver

Cal had entered a pie-eating contest and it was down to three contestants. The other two contestants had a combined weight of nearly six hundred pounds, compared to Cal's weight of one hundred seventy-five pounds.

The three remaining contestants had been given a five-minute break before the contest was to resume, and Cal and Pearlie were back in one corner of the room, talking quietly.

"I don't know if I can do it," Cal said. "I'm stuffed."

"You're stuffed?" Pearlie said. "This is pie we're talkin' about, Cal. In all the time I've known you, I've never known you to pass up a piece of pie."

"This isn't a piece of pie, Pearlie, it's a whole pie. And I've already eaten three."

"Then what's one more? Here, let me rub your

stomach, that'll move some of what you've already eaten aside and give you a little more room."

"All right, gentlemen, the time is up," the judge called. "Please return to the table."

Initially, there had been several tables, but the final three contestants were moved to one round table and seated across from each other. A pie was put in front of each of them.

"All right, gentlemen, you may commence," the judge said.

One of the heavy contestants stared at the pie for just a moment, then without so much as touching it, he stood up and walked away. That left only two people.

The two began eating their pie. Cal called out to the judge and pointed to the pie the big man had left behind on the table. "Hey judge, since he's not going to eat that pie, can I have it when I finish this one?"

The spectators who were gathered around the table laughed and exclaimed in amazement. "There's no bottom in that man's stomach!"

When Cal asked for the abandoned pie, the the other contestant got a very sick look on his face, then pushed away from the table. "I quit," he said.

Everyone cheered, but the judge held up his hands to call for quiet. "You must take at least one more bite to be declared the winner," he said to Cal.

Smiling, Cal not only took another bite, he consumed half the pie, then held his hands up over his head in triumph.

The crowd cheered and offered their congratulations as Cal was crowned the "pie-eating champion of Colorado."

After what seemed an interminable length of travel—he'd had no idea America was so large—Garneau reached Denver. From there, he took a train to Pueblo, and from Pueblo he began the final leg of a journey that had started in Dijon almost a month earlier.

Six and one half days after he left New York, Garneau arrived in Big Rock at six o'clock in the morning. He was tired from the overnight trip, for there had been no sleeping arrangements on the train. He inquired of the station agent where he might find a hotel.

"Well sir, we've got two of 'em," Phil Wilson replied. "We've got the Big Rock and the Dunn. One's just about as nice as the other, so I wouldn't know which one to recommend."

"Which is the closest?"

"That would be the Big Rock. You just go down Tanner Street for one block, and it's on the corner of Tanner and Center Street."

"*Merci.*"

Although the Big Rock Hotel was but one block away, Garneau arranged for him and his luggage to be transported there. He was very tired, and wanted nothing more than to go to bed, but he knew there was something he had to do first. Before he could rest, he had to go to the bank.

He looked at his two cases on the floor of his room. One contained clothes, and a casual look into the other would suggest it also contained nothing but clothes. However, under the first layer of clothes, were forty-seven bound packets of hundred dollar bills, one hundred bills in each packet.

Garneau had been very nervous with the money in his possession for the last month.

Finally, when he was certain the bank was open, he took the suitcase containing the money and walked downstairs. As he started across the lobby, the desk clerk called out to him.

"Sir? Is something wrong with your room or our service? Are you leaving?"

"I'm not leaving," Garneau said. "Monsieur, could you direct me to the bank, *s'il vous plaît?*"

"Certainly." The desk clerk pointed. "Just go this way one block to Ranney Street, turn left one block to Front Street. You can't miss it. It's the third building on the right, next to the Dunn Hotel."

"*Merci,*" Garneau replied.

Although it was the middle of the day, and he was in the middle of town, Garneau was nervous as he carried the suitcase to the bank. He felt a sense of relief when he reached the bank a moment later. When he stepped inside, he stood for just a moment as he had a long look around.

"Yes, sir, may I help you?" a man sitting at a desk just inside the door asked.

"*Oui.* I am just moving here and would like to open an account, *s'il vous plaît.*"

"I can do that for you, sir," the man said, picking

up a printed form and a pen. "How much would you like to deposit in the account?"

"Four hundred and seventy-five thousand dollars," Garneau said.

"What?" the bank clerk gasped. "How much did you say?"

"Four hundred and seventy-five thousand dollars," Garneau repeated. He sat the suitcase on the desk and opened it, then began removing the packets of money."

"No, sir, not here," the bank clerk said. "Come into the back with me to speak with the president of the bank. I don't think it is good to show so much money in public."

Joel Montgomery looked at the money that was piled up on his desk.

"We can handle your deposit, Mr. Garneau—"

"Colonel Garneau," Garneau insisted.

"Yes, sir. Well, here is the thing, Colonel Garneau. We can handle your deposit, but there is no way we are going to keep all that money here. We are going to have to lay off ninety percent of it to other banks."

"Why?"

"The risks. We are capitalized at fifty thousand dollars, and it would be much too risky to keep this much money in one bank, so over the next few days we will be making deposits in other banks. That it won't all be kept in this bank will not affect you. You will still have a demand account, and can draw against it at any time."

"*Merci,*" Garneau said.

Half an hour later, he left the bank with one hundred dollars in small denominations in his pocket, along with a deposit slip for the four hundred seventy-five thousand dollars he had left at the bank. He returned to his room at the hotel and slept through the rest of the day.

Waking up that evening, Garneau decided to walk through the town to get a look at the rather quaint place that was to be his new home. He took his dinner at Delmonico's, then went next door to Longmont's, which he perceived to be a drinking establishment.

"What will you have, sir?" the bartender asked.

"I don't suppose you would have any cognac, would you?"

The man standing at the far end of the bar overheard Garneau's accent and his order. He smiled and came toward him. "*Bonsoir, monsieur. Par votre accent, je suppose que vous êtes un homme de bonne taste. Vous demandez pour le cognac, j'ai J.V.C. Aumasson.*"

"How delightful," Garneau said. "You speak French, though with an accent I can't place. As I am in America now, I wish only to speak English. And J.V.C. Aumasson is a most delightful cognac."

"Very well. We will speak English. My name is Louis Longmont, and I own this establishment. The first cognac is on the house."

"*Merci,* Monsieur Longmont. And my name, sir, is Colonel the Marquis Lucien Garneau."

"What brings you to Colorado, Colonel Garneau?"

The bartender served the cognac, and Garneau

swirled it about, used his hand to waft the fragrance into his face, smiled, and took a sip. "Marvelous. I have come to this place to buy land and raise cattle."

"Well, there is land for sale. And this is good cattle country. In fact, we have one of the largest and most successful ranches in the nation right here. It is called Sugarloaf, and is owned by Smoke Jensen. I'm sure you have heard of him."

"Smoke? *Fumer?*"

Louis nodded. "'*Fumer,*' yes. 'Smoke' is not his real name. His real name is Kirby, but everyone calls him Smoke."

Garneau shook his head. "What an odd name."

"How long have you been in America?"

"I have been in this country for a fortnight only."

"Well, that explains it. Anyone who has been here for six months or longer has heard of Smoke Jensen. We don't have marquis and lords and such, but if we did, Smoke Jensen would have a title for sure."

"He sounds quite successful. I should like to meet him."

Louis looked toward the door and smiled. "Well, speak of the devil. Smoke just came in."

"Smoke!" someone called, and he was greeted by at least half a dozen others.

"Smoke, over here," Louis called.

Acknowledging the greetings, Smoke shook hands with a couple and waved at the others. Then, with a broad smile he went over to Louis. "It looks like business is good tonight."

"Business is good every night, as you would know

if Sally didn't keep you on such a tight leash," Louis teased. "How is it she let you come to town tonight?"

"She is on the school board, remember? There's a meeting down at the school tonight."

"I thought it must be something like that. Smoke, this is Colonel the Marquis Lucien Garneau. Colonel Garneau, this is the man I was telling you about. Smoke Jensen."

"It's a pleasure to meet you, Mr. Garneau."

"That would be Colonel Garneau," Garneau said.

"I beg your pardon, Colonel."

"I understand you are the largest and most successful rancher in the county," Garneau said.

"I've been fortunate," Smoke said.

"Well, Monsieur Jensen, I give you fair warning. My personal motto is *secundus nulli*. That is Latin for—"

"Second to none," Louis said.

Garneau glared at Louis, showing displeasure over being one-upped. But he regained his composure quickly. "Yes. And I am not used to being second to anyone. I will soon have a ranch that is larger."

Louis laughed.

"You find that humorous, *Monsieur*?" Garneau asked rather sharply.

"Not humorous, so much, as impossible," Louis said.

"Why is it impossible?"

"Because there isn't enough available land left in Eagle and Pitkin counties combined, to build a ranch larger than Sugarloaf."

"I will find the land. Thank you for the cognac." Garneau took a coin from his pocket and slapped it onto the bar. Then, turning, he walked away and left the saloon.

"Now that is one odd duck," Smoke said.

"He is a marquis," Louis replied. "I think that to be a marquis, one must first be an odd duck."

Smoke laughed.

When Garneau awakened the next morning, he donned the uniform of a colonel in the French Cavalry. Although he never advanced above the rank of captain, he felt that passing himself off as a colonel would be more impressive. Inquiring at the hotel desk, he was directed to the land office, which was just around the corner from the hotel on Ranney Street.

When Garneau stepped into the building the clerk looked up, then registered surprise at seeing Garneau in uniform. "May I help you?"

"I am Colonel the Marquis Lucien Garneau, and I have come to buy land," Garneau said.

"Yes, sir, if you'll wait here for just a moment." The clerk stepped into another room, then a moment later reappeared. "Mr. Perkins will see you, sir."

Pete Perkins was a small man with a red face and an oversized nose. He invited Garneau to have a seat. "I understand that you want to buy land."

"*Oui.*"

"How much land are you interested in buying?"

"How much does the land cost?"

"It is about five dollars per acre."

"How much land does Monsieur Jensen have?"

"Oh, heavens, I don't know. I would guess he has around thirty thousand acres or so."

"Then I shall want thirty thousand acres as well."

Perkins chuckled and shook his head. "There aren't that many acres of unowned land available in the whole valley."

"How large is Eagle County?"

"Just over one million acres."

"You say that there are one million acres in the county, but I can't buy thirty thousand acres?"

"Oh, there might be that many acres, perhaps even more, but it wouldn't be contiguous. There are too many ranches and farms of one to three sections of land."

"Suppose enough farmers and ranchers contiguous to land that I buy could be persuaded to sell their land. Would it be possible to put together a ranch of the size I am seeking?"

"Well, yes, if you could convince enough of the smaller owners to sell. But I'm not sure you can do that. The small ranchers and farmers are doing remarkably well. I don't see any of them selling out, let alone enough for you to do what you want."

"Please buy as much land for me as you can, and let me worry about the adjacent land owners."

Perkins did some math on a sheet of paper, then whistled. "Colonel Garneau, this is going to require quite a sizeable outlay. With just the land I know is available, we are talking about at least eighty-seven thousand dollars."

"If you wish, you may go with me to the bank and inquire as to available funds," Garneau said.

Perkins stood, then retrieved his hat from the hat rack. "The bank is just around the corner." He exited the bank and Garneau followed.

"Colonel Garneau!" the bank president said when Garneau and Perkins stepped into the bank a few moments later. "What can I do for you?"

"You can inform Monsieur Perkins that I have sufficient funds to buy land," Garneau said.

"Mr. Perkins," the bank president said, "it would not be ethical for me to disclose just how much money Colonel Garneau has on deposit with us. Suffice it to say that he is good for any amount of land you can find for him to purchase."

Perkins smiled at the Frenchman. "Colonel Garneau, I can see that you and I are going to have quite a profitable relationship."

CHAPTER FOUR

DIED

Early on the morning of August 25th,
GEORGE MUNGER, *owner*
of the successful ranch, Long Trek.

Death is a solemn event, but one which all must meet sooner or later. Sometimes the pain and sadness occasioned by its touching the hearts of the bereaved is of more than an ordinary character. It is so in this case. George Munger's six thousand acre ranch, Long Trek, is the envy of all in Eagle County who have taken up that profession.

Munger arrived in Colorado nine years previous, and in that time not only began a successful ranch, but fathered two children, a boy, Seth, and a daughter, Meg. His widow, Ann, was the apple of his eye. He had spoken to others of his hope to raise Seth to be of great help on the ranch and to prepare him for eventual ownership, but that is not to be.

Barely two weeks have gone by since George Munger took ill, and though he initially passed it off as something of no consequence, the illness quickly took control, and he died. His last wish was that his widow sell the ranch and move back to Ohio where she has family, believing that a woman alone and raising two children would have a better life there than she would find here.

Mrs. Munger acquiesced to her husband's last wishes by placing the ranch on the market. As it was adjacent to land recently bought by Colonel the Marquis Lucien Garneau, the Frenchman made her a generous offer and she accepted. Out of respect for its previous owner, Colonel Garneau will keep the name Long Trek, and states that whatever property he may henceforth acquire will be assimilated into and retain the name Long Trek.

Mrs. Munger can take comfort in the knowledge that while the body may be committed to the tomb, there is a bond that reaches beyond the grave and it will ever hold her in affectionate embrace.

Lucien Garneau bought Long Trek, complete with house and outbuildings. Over the ensuing four months, he bought several more acres contiguous to Long Trek, so by spring he had 15,000 acres, making Long Trek the second largest ranch in the valley. Every ranch he had bought had been one the owners were willing to sell. But his 15,000 acres were locked in by at least eight other ranchers, all who had property that abutted his, none who wanted to sell.

"I don't believe you're goin' to get anyone else to sell out to you, Colonel." Otis Nance had been foreman of Long Trek when it was owned by Munger, and he had stayed with the ranch when Garneau bought it.

"They will sell," Garneau said. "I will have the biggest and the best ranch in the entire valley."

"Well, I tell you, Colonel, you might talk enough of 'em into sellin' out to you to wind up bein' the biggest ranch in the area, though that ain't likely. And it's even less likely that you'll be the best."

"And why not, if I may ask?" Garneau replied, obviously miffed by the comment.

"First of all, 'cause you cain't grow no more 'lessen you can get some of the folks around you to sell their land to you, which I can tell you right now, there ain't no more of 'em goin' to do it. And then even if you can wind up with more land, well, sir, I've worked some over at Sugarloaf and it's about the best run place I've ever seen. And it ain't just Smoke Jensen, it's his wife, 'n the men that work there. Jensen, he don't let all his people go in the wintertime like most of the other ranchers, and so the ones that's workin' there, stays just real loyal to him."

"Then perhaps you should go back to work for him," Garneau said angrily.

"There ain't no need for you to go gettin' all riled

up now. I was just tellin' you the truth 'cause I thought you might want to know," Nance said.

"Leave my ranch, now, Monsieur Nance," Garneau ordered.

"Wait a minute. Are you firin' me?"

"I am."

"Then in that case, you owe me half a month's wages," Nance said, realizing that he wasn't going to be able to talk Garneau into keeping him on.

Two days later, Nance was in the Four Flusher Saloon in Wheeler, Colorado, drinking beer and still complaining about being fired. "I got fired for tellin' the truth. A fella ought not to ever get fired for doin' nothin' more than tellin' the truth. The problem is the colonel has more money than he's got sense. He's tryin' to buy up the whole county, only there ain't no more people goin' to sell to him."

The bar girl Nance was talking to was paying attention to him only as long as she could entice him into buying more drinks. But a solitary drinker at the next table over was listening, and he turned to Nance. "Who is this man you are talking about?"

"He's a Frenchman, by the name of Garneau. Lucien Garneau. Calls himself a marquis, and he likes for folks to call him Colonel. I think a marquis is supposed to be like a lord or something."

"And he's a rich man? This Garneau?"

"Oh yeah, he's rich all right."

Deekus Templeton smiled. It was good information to know.

"The thing is, he's wantin' to make his ranch the biggest and the best in the valley, but I told him, he ain't never goin' to get the better of Smoke Jensen."

"Who?"

"Smoke Jensen. You've heard of him, ain't you? Hell, I thought ever'one had heard of Smoke Jensen."

"Yes, I've heard of him."

Smoke, Templeton knew, was the one who had prevented his train robbery, but he thought it best to suggest that he had only marginally heard of him.

"Well, Smoke Jensen is the one who owns Sugarloaf. I told Garneau that there weren't no way he would ever make his ranch bigger. Hell, he can't, 'cause he can't grow no more. Puddle and all them other little farmers and ranchers has got their land right up next to his, and if they don't sell to him, then there ain't nowhere else he can go."

"Has he tried to buy them out?" Templeton asked.

"Oh, yeah. He's tried a bunch of times. And he got Turner an' Daniels to sell out to him. But there ain't nobody else goin' to sell to him."

"Darlin', do you want to sit here all day and talk to him? Or do you want to buy me another drink and talk to me for a while?" the girl asked.

"Ha! That's an easy question to answer," Nance said. "Get yourself another drink, then come back and sit with me."

Templeton left the saloon then. He had been thinking about how to get even with Smoke Jensen ever since he had interrupted the train robbery. It just might be the way he could do that. Not only would he be able to get even with Jensen, he could make some money as he was doing it. And if this Garneau man was rich, there just might be a way to make a lot of money.

Long Trek Ranch

Templeton passed through the gate that arched over the road leading up to the main house. The name of the ranch, LONG TREK, was burned into the wood, and to either side of the name was a fleur-de-lis, though Templeton had no idea what it was, or what it meant.

As he rode past the bunkhouse he saw three men out front, sitting in chairs that were tipped back against the front wall. None of the three made any effort to greet him. Tying his horse off at the hitching rail in front of the main house, he stepped up onto the porch and knocked on the door. It was opened a moment later by a short, red-faced man wearing a jacket and tie.

"Mr. Garneau?" Templeton asked.

"I am Garrison Reeves, sir. I am Colonel the Marquis Garneau's valet," the man replied in a very English accent.

"His what?" *Valet* was not a word with which Templeton was familiar.

"Do you wish to speak with Colonel Garneau?"

"Yes."

"Your name, sir?"

"Templeton. Deekus Templeton."

"You may wait in the parlor."

Templeton was shown into the parlor and as he

waited, he saw, in a felt-lined case, two pistols, though they were unlike any pistol he was familiar with. He picked one of them up for a closer examination. It didn't have a cylinder, and when he pushed a button on the side, the barrel dropped down. It was a single shot, breech-loading pistol.

"That is a perfectly matched pair of dueling pistols by Gastinne Renette, and they are very valuable."

Turning, Templeton saw a tall, dark-haired man with eyes so light blue they were almost colorless.

"Who would duel with something like this?" Templeton asked. "Hell, the barrel is so long you'd have a hard time gettin' it out of your holster."

"When a gentleman duels, the pistol is already in his hand. There is no need to withdraw it from a holster."

"The hell you say." Templeton shook his head. "I've never heard of a gunfight like that."

"It isn't a gunfight, Monsieur. It is an *affaire d'honneur.* Mr. Reeves told me you wish to speak to me."

"You are Mr. Garneau?"

"I am Colonel Garneau."

"Yes, sir. Well, Colonel, I'd like to come to work for you."

"I have too many employees now. I have no need for more cowboys."

"Yes, well here's the thing, Colonel. I'm not exactly what you would call a cowboy," Templeton said.

"Then if you aren't a cowboy, why do you ask for employment? What are you, a cook?"

Templeton chuckled. "No, I'm not a cook either.

I'm what you might call someone who makes things happen."

"I don't understand. What does that mean . . . you are someone who makes things happen?"

"I've heard you want your ranch to grow larger, but you are blocked in by some small ranchers who won't sell out to you."

"They are cretins," Garneau said.

"Well, Mr. Garneau, I believe I can convince those folks to sell to you. And not only that, I can get 'em to sell to you at a price that's less than what their land is worth."

"That is most interesting," Garneau said, paying a bit more attention to what Templeton had to say. "You can convince all eight to sell?"

"We won't have to convince all eight of 'em. All we have to do is convince two or three to sell, and the others will fall into place. I can do that."

"And how, exactly, are you going to do that?"

"By hunting down cattle thieves," Templeton said.

"I don't understand. How does hunting down cattle thieves have anything to do with my intention to grow my ranch?"

"Well, if cattle are disappearing from your ranch, don't you have a right to go after the people who are stealing them?"

"I suppose so," Garneau replied, still not sure where Templeton was going with this.

"It has been my experience these small ranchers

can only survive by stealing cattle from the larger ranchers."

"And you think the smaller ranchers are stealing cattle from me?"

"We can make sure they are," Templeton replied with a smile.

Garneau nodded. Finally, he understood. "I see. And you can take care of that problem for me?"

"That depends on how particular you are about how I go about it."

"How particular I am? I don't understand, Monsieur Templeton."

"I mean, what if something was to happen to one of the people who have been stealing your cattle. Something bad enough to make him want to sell?"

"Am I to assume you can make that happen?"

"I can and I will, if that's what it takes to get someone to listen to reason," Templeton said.

"I see."

"How would you feel about that, Colonel Garneau?"

"I am more interested in results, Templeton, than I am in how those results are obtained."

Templeton smiled. "Then I am your man."

"What sort of compensation will you require?"

"Ten thousand dollars, plus expenses," Templeton said.

"Ten thousand dollars?" Garneau replied with a gasp. "You think most highly of yourself, Monsieur."

"Plus expenses," Templeton said again.

"And just what would these expenses be?"

"I'd say about two thousand dollars," Templeton said. "I would need that money up front. You don't have to pay the ten thousand dollars until you have acquired all the land you need."

"Very well, Monsieur Templeton. Return tomorrow, and I will have the expense money for you. How soon will you get started on your . . . project?"

"First things first, Colonel. I have to take care of someone who might be a problem."

"Who would that be?"

"Now, Colonel, you really don't want to know that," Templeton said. "The less you know about what I'm doing, the better off you will be. This way, none of it will come back on you."

"Yes," Garneau said with a nod of his head. "Yes, I believe you may be correct."

"I'll be here tomorrow for the expense money."

CHAPTER FIVE

A MEETING
of the
EAGLE COUNTY CATTLEMEN'S ASSOCIATION
~ Monday Next ~
County Courthouse
Red Cliff, Colorado

The signs had been posted in all the towns of Eagle County: Mount Jackson, Dillon, Frisco, Wheeler, Eagle Park, Mitchell Wells, Swan, Preston, and Big Rock, so it was well attended by the larger landholders of the county.

Smoke got a cup of coffee from the table in the back of the room, then took his seat as Wes Gregory, president of the Cattlemen's Association called the meeting to order. "Gentlemen, the purpose of this special-called meeting is twofold. First, it is to introduce you to our newest member, Colonel the Marquis Lucien Garneau. Colonel Garneau, as some of you may know, bought Long Trek from George Munger's widow and has subsequently added to it, so it is accurate to say he is now one of the larger landholders in our county. The second reason I have called this meeting is because Colonel Garneau has encountered a problem all of us have faced from time to time, and if what is happening at Long Trek is any indication, we may all be facing it again, soon."

"What problem would that be, Joel?" Adam Dickerson asked.

"Cattle rustling."

"Cattle rustling? Why, I ain't had no problem with that, other than some transient killing a steer now and then for meat."

"Perhaps I had better let Colonel Garneau talk," Gregory said.

"*Merci*, Monsieur Gregory," Garneau said, then he smiled at the audience. "And I promise you, saying thank you to Mr. Gregory will be the last French I use. I will speak only in English, because I want to make certain everyone understands the severity of the problem.

"I have been here but a short time. I bought the ranch from the widow of George Munger, along with all the livestock. I have added to the size of the original ranch by purchasing property adjacent to the ranch. I can expand no farther, because the holdings of small ranchers and farmers have me blocked.

"That would not be a problem except for this." Garneau held up a finger to emphasize his point. "I am losing cattle at an alarming rate, and I am convinced the culprits are those same small ranchers and farmers who have me locked in."

"Garneau, I think you may be mistaken there," Smoke said. "I know all the ranchers and farmers you are talking about—they have been my neighbors for some time. Speer, Woodward, Turner, Babcock, Logan, Clayton, Daniels, Keefer, Drexler, Butrum, and Puddle. Why, you couldn't ask for a finer neighbor that Humboldt Puddle. Anytime anyone runs into trouble, Mr. Puddle is the first one to offer help."

"Perhaps, Monsieur Jensen, it is because you are a long-time, established resident that they leave you alone. Perhaps it is only because I am new here, and I am a foreigner, that I have been singled out."

"Have you gone to the sheriff about it?" Dickerson asked.

"The sheriff is as Monsieur Jensen, I'm afraid. He thinks his neighbors can do no wrong," Garneau said. "But I don't need the sheriff. I am in the process of putting together my own *régulateurs*."

"Regulators? You mean, vigilantes?" Dickerson asked.

"Yes, to guard my cattle and to stop the thievery."

"Look here, Garneau, are you expecting us to join you in hiring a bunch of vigilantes?"

"No, no, that isn't at all necessary," Garneau said. "I just want to make you aware of the problem . . . and how I plan to solve it."

Big Rock

When Smoke stepped into Longmont's Saloon three days later, he saw Tim Murchison, the owner of the leather goods store, and Dan Norton, the lawyer, sitting at a table with Louis Longmont, and he walked over to join them.

"Hmm," Louis said. "What are you doing here at this hour? Another school board meeting?"

"Do you think the only time I can come in at night is when Sally is at a school board meeting?"

"Yes."

"Well, you're wrong," Smoke said. "I also come in when she's at a garden meeting, like tonight."

The others laughed.

"Smoke Jensen, there's not a gunman in the country that you won't face down, but I think Sally's got your number," Murchison said.

"Listen, have you ever seen Sally with a gun?" Louis asked. "She's as good as anyone I know."

"I believe you there, my friend. I have seen her give shooting exhibitions," Norton said.

"How did the Cattlemen's Association meeting go up in Red Cliff the other day?" Murchison asked.

"It seems our newest rancher is being plagued with cattle rustling," Smoke said.

"Cattle rustling? That's strange. I haven't heard anyone else talking about cattle rustling. Have you had any trouble with it?" Norton asked.

"No, I haven't."

"Hmm." Louis was staring at the entrance. "There are three men I haven't seen before."

Smoke looked toward the front of the saloon as three men entered. "Probably more cowboys coming to work for Garneau. He's bringing them in from everywhere," Norton said.

"Uh-uh. Those men aren't cowboys," Smoke said.

"What do you mean?"

"Look at their hands. Most working cowboys have hands that are callused or crooked fingers from being broken. Those men have smooth hands. They've never done any real work."

"And look how they are wearing their guns," Louis said.

In cut-down holsters, their guns hung rather low from the hip. They carried themselves with the swagger of someone who not only knew how to use a gun, but had used it.

"Barkeep!" one of them called out. "Three beers. And which way to the Long Trek Ranch?"

"I'll be right with you, sir."

"No, by God, you'll be with us now," the man said belligerently.

"Sir, I am with a customer."

"Well, what the hell do you think we are?"

"I'm sorry, sir, please be a little patient. I'll be with you shortly," the barkeep said.

"Is that a new bartender?" Smoke asked.

"Yes," Louis responded, paying close attention to what was going on at the bar.

The man slammed his fist on the bar. "By damn, I said you'll be with us *now!*"

"Monsieur," Louis called over to him.

The belligerent man looked over toward the table where Louis, Smoke, Murchison, and Norton were sitting. "Are you talking to me?"

"I am, sir. The Long Trek is five miles west of town. I suggest you go there now. If you want a drink, you might be happier with the service at the Brown Dirt

Cowboy. That is another saloon one block east of here, on the corner of Front Street and Sikes," Louis suggested.

"Yeah? Why should we go to another saloon, when we are already in a saloon?" He turned back toward the bar. "Barkeep, are you comin' down here, or do I have to do something to get your attention?"

"Perhaps I was too subtle for you," Louis suggested.

"Too . . . what?" the man replied, his face screwing up in confusion over the word *subtle*.

"I will say it in words even someone like you can understand. Get out of my establishment."

"Your establishment? You mean you own this place?"

"I do."

"You ain't all that careful about how you treat your customers, are you?"

"The customers I value, I treat very well. The others, I ask to leave. As I am asking you."

The belligerent one turned toward Louis then, and the two men with him stepped out beside him. All three faced Louis. They were standing, and Louis was sitting, which put him at a significant disadvantage if the situation developed any further.

"Suppose we don't want to leave, what are you going to do about it?"

"I will force you to leave."

The man smiled an evil smile. "Is that so? Now just how are you going to do that? You seem to have gotten yourself into a little pickle, here. I mean, you are sitting down, and we're standing."

"I believe you wanted my attention, sir?" the bartender said at that moment.

"Not now. I may have some business with this man."

The loud sound of two hammers being pulled back was heard, and the belligerent one got a shocked expression on his face, then turned toward the bartender. He was holding a sawed off, double-barreled twelve-gauge shotgun about twelve inches from the belligerent one's head. "And I've got business with you. I believe I could get all three of you with one shot."

"No, wait!" the man shouted, holding his hand out. "Look here, now. There ain't no need in this goin' on any further. It was just a little misunderstandin' is all. If the man don't want our business, we'll take it down to that other saloon he was talkin' about."

"That would be the Brown Dirt," the bartender said. "And as Mr. Longmont explained, it is one block east, then south on Sikes Street. You can't miss it. It's rather loud and unruly, just your kind of place."

"All right, all right. We'll go."

"Thank you," Louis called out to the three men. "I would appreciate that. Oh, and if you three would like to come back in here again sometime . . . and act like gentlemen . . . I would welcome your business."

"We ain't never acomin' back here. Come on, let's go," the man mumbled to the other two, and laughter from the bar patrons chased the three men out.

"If those three men aren't cowboys, why do they want to find the Long Trek?" Norton asked.

"Over the last several days, I've noticed quite a few men like that have gone to work for Garneau," Murchison said.

"What on earth for?" Norton asked.

"Garneau is recruiting a private army to, as he explains it, control the cattle rustling," Smoke said.

"What a dumb thing for him to be doing." Louis looked toward the bar and waved the barkeep over.

"Yes, Mr. Longmont?"

"Mr. McVey, I want to introduce you to some friends of mine," Louis said. "Smoke, Dan, Tim, this is my new bartender, Johnny McVey."

"What happened to Poke?" Norton asked.

"He still works here. He won't come in until eight o'clock tonight," Louis answered. "He and Johnny are splitting the time."

"Well, Mr. McVey, you looked as if you were at home with that scattergun," Smoke said.

"Yes, sir, I've deputied some, and I've been a shotgun guard on a stagecoach," McVey said.

"It certainly came in helpful a few minutes ago," Smoke said.

McVey smiled. "Not really. The three of them standing were no match for the two of you, even if you were sitting down. I don't think they had any idea who they were dealing with. What I got was a cheap moment in the limelight."

"You wouldn't think to look at him that he is a pianist, would you?" Louis asked.

"So, you're a piano player, are you?" Murchison asked.

"No, sir. I'm a pianist," McVey said.

Murchison looked confused. "What's the difference?"

"A piano player plays *Buffalo Gals*. A pianist plays *Tchaikovsky's Piano Concerto Number One*."

"Smoke!" Norton shouted.

The three belligerent men had come back into the saloon, bursting through the batwing doors with their guns in their hands. Dan Norton, Tim Murchison, and Johnny McVey, none of whom were armed, dived for the floor. Smoke and Louis came up from their chairs, bringing their pistols to bear.

The saloon was filled with women's screams, the shouts and curses of men, and the bang of gunfire as all five guns were brought into play.

One of the bullets from the three intruders hit the sleeve garter Louis was wearing, cutting it in two. Because it was elastic, it flew from his arm and hit Norton in the face.

"I'm hit!" Norton yelled.

Another bullet smashed Norton's mug, sending out a spray of beer and tiny shards of glass. The third bullet hit the heating stove, cold for the summer, then went screaming off to bury itself in the wall.

It wasn't hard to track the three bullets fired by Smoke and the two fired by Louis. All three of the intruders went down with fatal wounds.

For a long a moment after the explosive sounds of the gunshots were gone, there was absolute silence in the saloon. Gun smoke curled upward, then formed a cloud that hung just under the ceiling, the acrid smell burning the eyes and noses of the witnesses and participants alike.

Smoke and Louis, with smoking guns still in their hands, approached the three men, all three of whom were now prostrate on the floor. Smoke prodded one of the shooters with the toe of his boot and got no response.

"Whoa, that was something!" one of the bar patrons shouted.

"Are they dead?" another asked.

"I'll say they're dead. They're deader 'n crap. Hell, I can tell that from way over here," another said, and after that, the saloon was alive with excited chatter.

"You don't mind if I look, do you?" Doc Urban asked. He'd been sitting in a card game on the other side of the room and had come over to examine the bodies."

"I'm tellin' you Doc, you don't have to examine 'em. They're deader 'n crap. I can tell that from way over here."

Doctor Urban squatted down beside the three men and felt the carotid arteries of each of them.

"What about it, Doc?" Louis asked.

"In my medical opinion," Doctor Urban said, "these three men are deader than crap."

Nervous laughter broke out in the saloon, and they were still laughing when Sheriff Carson came sprinting into the saloon with his pistol in his hand.

"You're a little late, Sheriff. It's done all been took care of," one of saloon patrons said.

"Are they dead?" Sheriff Carson asked.

"Indeed they are," Doc Urban said. "Oh, Dan, I'm sorry. You said you were hit?"

"Uh, it wasn't anything," Dan said.

"Maybe I should look at it anyway. Sometimes the most minor wounds can be quite troublesome. You may as well get it treated."

"Like I said, it wasn't anything. It was—uh—this." Dan held up the severed sleeve garter. "This hit me in the face."

Those close enough to see, laughed again.

"What happened here?" Sheriff Carson asked, eventually getting the story, though so many were trying to tell it at the same time it took a few minutes before he got the entire story. "Anybody know these men?"

Nobody knew them, so he went through their pockets. In every man's pocket he found the same thing. A recruiting poster.

Men Wanted

To Stem the Rising Tide of Cattle Rustling

Must be Proficient with Firearms

Apply at Long Trek Ranch

Big Rock Colorado

Will Be Well Paid

Cattle rustling?" Sheriff Carson asked. "What cattle rustling would that be?"

CHAPTER SIX

Loy Babcock was having his lunch when there was a loud knock at his door. "I wonder who that could be?" He got up from the table.

"Loy, be careful," Millie said.

"Be careful of what? It's just someone knocking on the door." He opened the door and saw Deekus Templeton standing there. Behind him were four men, all of whom were mounted. With the four mounted men was a steer with a rope around its neck.

"Can I help you?" Babcock asked.

"You mean instead of, can you help yourself?" Templeton asked.

"What do you mean, help myself. I don't know what you are talking about."

"I'm talking about the fifteen head of steers that are mixed in with your cattle. You tried to change the brand, but you did a sloppy job."

"You're crazy! I don't have any Long Trek stock!"

Templeton turned and called, "Bring that steer up here, Nixon."

The man called Nixon dismounted, then led the steer up to the front of the house.

"What do you call this?" Templeton asked. "Look at this brand." He stepped down from the porch, pointing out the very clumsy attempt to change the LT brand into a Bar-B. The LT was still clearly visible.

"That's not my steer," Babcock said.

"You damn right it's not your steer," Templeton said. "That's the whole point. So what was this steer doing on your ranch? This one and fourteen others just like it."

"I don't know how they got here. Maybe they wandered over here. Cattle do that, you know. They start following the grass or the water, and there's no tellin' where they are likely to turn up," Babcock said, growing a little more frightened.

"Uh-huh. And I suppose after they quit wanderin' around, they also branded themselves."

"I'm tellin' you, I don't know how those steers got on my land. And I don't know how they got branded, but I didn't have anything to do with it."

"You're lyin'," Templeton said. "Well, I'm tellin' you right now, your cattle rustlin' days are over."

Nixon, who had been coming closer, suddenly dropped rope over Babcock, then cinched it up tight.

"What are you doing?"

"We're going to make certain you never steal anybody else's cattle."

Nixon jerked him down from the porch, then dragged him toward the barn.

"Get 'im up in the hayloft," Templeton ordered.

"What are you doing? Let my husband go!" Millie Babcock shouted.

"You'd better stay out of this, missus!" Templeton said.

Millie stepped back into the house, then came back out onto the front porch, holding a rifle."

"You let my husband go!" she shouted, raising the rifle to her shoulder.

Templeton shot her, and she fell.

"Millie!" Babcock screamed.

"Get 'im up there. Get the job done!" Templeton ordered.

Two of the four men climbed the ladder to the hayloft in the barn. Then they grabbed the rope and literally pulled Babcock up. When they got him into the loft, they took him over the open door, tied one end of the rope around the protruding hay hoist, and looped the other end around his neck.

"You got any last words, cattle thief?" Templeton asked.

"I didn't steal your cows," Babcock said. "You killed Millie so I have nothing to live for, but I'll be damned if I let you kill me."

Babcock leaped out of the door himself, hit the end of the rope, then swung back and forth as he gagged. Templeton and the others watched until he quit swinging.

"Get the rope off him," Templeton said.

"You mean cut him down?"

"No, leave him up there. Just take off the rope we used to tie him up," Templeton said.

He walked back over to the porch, where the body of Millie Babcock lay. He picked up the rifle, fired one round from it, then tossed the rifle onto the ground halfway between the house and the barn. "Let's go."

"What about the steer we brought over?" Nixon asked.

"Take him back to Long Trek. We don't need him anymore."

From the *Big Rock Journal*:

Terrible Tragedy

Loy Babcock and Wife Found Dead

Yesterday, Charles Woodward, whose land adjoins the Babcock spread, grew concerned that it had been some time since he had seen his neighbor. Riding over to see if anything was wrong, he came upon a most grisly scene. Loy Babcock was found hanging from the hay hoist at his barn, and his wife, Millie, was dead of a gunshot wound on the back porch. Halfway between the porch and the barn, was found Babcock's rifle, with one bullet having been fired.

Tom Nunnley, the county coroner, has ruled the deaths as murder suicide.

"It appears that Mr. and Mrs. Babcock got into an argument, resulting in Mr. Babcock shooting his wife," Nunnley said. "Then, unable to live with what he had done, Mr. Babcock took his own life."

> Interment will be in the Garden of
> Memories Cemetery in Big Rock tomorrow
> at two o'clock, post meridiem. There will be
> no church services.

"I don't give a damn what Nunnley says," Woodward told the others after Babcock and his wife were buried side by side. "I know damn well Loy didn't kill Millie. Why, you ain't never seen a couple that loved one another like them two did."

"Then what do you think happened?" Humboldt Puddle asked.

"I don't know. Could be, a group of outlaws come by to see what they could rob."

Chris Logan shook his head. "Can't be that. Sheriff Carson found sixty-two dollars in the sugar bowl. Don't you think if it was robbers, they would've took the money?"

"Maybe they didn't find it," Woodward said.

"How could they not have found it? Damn near ever'one I know keeps their money in a sugar bowl," Logan said.

"I don't know why they didn't find it. Maybe they wasn't even robbers in the first place. I just know that Loy wouldn'ta kilt Millie."

One of Babcock's neighbors who went to the interment was Lucien Garneau. After the burial, he went to the land office to see Pete Perkins.

"You didn't waste any time getting here," Perkins

said. "Babcock's body isn't even cold in the ground yet."

"I'm thinking of his next of kin," Garneau said. "Surely he has someone who will inherit his land. I want to find out who that is, and make them an offer on the place. I'm sure they will be aggrieved by his death, but perhaps some money would help ameliorate that grief."

"I will see what I can do," Perkins said. "Robert Dempster should be able to find out who the next of kin might be."

Robert Dempster was a morbidly obese man. As he sat behind his desk listening to Garneau, he was eating a sugarcoated cruller. He took the last bite, then sucked the ends of his fingers. "I'll see what I can find out."

Garneau nodded and left the office.

"There is no need to find out who the next of kin is," Dempster said after two days of investigation. "In thirty days taxes will be due on every piece of property in the entire county. Babcock won't be here to pay the taxes, so title to the land will pass to whoever pays those taxes."

"How much will that be?" Garneau asked.

"That little bit of information comes under the heading of my legal fee," Dempster said.

"All right. How much is your legal fee?"

"One hundred dollars."

"Come to the bank with me, and I'll pay you."

Half an hour later, in exchange for the one hundred

dollars he had received from Garneau, Dempster handed over a piece of paper. "Go to the county assessor and pay him the amount on this form, and he will hand over a deed of possession to you."

Garneau looked at the form. "What? This can't be right!"

Dempster chuckled. "Believe me, it is right. Do you see now, how advantageous it is for you to have a good lawyer?"

"This says sixty-two dollars."

"That's right. For sixty-two dollars you will own what was Babcock's ranch."

Two days later, Charles Woodward saw black smoke curling into the sky and he called out to his wife. "Sue, it looks like there's a fire over at the Babcock ranch."

"How in heaven's name could a fire get started over there?" Sue asked. "There's nobody there."

"I'm going to go check it out."

"Why? I mean if nobody is there, what difference does it make?"

"I'm just curious, that's all."

Woodward reached the Babcock place in about twenty minutes. He saw a wagon loaded with furniture he recognized from his many visits with the Babcocks. He also saw that not only the house was burning, but so were the barn, the implement shed, and the little building where the hired hands stayed during the season. Four men stood around, watching the buildings burn. They watched Woodward as he rode up and dismounted.

Woodward recognized Templeton. "I was going to say that you did a good job of getting the furniture out before it was burned along with the house. But it looks like you took it out before the house caught fire."

"Of course we did," Templeton said. "Just because we are burning all the buildings, doesn't mean we have to burn the furniture too."

"Are you telling me that you burned the buildings?"

"We sure did."

"Why would you do that?"

"Once Colonel Garneau bought the ranch, he was only interested in the land," Templeton said. "The buildings were just in the way."

"What do you mean Garneau bought the ranch? Bought it from who?"

"You'll have to ask the colonel that," Templeton said. "All I know is, he now owns the place. And that means you are trespassing, by the way. What are you doing here, anyway?"

"I came to see about the fire."

"Well, you've seen about it. I suggest you get off the colonel's property."

Disgruntled, Woodward returned to his home.

"What caused the fire?" Sue asked as he came in the door.

"Garneau caused the fire," Woodward said. "Sue, that man Templeton, the one who works for Garneau, says Garneau owns the ranch now."

"What? How can that be possible? Why didn't it

pass to Loy's younger brother? You know what store he set by that boy."

"I don't know, but something is fishy here. I don't know how Garneau got possession of the land, but I'd be willing to bet that it was something crooked. And I'll tell you something else. I wouldn't be surprised if Garneau didn't have something to do with Loy and Millie gettin' killed."

"Oh, Charles, don't ever say that to anyone. Why, if it got back to Garneau that you were accusing him . . . I don't know what he would do."

"I'll tell you what I'm going to do," Woodward said. "I'm going over to Humboldt's, and see if he won't call a meeting of all the small farmers and ranchers. I don't know where Garneau is goin' with all this, but I sure don't like the looks of it."

CHAPTER SEVEN

Humboldt Puddle agreed to host a meeting, and word went out to every rancher and farmer whose land was adjacent to Long Trek Ranch.

He was the oldest of the landowners, and his ranch, *Carro de Bancada*, consisted of four sections, making him the largest property owner of the group. Because of his age, property, and the fact that he was a natural leader, the others tended to look to him for direction. It was natural, then, that the meeting took place in his house.

Otto Speer was the first to arrive. He was a German who had come to the U.S. just before the Civil War. He'd fought in the war on the side of the North, and after the war, brought his family to Eagle County to homestead a half section of land.

Woodward arrived next. He was from Georgia and had fought for the South. When the war ended, there was little left for him to go back to, so he, his wife, and daughter had come to Colorado to homestead. Despite the fact that they had fought on opposite sides, Woodward and Speer were friends. Lucy, who was a very pretty eighteen-year-old, came to the meeting with her parents and offered to look after the youngsters who came.

Herman Drexler was next to arrive. He and his wife had come to Colorado from Pennsylvania. They had a twelve-year-old son named Jimmy. Even though Drexler and his wife came by spring wagon, Jimmy rode Duffy, the horse he had gotten for his birthday. He wanted to show Duffy off to the others.

Jimmy showed Duffy first to the two young boys of Chris Logan, giving them a ride, one at a time. Logan had been a first sergeant in the Seventh Cavalry, making Custer's last scout with him. He was with Reno during the battle, and thus avoided the fate that befell so many of his friends. Logan's nearest neighbor was Marvin Butrum. Butrum was also married, with two young daughters, and on occasion Logan and Butrum discussed whether or not their children would marry each other when they grew up.

Tom Keefer was the remaining neighbor. He had a spotted past, and though his neighbors may have wondered about him, he proved to be affable and helpful, so no one questioned him. Nobody knew he had once been a road agent down in Texas, and it was money he stole from a stagecoach shipment that gave him the start he'd needed in Colorado. Keefer wasn't married.

Puddle had been married when he came to Colorado, but his wife, Martha Jane, had died two years ago without ever having borne a child. Because he lived alone, the wives of his neighbors brought food so there was a potluck dinner before the meeting. Finally, when the last biscuit had been buttered and the last pork chop eaten, Puddle invited the men into his parlor to talk.

"I'm goin' to have to do somethin'," Logan said. "Ever since Burt Daniels sold out to the Frenchman, my stock has been cut off from water. Frying Pan Creek ran through Daniel's land and on to mine. Me 'n Daniels had us an arrangement where we was sharin' that water. Daniels always made certain the creek was flowin', but the water has stopped, and I believe the Frenchman has blocked it, of a pure purpose."

"What are you doin' for water now, Chris?" Otto Speer asked.

"I'm keeping the waterin' troughs filled with water from my well, but I'm afeared the well's goin' to run dry."

"Tell you what, you can run your cattle across my range. I've got plenty of water," Speer said.

"That's damn neighborly of you, Otto," Logan said.

"And that's how we're goin' to get through this," Humboldt Puddle said. "If we're good neighbors to each other, and help each other out when it's needed, the Frenchman will get the idea that he can't just buffalo us like he's tryin' to do."

"Hell, the man has more land now than anybody else," Woodward said. "What does he want to do? Own the entire county?"

"He doesn't have more land than anyone else," Keefer said. "That's the problem. Smoke Jensen has the most land, and I've heard it said the Frenchman won't stop until Long Trek is bigger 'n Sugarloaf."

"Well, that's not going to happen. He's locked in now. He can't grow any bigger."

"Not unless he gets our land," Puddle said. "And that's what he's after now. He wants to buy us out . . . or force us to leave."

"Well, he'll play hell gettin' my land," Woodward said. "'Cause I ain't sellin'."

"No, and sell my land *werde ich nicht tun,*" Speer said.

"What did he just say?" Logan asked.

"He said he would not sell his land," Woodward said.

"Well I'm willin' to stay as long as all the others are," Drexler said.

"I'd like to see us all make that pledge," Puddle said. "I think if we stay together, the Frenchman will quit trying, and will leave us alone."

"I'm willin' to make that pledge," Logan said, and he stuck his hand out. One by one the others extended their hand, until an eight-armed star was formed.

Geneva, Switzerland

For five months Inspector Laurent had conducted a diligent search and inquiry of every bank in France, looking for a major depositor, but none could be found. When he was about to report to General Moreau that he had come to a dead end, he got a break. He received a letter from the director of France's international currency exchange.

Monsieur Inspector Laurent,

I am informed that you have been making inquiries of all banks and financial institutions with regard to large and unexpected monetary deposits. In accordance with your investigation, I can tell you we have recently received a transfer of two and one half million francs from the Swiss National Bank. The paperwork accompanying the transfer indicated this amount was the result of a transaction with one Antoine Dubois.

I hope this information will be of some assistance to you in your investigation.

> *Most sincerely,*
> *Jean Arnaud*
> *Minister of Finance*

That was it! Laurent knew Dubois was dead. If someone made a money exchange in Geneva using the name Dubois, it had to be Mouchette!

Two days after Laurent received the letter, he stepped off a train in Geneva, Switzerland, then went straight to the Swiss National Bank.

"Yes, Monsieur Inspector, a French gentlemen by the name of Antoine Dubois did present exactly two and one half million francs for monetary exchange."

"Was this the man?" Laurent asked, showing the bank officer a photograph of Pierre Mouchette.

The bank official looked at the photograph. "*Oui,* Monsieur, I believe this may be the man. But he was not in uniform. He said he was a French businessman. He exchanged the francs for American dollars."

"*Merci,* Monsieur, you have been a great help."

When he left the bank, Inspector Laurent wore a big smile. He had traced Mouchette to Switzerland. Mouchette had exchanged two and one half million francs, which was the exact amount of money taken, and had passed himself off as Sergeant Dubois. It was all the evidence Laurent needed. That the bank official identified the photograph was but corroboration of what he already knew.

Mouchette had made the exchange for American dollars. That could only mean he had gone to America. It would be harder to find him, but Laurent was convinced that he would find him. And he would take him back to France to face the guillotine.

Sugarloaf Ranch

Sally and Smoke were in the kitchen. She laughed as she read a letter from Cal.

"What is it?" Smoke asked from the table where he sat drinking a cup of coffee.

She read aloud. "Miss Sally, me and Pearlie don't mind being here in Denver all that much, what with there being a lot to do and we know that Smoke needs us over here. But what is so hard is that we ain't had nary one bite of your bear sign in so long we've near 'bout forgot what they taste like. Could you cook some up and put 'em in a box, then put 'em on a train and have 'em sent here. Wouldn't take more 'n a day to get 'em here by train, and more 'n likely they'd still be good to eat when they got here."

Smoke laughed. "I'll tell you what is hard."

"What's that?"

"For you to read that letter exactly as Cal wrote it. I mean with bad grammar and all. It had to be almost more than you could do."

Sally laughed as well. "It did hurt me to misuse grammar. But I thought if I didn't read it exactly as Cal wrote it, it would lose something."

"Are you going to make some bear signs for them?"

"Now, how can I turn down a heartfelt request like that? Yes, I'm going to make some for them."

"Uh, would you, uh . . ."

Sally laughed again, interrupting Smoke in mid-request. "Of course I'm going to make a few extra." Sally looked through the window.

"Oh, there's Mr. Puddle coming up the road. I wonder what he wants."

"Only one way to find out." Smoke stepped out onto the porch to meet Puddle. "Hello, Humboldt. Climb down and come on into the house for a cup of coffee."

"Thank you." Puddle swung down from the saddle. He was in his mid-fifties, with a full head of gray hair and a gray beard. He wasn't a very big man, but he managed to project a persona bigger than his physical stature.

Sally greeted him when he came in. "Hello, Mr. Puddle. Welcome to Sugarloaf. Why don't you and Smoke go on into the parlor," she invited. "I'll bring you some coffee."

"Thank you kindly, Sally," Humboldt replied, taking advantage of his age to address Sally so.

"What's on your mind, Humboldt?" Smoke asked when the two men were seated.

"Smoke, just how much do you know about this fella, Garneau?" Puddle asked.

"Not too much," Smoke said. "He doesn't seem to be a man you can get friendly with."

"You got that right. You know, don't you, that he has taken over Babcock's place."

"Yes, I heard that he had."

"Do you know how he got that ranch?"

"I haven't heard, but I expect he pulled some sort of deal," Smoke said.

Puddle grunted. "I'll say he did. He paid the taxes on it. That's it, Smoke. He paid the sixty-two dollars tax on the land, and got title to it. And you know the real ironic thing? They found sixty-two dollars in the sugar bowl in Loy's house. He had the money for the tax and was going to pay it.

"I read in the paper that it was a murder suicide," Smoke said.

"You'll never get me to believe that," Puddle said. "Not in a thousand years would I believe that."

"I didn't know Babcock that well."

"Well, believe me, he wouldn't do a thing like that. It just seems damn convenient to me that both he and Millie wind up dead, and Garneau winds up with title to their property. He's already bought out Daniels, and he's been tryin' to buy ever'one else out, but I've managed to hold ever'one together so far."

"I don't doubt it. You're a man people listen to," Smoke said.

"Yes, sir. But here's the thing. Am I right in tellin' ever'one else to hold on? I mean, when you get right down to it, it ain't none of my business. And even if Garneau didn't have anything to do with killin' Babcock, it is still gettin' pretty ugly."

"How?"

"Well, you take Logan's property for example. Once Garneau got his hands on Daniels' ranch, he damned up Frying Pan Creek. Daniels was lettin' it go on through so's Logan had water, but now he has none."

"That's not good."

"No sir, it ain't. And I'm afraid it's goin' to get worse. I guess what I'm wantin' to hear from you, Smoke, is if I'm doin' the right thing by keepin' ever'one together."

"What are the others saying? Are they wanting to sell out?"

"No, sir. We had a meetin' at my house, and ever'one came. And ever'one of 'em said they was plannin' on stayin'."

"Then you aren't forcing them into anything, Humboldt. You are leading them. And any successful group has to have a good leader. I'd say you're doing the right thing."

Puddle smiled. "Thank you, Smoke. To be truthful with you, I think I rode over here just to hear you say that."

Sally came into the room then. "My first batch of

bear signs will be out shortly, Mr. Puddle. I do hope you will stay long enough to have one."

"Miz Jensen, if that's the delicious thing I been smellin' ever since I got here, I ain't likely to leave 'less I get told to leave."

Sally chuckled. "We're not about to do that."

"Then yes ma'am, it'll be a pleasure to stay.

CHAPTER EIGHT

Long Trek

"Colonel, I'm goin' to be gone for a few days," Templeton said. "I'll check in with you when I get back."

"Where are you going?"

"I'm goin' to take care of what could be a problem for us. Believe me, you're better off not knowin' anything about it."

"All right. I won't interfere," Garneau said.

Red Cliff, Colorado

Templeton was in town to meet with a man named Jake Willard. A tall man with a narrow face and a badly burned, disfigured cheek, he was a gunman who killed for money. Templeton had money, and he wanted someone killed.

He found him sitting in the back of the Moosehead Saloon, drinking beer and dealing poker hands to himself. "Willard." Templeton pointed to a chair. "May I sit down?"

Willard nodded, and Templeton took a seat.

"Didn't you once tell me you would like to go up against Smoke Jensen?"

"If the conditions are right."

"By conditions, do you mean money?"

"Money is one of the conditions I mean. I would also like to have an edge. A man is a fool if he goes into a gunfight without an edge, especially if it's ag'in someone like Smoke Jensen."

"Suppose I get something set up for you where the conditions are right? Would you be interested?"

"How are you going to make the conditions right?"

"I'll pay someone to back your play."

"How much will you pay me?"

"One thousand dollars, after it's done," Templeton said.

Willard took the last swallow of his beer, then wiped his mouth with the back of his hand.

"All right. Let's do it."

Big Rock

Smoke and Sally had come into town in the spring wagon. Sally was planning on doing some shopping, stopping first at Foster and Matthews Grocery, then Goldstein's Mercantile, and finally the dress shop.

"Are we going to have any money left when you are finished?" Smoke asked.

"Kirby Jensen, you have enough money to buy every store in this town. I imagine you'll have some left when I'm finished." Sally smiled. "Not much," she teased. "But some."

Smoke stopped in front of the grocery store, then handed the reins to Sally. "I'll let you keep the spring wagon so you have a place to put everything you're buying. I'll be at Longmont's," he added as he hopped down, then started up Front Street.

"Tell Louis I said hello."

As he passed Murchison's Leather Goods store, Tim stepped out to speak to him. "Smoke, I have those boots you ordered."

"Good, I'll pick 'em up on the way back."

"No need, I saw you and Miz Sally come into town. I'll just take 'em down and put 'em in your wagon."

"Thanks, Tim."

"Where's Pearlie and Cal? I haven't seen either one of 'em in coon's age."

"I've got them both in Denver, running the abattoir for me."

Murchison chuckled. "I don't suppose they are any too happy about that."

"All in all, I think they would rather be back on the ranch," Smoke said. "And I expect I'll have them both back before too much longer."

"Tell them I asked about them."

"I will."

Templeton had climbed up to the top of the McCoy Building, which was the highest building in town. From there, he had seen Smoke approaching the town, even when the wagon was still far out on Gold Park Road.

He had a good view of Front Street by looking across the top of the Dress Shoppe, and he watched Smoke talking to Murchison in front of the leather goods shop. Templeton stayed there until he saw Jensen go into Longmont's Saloon.

Climbing down from the top of the McCoy Building, Templeton hurried down the street to the Brown Dirt Cowboy Saloon. There, he found Willard sitting at a table alone, drinking beer and dealing himself poker hands. His reputation was such that nobody would play cards with him. He looked up when Templeton approached his table. "Is he in town?"

"He just went into Longmont's. I knew he would go there, so I've got a man with a rifle up on the balcony. All you have to do is call Jensen out."

"Who's goin' to kill 'im? Me or the man up on the balcony?"

"You're goin' to be the one that kills him," Templeton said. "All my man is going to do is get his attention."

"How?"

"Once you call him out, my man will cock his rifle. That'll make Jensen look around. You said you wanted an edge? That's the edge. When he looks around, that's when you'll kill him."

Willard smiled, giving him an even more skull-like appearance. "All right." He stood and loosened the pistol in his holster. "I had me a plate of beef and beans a while ago. And this beer. You take care of my tab. And have the thousand dollars ready as soon as I do the job."

"I've got the money out in my saddlebag."

"I want to see it," Willard said.

Templeton nodded, then started back toward the door with Willard right behind him. When they reached Templeton's horse, he opened the saddle-bag flap.

"You can look in. I don't plan to flash that much money in public."

Willard looked into the bag, satisfied himself that the money was there, then nodded. "Don't you be goin' anywhere. I'll be back for my money in a couple minutes."

Smoke was standing at the bar, having a drink with Sheriff Carson when Jake Willard stepped in through the front door. "Jensen! I'm callin' you out!"

There was a quick scrape of chairs and tables as everyone scrambled to get out of the way. Only Sheriff Carson didn't move away from Smoke. The sheriff looked over at the bartender, who had ducked down behind the bar.

"Poke, would you draw me another beer, please?" he asked in a calm voice.

"Sheriff, are you crazy?" Poke hissed. "Get out of the line of fire!"

Sheriff Carson chuckled, then looked back toward Jake Willard, who was standing in the doorway with his arm crooked, just above his pistol.

"Don't you know who that is?" Sheriff Carson

asked, pointing to Willard. "His name is Jake Willard, a two-bit outlaw who is hardly worth the reward that's out on him. If he's serious about this foolish notion of challenging Smoke, then he's about to die. Now, how about the beer?"

Poke rose up just enough to take the sheriff's mug, then he drew another beer and handed it to him.

"Thanks." Carson blew the foam off, then turned and looked toward the gunman. "Willard, I'm glad you showed up. I have paper on you, and this keeps me from having to go look for you. Why don't you just take your pistol out real slow and put it on the table there? I'll take you on down the street to the jail and hold you until someone comes to get you."

"Do you really think I'm crazy enough to do that?" Willard asked.

"No, I think you're crazy enough to draw on Smoke and get yourself killed. And that's fine with me. Either way, it ends for you today."

Willard went for his pistol, shouting a challenge. "Draw, Jensen!"

Smoke beat the draw and fired a split second before Willard.

The gunman fired twice. His first bullet plowed into the bar right beside Smoke, and his second punched a hole through the floor as he fell.

Smoke stood in place, his pistol still ready, should Willard have any partners wishing to continue the confrontation. The smoke of the three discharges drifted toward the ceiling, joining the smoke of pipes, cigars, and cigarettes already gathered in a cloud.

"Did you see that?" someone asked in an awestruck voice.

"Well, yeah, I seen it. I'm here, ain't I?"

The response elicited nervous laughter from some of the others.

Outside, Deekus Templeton heard the shots and waited a moment to see if Willard came out. When he didn't, Templeton knew for certain it was Willard who had been shot. Joining the several curious people rushing into the saloon, he saw Willard lying dead on the floor. Tales of what happened were already buzzing around the saloon.

Templeton looked down at Willard and shook his head. No one with a rifle was on the balcony providing back up, nor was there ever intended to be. He had told Willard that only to give him the courage to face Jensen. To be honest, Templeton didn't think Willard actually had any hope of besting Smoke Jensen, but figured it was a chance worth taking, especially since no money would change hands unless he succeeded, and also, because it wasn't his own life put at risk.

Sally was just coming out of the dress shop when she heard shooting from the saloon. She knew, with a loving wife's intuition, it involved Smoke. And though she knew Smoke could handle himself in any fair encounter, she also knew there were people who would think nothing of shooting him in the back. It was for that reason she hurried to join the others as they ran toward the saloon.

Reaching the front porch she looked in over the swinging doors and saw Smoke standing just in front of the bar, still holding a smoking pistol. She breathed a sigh of relief to see that he wasn't hurt, then rushed in to embrace him.

"Are you all finished with your shopping?" Smoke asked calmly as he put his pistol away.

"Smoke! I come in here to see that you have been in a gunfight, and all you can say is whether or not I'm finished with shopping?"

Smoke smiled. "I'm sorry. Am I not supposed to ask such a thing?"

"You're impossible," Sally said with a laugh. She looked back toward the body, around which several had gathered.

"Who was he?"

"His name was Jake Willard."

"I've never heard of him. Is he someone who had a grudge for you?"

"Evidently so," Smoke said. "Though I don't know why."

"He was over in the Brown Dirt a few minutes ago," Templeton said. "I went over to talk to him, but he didn't give me any idea he was going to do something like this."

"What were you talking to him about?" Sheriff Carson asked.

"I'll be honest with you, Sheriff. I was discussing the possibility of him working for the Long Trek."

"As a cowboy?" Sheriff Carson asked.

"No, sir. As a private detective, so to speak, to see if we can't get a handle on all the cattle rustlin' that's goin' on."

"Smoke, have you had any problem with cattle rustling?" Sheriff Carson asked.

"No, I haven't."

"Neither has anyone else in the county, as far as I know. At least, nobody else has filed any complaints about it."

"When the Colonel met with the Cattlemen's Association no one else seemed to have a problem, either," Templeton said. "And I think I've got that all figured out, as to why."

"Why?" Sheriff Carson asked.

"I think it might be because Colonel Garneau is new. And he's a Frenchman. The rustlers probably think he is an easy target. Only they've got another think comin'. I'm makin' it my business to hire men who can deal with them."

"Like Jake Willard?"

Templeton shook his head. "I didn't hire him. As it turns out, I reckon it was a good thing I didn't."

The next day an article appeared in the *Big Rock Journal*:

Shootout n Longmont's Saloon

INITIATOR OF THE DEADLY ENCOUNTER KILLED

Jake Willard, who fancied himself a man of considerable skill with a pistol, learned to his sorrow yesterday that his skill was not the match of Smoke Jensen. Accosting Mr.

Jensen while he stood at the bar having a beer and engaged in peaceful conversation, Willard proved to be inadequate to the task he had set for himself. Smoke Jensen, in a move that was lightning swift, pulled his .44 and energized the ball that ended Jake Willard's life of crime. There was a one thousand dollar reward for Jake Willard, but Smoke Jensen, in a move of great generosity, has donated the money to the Holy Spirit Orphanage.

As there was no one to mourn Jake Willard, he was put unheralded, and with naught but the gravedigger in attendance, into a pauper's grave this morning.

Garneau read the article with interest, but made no connection between the incident and the conversation he had held with Templeton a few days earlier. He was not aware the attempted assassination had been concocted by the gunman.

The colonel read a few more articles, thinking he should keep up with the local news. He was about to put the paper down when he noticed something under a column with the heading INTERNATIONAL INTELLIGENCE BY CABLE.

NEW MYSTERY FROM FRANCE

Deceased Soldier Not Who They Thought

It has been some time since the charred remains of a French soldier were found near Dijon, France. Those remains were initially identified as Captain Pierre Mouchette. It was suspected that Sergeant Antoine Dubois had murdered Captain Mouchette, and absconded with as much as two and one half million francs. It is now known that the body found was not that of Captain Mouchette, but Sergeant Dubois himself. The inescapable conclusion is that Mouchette, in all violation of the honor of his office, the fiduciary responsibility to the army he served, and the betrayal of the sergeant who served him, is the murderer and thief.

The current location of the wretched Captain Mouchette is not known.

Garneau was disturbed that his ruse had been discovered, that the authorities in France knew it was Sergeant Dubois' body they had found, and that they had deduced he was the thief and murderer. But he found succor in the fact that the article clearly stated his whereabouts was unknown.

CHAPTER NINE

Brooklyn, New York

Malcolm Theodore Puddle was a shipping clerk for the Brooklyn Transit Company. It wasn't a job he particularly liked, but it paid well, and he was conscientious about his work. He was handling a bank shipment of ten thousand dollars in cash that had been delivered to him by an armed messenger. Malcolm had to stay beyond his usual quitting time, because the money could not be out of his sight until it was put on board one of the car floats, a barge that ferried railroad cars across the Hudson River.

Earlier, he had stepped into Henry's Café and arranged to have his dinner brought to him that evening. But it was getting close to seven and still no dinner. He was beginning to wonder if Henry had forgotten. Since it was something Henry had done for him many times, Malcolm decided he must have just gotten very busy at the last minute.

* * *

Sixteen-year-old Teddy Cline had the pork chop, roll, and a baked potato in a covered dish and started out the back door of the café. He didn't mind delivering the supper meal to Mr. Puddle, because Puddle always tipped well. The café was very busy, and he had gotten away late, so he hurried through the alley, which was the shortest distance between the café and the terminal. He could save time that way, but it always made him just a little uncomfortable.

Suddenly two men stepped out in front of him, and his worst fears were realized.

"What do you want?" Teddy asked. "I don't have any money. I don't have anything you want."

"Oh, I wouldn't say that." One of the men pointed to the covered plate. "We'll just take the supper you are carrying."

"No!" Teddy said, pulling the dish away as one of the men reached for it. "This is for Mr. Puddle over at the terminal."

"Yes, well, see, we want to meet Mr. Puddle, and we figure taking him his dinner will do it for us."

"You don't need to take him his supper. Mr. Puddle is a very nice man. If you want to meet him, all you have to do is go see him."

"How are we going to do that? The office is closed and the door is locked. We figured if we had his meal, when we knock, he would open the door to us. Isn't that how you get in?"

"Ha!" Teddy said. "I have a key. He left it with me earlier today when he ordered his meal."

"You're lyin'."

"No, I'm not. It's right here, see?" Teddy lifted the lid on the covered dish, and there, beside the pork chop, roll, and baked potato was a key.

"We'll just take that key." The man pulled a cloth from his pocket and held it over Teddy's nose and mouth. Teddy smelled a cloying odor, then everything went black.

"How long will he be out?"

"Long enough for us to get the money and be out of here." The man put the handkerchief and chloroform back in his pocket.

"Do you have enough of that stuff left to take care of Puddle?"

"Yes."

Malcolm Puddle was playing solitaire as he waited on his supper. Glancing up at the clock, he saw that it was getting close to eight. The car barge would leave at eight-thirty. If he had known it was going to take this long, he would have waited until after he got the money shipment on board, then gone to the café to eat.

He had just put a red seven on a black eight, when he heard the front door open. "Teddy," he called. "What has taken you so long, I'm about starved." He looked up, saw two men coming into the office, and didn't recognize either one. He stood up and backed away from the desk. "Where's Teddy?"

"Oh, he's back at the café. They got real busy and my friend Toby and I were coming this way anyway, so he gave us your supper. Oh, and the key," the man added, smiling and holding the key out toward Puddle. "He told me to be sure and give the key back to you."

Something about the two men made Malcolm feel a little wary of them, but he gave no indication. "Thank you. You can put the food and the key there on the desk."

"I'd rather not. Ol' Henry now, he was real particular about tellin' us to put the key directly in your hands, and if you don't mind, that's what I plan to do. Put it right in your hands."

Both men stepped around the desk toward him, and Toby took a cloth and a small bottle from his pocket. Malcolm had no idea what it was, or what Toby had in mind, but he didn't like it. "I told you, put the food and the key on the desk. Except for deliveries, no one is allowed in here."

"Ah, deliveries. You mean like the ten thousand dollars delivered to you today?"

Malcolm realized his suspicions were well founded, and he moved away from the desk into an open area.

"Grab him, Sid," Toby said.

Malcolm stood five-feet-nine-inches tall and weighed 155 pounds. Sid and Toby were longshoremen, over six-feet tall with a good two hundred pounds of muscle. They didn't expect any problem with Malcolm.

But they got it. Malcolm was a middleweight boxer

who had twenty-three fights under his belt, and not one loss.

As Sid approached, Malcolm snapped a quick, hard, left jab to the dock man's nose. He felt the nose go under the blow, and Sid let out a yell of pain. Enraged, he raised both hands over his head and rushed toward the clerk. Malcolm ducked under the upraised arms, then sent a hard right into Sid's solar plexus. With a painful expulsion of breath, Sid fell to the floor with the breath knocked out of him.

Toby watched in disbelief as the little clerk of a man handled Sid.

"Why, you little creep!" Toby swung a powerful, roundhouse right, which Malcolm danced away from. The dock man swung again, and missed again when Malcolm bent back at the waist to let the fist fly by him.

That missed blow left Toby open, and Malcolm sent a whistling right into Toby's ear. Out of the corner of his eye, he saw that Sid was on his hands and knees, with his head lowered almost to the floor.

"Sid! Sid! Get up and help me!" Toby shouted, trying, unsuccessfully, to connect with another roundhouse right.

Malcolm danced over to Sid and kicked him in the side of the head. Sid went down and out.

Toby roared in a rage and decided to quit trying to hit Malcolm, planning to get him in a bear hug instead.

Malcolm knew if the big oaf got his arms wrapped around him, that would be the end of it. He would have only one shot and it had to be a good one.

As Toby rushed toward him, Malcolm skipped to his right. Then, putting everything he had in his left fist, he drove it into Toby's Adam's apple. The big man gasped for breath and threw both hands over his throat. He dropped to both knees, his breathing coming in hoarse gasps.

"Wow!"

Looking toward the voice, Malcolm saw the café delivery boy. "Teddy, are you all right?"

"Yes, sir. They held something over my nose, and it made me pass out. But I'm all right now. Wow, Mr. Puddle, you sure can fight."

Malcolm picked up the bottle and sniffed it. "Chloroform."

"I'm sorry I let them take the key away from me."

"It wasn't your fault. I'm just glad you are all right. Do me a favor will you, Teddy? Run down to the corner, and tell Officer Casey what happened. Ask him to come here."

When the policeman showed up a couple of minutes later, Malcolm was sitting calmly at his desk, eating his dinner, while the two big men were sitting on the floor, one gasping for breath, the other holding his head.

"Holy Mary," the policeman said. "And would you be for tellin' me what this is all about?"

"Let's just say I had some unwanted visitors," Malcolm replied. "I think they were intent on robbing me."

"I used the call box to contact the station. There'll be a paddy wagon here shortly. Are you all right?"

"I'm fine, thanks."

"You should have seen him, Officer Casey. He whupped both of them," Teddy said excitedly.

"I should say he did," Officer Casey replied.

"Oh, I'd better get back. Mr. Wright is going to wonder what happened to me."

"Oh, Teddy, wait," Malcolm called. "I didn't tip you for bringing my supper."

Long Trek

"I think it is time to move on to the next step," Templeton said.

"What step would that be?"

Templeton smiled. "Now, Colonel, my job is not only to convince these people to sell to you, it is also to keep your name out of anything that might happen. Believe me, you will be better off if you don't have any idea about the details of how I go about getting them to sell."

"Yes, yes," Garneau said, nodding. "I think you are right."

"Now, I'm going to ask you to do something that is for your own good. I am told that you . . . uh . . . sometimes visit the girls at the Brown Dirt Cowboy."

"Is that any business of yours?" Garneau snapped.

Templeton held both his hands out, palms forward. "It's none of my business at all. But, if you ever had any interest in spending the night with one of the girls there . . . let's say to have someone who could tell the sheriff where you were in case you had to establish an alibi . . . well, tonight would be that night."

Garneau stared at Templeton for a long moment.

"I see. That is to keep my name out of whatever you have planned?"

"Yes, sir, that's it exactly."

"There is a young woman named Amy," Garneau said. "I think spending the night with her could be quite pleasurable."

Garneau went into town by carriage. It was painted green and trimmed in yellow. On each door of the carriage was the fleur-de-lis, over which, written in yellow, was the name LONG TREK. Whenever he went to town his arrival was noticed, and it was no different this time.

The carriage stopped first in front of Longmont's, and the driver, after hopping down to open the door for Garneau, retook his position on the seat while Garneau went inside.

"Monsieur barman, a drink for everyone present, *s'il vous plaît.*"

With a cheer, patrons rushed to the bar to claim their drinks. Garneau spoke to no one, nor did he buy a drink for himself, though he did step up to the bar and pay for the drinks that had been delivered. After that, he left.

Louis stepped up to the bar. "Tell me, Poke, did he pay for everything?"

"Yes, sir, he did."

"I wonder what that was all about? Why would he come in here, buy drinks for the house, then leave?"

"I don't know," Poke replied. "But now that you mention it, it is rather strange, isn't it?

* * *

Two blocks away, the carriage stopped in front of the Brown Dirt Cowboy Saloon. Again the driver hopped down to open the door for Garneau. "Shall I wait here for you, Colonel?"

"No. Go board the team in the livery and park the carriage there for the night."

"No need on you wastin' your money doin' that, Colonel. If you're goin' to spend the night in town, I can drive back out to the ranch and come back to pick you up in the mornin'. I don't mind doin' that. Just tell me what time you want me to come back."

"Monsieur Calloway, I want you to do exactly as I tell you to do," Garneau said sharply. "Board the horses in the stable and park the carriage out on the street where it can be seen. Do you understand that? I want the carriage out where it can be seen."

"Yes, sir. I understand that," Calloway said, though the expression on his face indicated he had no idea why Garneau had made such a strange request.

"Here is money for boarding the team, for your dinner, and for your accommodations for the night. You may stay at the hotel of your choosing."

"I suppose I'll stay at the Big Rock Hotel. It's the closest to the stable."

"Very good. You may call for me tomorrow morning at eight o'clock," Garneau said.

Leaving the driver to carry out his instructions, Garneau stepped into the Brown Dirt Cowboy and, as he had over at Longmont's, bought a round of drinks for everyone in the house.

As everyone was happily drinking, Garneau called Amy over to him. "My dear, I should like to engage your services for the evening."

Amy smiled. "I'll be with you soon, Colonel. I've already told another man I will spend a little time with him. He's first."

"Who is the man?"

"He's just a customer. His name is Paul, and he works at the wagon yard."

"Point him out for me, if you would, please."

"Oh, Colonel Garneau, you aren't going to cause any trouble, are you?"

"Not a bit, my dear. Please, bring your young man over to see me."

"All right," Amy said with some hesitation.

A moment later a young man, barely in his twenties, came over to see Garneau. "You wanted to talk to me?"

"I do, indeed. I want Amy's services for the entire night. I want to ask you to engage another *putain*."

"Another what?"

"Putain, uh, *prostituée*. Another young woman."

"But I want this one," Paul said.

"Would this convince you to change your mind?" Garneau handed Paul a twenty-dollar bill.

Paul looked at it, then smiled broadly when he saw the size of it. "Yes, sir. Yes, sir, I reckon this could make me change my mind. Sorry, Amy."

"That's all right, Paul," Amy said. "There will be other times for us."

"Yeah," Paul said, the smile still on his face. "There will be other times."

CHAPTER TEN

The Drexler farm

On a low hill, Templeton sat in his saddle, looking down upon the farm of Herman Drexler. The house and barn were clearly visible in the moonlight. There was no bunkhouse; Drexler's farm was too small for him to have employees. Drexler, his wife, and his young son worked the farm by themselves.

There was no movement in or around the house, which was good. Templeton reached down to make certain the can tied to the saddle horn was secure as he rode down toward the barn. He stopped on the opposite side from the house, so if someone happened to be looking out the window they wouldn't see him.

Dismounting, he reached up to take the can down. Opening the lid, he started splashing the liquid onto the wide, weathered boards. From inside the barn he heard a horse whickering in curiosity. When the can was empty he tossed it aside, then lit a match and held it against one of the soaked boards. The kerosene caught quickly and flames spread up that board, then leaped over to the other boards that had been splashed with kerosene.

He heard the whinny of a horse inside the barn as he remounted, then rode away, keeping the barn between him and the house. After he had ridden a couple hundred yards away he turned back for another look. The entire backside of the barn was ablaze, and flames had leaped up to the roof, which was also burning.

Twelve-year-old Jimmy Drexler awakened in the middle of the night to see the walls of his bedroom glowing. For a moment he was confused as to what was causing the glow, then he heard the whinny of horses. Jumping out of bed, he ran to the window and saw that the barn was on fire.

"Papa! Mama!" he shouted. "The barn is on fire! The horses!"

His shouts awakened his father, who, from his bedroom, had no visual indication of the fire. "What is Jimmy yelling about?" he asked groggily.

Jimmy came running into his parent's bedroom. "Papa! The barn is on fire!"

"What?" Drexler shouted, leaping up from the bed. Running to the window he could hear the panicked whinnying of the horses trapped inside the barn.

"I've got to save Duffy!" Jimmy shouted.

"Jimmy, don't you go into that barn!" Mary Drexler shouted.

"I've got to, Mama! Duffy is in there!"

Drexler didn't bother to put on pants over the long johns he was sleeping in, but he did pull on his boots. He rushed outside, just in time to see Jimmy running into the barn. By that time, the barn was fully involved in flames.

"Jimmy, no!" Drexler screamed. He ran to the door of the barn intending to drag his son out, but the flames were so intense he couldn't go any farther. "Jimmy get out of there!" he screamed at the top of his voice. But his scream was drowned out by the loud crash of the blazing barn falling in on itself, and Drexler had to leap away to avoid having the barn collapse on him. He stood in numbed shock, looking at the fire which he knew was a funeral pyre for his son.

As the sun came up the next morning, the air was full of the smell of smoke and the odor of burned flesh. Several of Drexler's neighbors, drawn by the smoke, were at the Drexler house. The women were in the house comforting Mary Drexler. The men were outside with Drexler, looking at the blackened and smoldering remains of the barn. The bodies of the horses and the cow were easily seen as they were large enough to stand out.

It took a while before they actually located young Jimmy's body. They found his charred remains on the ground, his arm toward one of the charred horses as if he had been holding a rope to lead him out. If there had been a rope, it had been totally consumed by the fire.

"What ever possessed him to run into the barn when it was on fire?" Woodward asked.

"He ran in to save the horses," Drexler said. "His horse."

"He was a brave young man," Keefer said. "Not much comfort there, I know. But you can be proud of his courage."

"I don't want his mother to see him like this," Drexler said as he looked at the blackened remains.

"Don't worry. We'll get him out of there, and in a nice coffin before she has a chance to see him," Humboldt Puddle said.

"Mr. Puddle? Drexler? Come here. You might want to see this," Woodward called.

The two men answered the call.

"What is it, Charles?" Puddle asked.

Woodward pointed. "That's a kerosene can. There's no doubt in my mind but that this fire was started."

"Started by who?" Drexler asked.

"Who has been trying to run the rest of us out of the valley?"

"The Frenchman," Puddle spit out.

Garneau was awakened the next morning by a buzzing fly. He waved at it a couple times trying to ward it off, until finally he was fully awake. He watched the fly until it landed, then, cupping his hand he swung it over the fly, catching it when it flew up. He pulled both wings off, then lowered the sheet covering Amy, exposing her naked breast. He put the fly on her nipple and watched with interest as it crawled over her breast.

Amy twitched and groaned, then suddenly slapped at her breast, sitting up quickly.

"What?" Garneau asked as if he had just been awakened by her activity. "What's wrong? What are you doing?"

"I don't know," Amy said. "Something was crawling on me."

"*Mon Dieu,* you gave me quite a start there, waking me like that."

"I'm sorry."

"*Ce n'est rien.* It is nothing. It's time to get up anyway. Amy, *ma chère,* because you provided me with such a delightful night, I would like you to be my guest for breakfast at Delmonico's."

"Really? You want to take me to Delmonico's? Mr. Brown serves breakfast here, you know."

"Yes, I know. Biscuits and some sort of sauce that I think is called gravy. Food that is hardly fit for a *cochon,* and certainly not fit for human consumption. At Delmonico's, we can have a baguette with jam and butter, and *café crème,* which is what a proper breakfast should be."

When they stepped into Delmonico's a short while later, everyone seemed to be engaged in quiet conversation.

Garneau ordered their breakfast.

"Yes, sir. I'll have it right out," the waiter said.

After the waiter left, Garneau spoke to someone at the table nearest his. "Tell me, Monsieur, everyone seems quite subdued this morning. Why is that? Has something happened?"

"You mean you haven't heard about it?"

"I'm afraid not."

"It's the Drexler boy."

"The Drexler boy? I beg your pardon, who is the Drexler boy?"

"Jimmy Drexler. He is the son of Herman Drexler, a farmer just out of town. Or rather I should say he *was* the son of Herman Drexler."

"Was? Oh, I see. You are saying the boy died?"

"He didn't just die. He was burned to death."

"Oh, heavens!" Amy said. "How horrible!"

"Yes, ma'am, I reckon it was. You see, the thing is, their barn caught on fire last night, and young Jimmy . . . well, for some reason, he ran into the barn. Most likely, it was to save the horses. Anyway, the barn fell in on him, and, as I say, he was burned to death."

"What a terrible thing," Garneau said as their breakfast was delivered. He smiled broadly. "Ah, the baguette looks wonderful."

Big Rock

Although Garden of Memories Cemetery was between St. Paul's Episcopal Church and Ranney Street Baptist, it wasn't affiliated with any specific denomination. It was crowded on the morning they what was left of young Jimmy Drexler was laid to rest. Mary Drexler, wearing a black dress and a long black veil sat in a chair next to the open grave, clutching a tear soaked handkerchief in one hand, while with the other hand she squeezed Herman's hand.

Sue Woodward stood behind Mary, with her hand resting on Mary's shoulder. Over one hundred people attended the funeral—a considerable number of townspeople, nearly all of the county ranchers and farmers, including Smoke and Sally, and some of the original cowboys who had worked on Long Trek when George Munger owned it. Conspicuous by his absence was Lucien Garneau.

The pallbearers lowered the pine box, which had been closed for the entire service, into the open grave, then pulled the ropes back up. Pastor E. D. Owen from the Ranney Street Baptist Church stepped up to the grave. "For as much as it hath pleased Almighty God in his wise providence to take out of this world the soul of our deceased brother, Jimmy Drexler, we therefore commit his body to the ground; earth to earth, ashes to ashes, dust to dust; looking for the general Resurrection in last day, and the life of the world to come."

He invited Mary and Herman to drop the first handfuls of dirt onto the coffin. As she heard the dirt fall onto the pine box, Mary let out a sob and turned to bury her head in Herman's chest. They stepped away as several others dropped dirt onto the coffin.

"Someone set fire to Drexler's barn, there's no doubt about that," Doc Urban said later that afternoon after several of the town folk and some of the county people gathered in Longmont's. "In my mind, whoever burned the barn also killed the boy. Jimmy set a world of store by that horse of his. Duffy, he called him. I remember the day he got him. He rode all the way into town just to show his horse off."

"I remember that too." Mark Worley was a self-employed contractor who did carpentry work around town. He was also a part-time deputy to Sheriff Carson. He sat at a table with Smoke, Doc Urban, and Louis Longmont.

"How do you know it was arson?" Longmont asked, lifting his wineglass to his mouth.

"Because they found an empty kerosene can behind the burned out barn." Doc Urban took a swallow of his wine before he spoke again. "That arrogant Frenchman did it. Of that, I've no doubt."

"Whoa, hold on. I am French!" Louis protested.

"You aren't French, Louis. You are a Coon Ass Cajun from Louisiana," Doc Urban said, chuckling.

"But my heritage is French," Louis said.

"Is it?" Doc Urban challenged.

"Well, Coon Ass Cajun French," Louis admitted with a smile.

The others around the table laughed.

"I would have suspected Garneau as well, but it couldn't have been him," Worley said, taking a sip of his beer.

"How do you know it couldn't have been him?" Doc Urban asked.

"Because on the night the Drexler barn was burned, he was at the Brown Dirt Cowboy. He spent the night with Amy Kirsley. They had breakfast together at Delmonico's the next morning. Everyone who was in Delmonico's that morning has said he was there, and that he seemed surprised when they told him about the fire.

"Besides which, that carriage of his, you know the green and yellow one with that fancy design on the doors? Well sir, it sat out in front of the livery all night long. I was deputy that night, and I seen it there."

Smoke set down his beer glass. "Does he spend many nights at the Brown Dirt?"

Worley shook his head. "We asked Emmett Brown, and he said that was the only night Garneau had ever spent there. Brown owns the place, so he ought to know."

"Did you say the girl with him was Amy Kirsley?" Louis asked.

"Yes. Why?"

"Amy used to work here, but she started doing a little business on the side, if you get my meaning. I don't let the girls who work here do that, so she left and went down to work for Emmett at the Brown Dirt. Wait a minute, Olivia said something about Amy just this morning."

Louis looked around the room until he saw Olivia standing at a table with a bunch of cowboys, smiling and joking with them.

"Olivia?" Louis called, summoning her over.

The girl excused herself and came over to Louis' table.

"Olivia, didn't you say you saw Amy Kirsley in Goldstein's Mercantile the other morning?"

"Yes, I did, why."

"What was it you said about her?"

"Oh. I said she was buying one of those expensive new hats the mercantile got in. And I was just wondering where she got the money."

"Thank you," Louis said. When Olivia left, he looked at the others. "Maybe Garneau paid her to say that he was with her?"

"Except Emmett Brown also says the Frenchman was there all night," Worley said.

"That's convenient for Garneau, isn't it?" Doc Urban asked.

"Yes," Smoke said. "You might say it is almost too convenient. Convenient as if he purposely stayed the night just to establish an alibi."

"Well, what is the sheriff going to do about it?" Worley asked. "Next to you, Smoke, the Frenchman is now the largest rancher in the entire county. I can't see the sheriff arresting him on suspicion."

"No," Smoke said. "But we can keep an eye on him. I'm sure he didn't burn the barn himself, but I wouldn't put it past him to have hired someone to do it."

"Smoke, how much do you know about this man he has working for him? Deekus Templeton. Had you ever heard of him before he came here?" Worley asked.

Smoke shook his head. "No, I can't say as I have."

"Well, I've been hearing things about him. You know how people talk, and as much as I get around town, putting in a cabinet here, or a new window there, I hear things an ordinary sheriff or deputy might not hear. There's no proof, mind you, and as far as I know he was never arrested, or even suspected of it, but there are stories that he once rode with the James gang."

"The James gang? You mean Jesse James, back in Missouri?" Doc Urban asked.

"That's what I've heard," Worley said. "But, like I said, there's no proof of it. Just rumors."

"That's interesting," Smoke said.

"Yes, and what makes it more interesting is that whenever one of the small ranchers is approached and made an offer, it's Templeton who has been doing it. And they all say the same thing about him."

"What's that?" Louis asked.

"They say he scares the bejesus out of them."

"Has he ever threatened them in any way?" Smoke asked.

"No, Sheriff Carson asked that very same question. They all say Templeton hasn't done anything to actually threaten them, but there's just something about him that scares them nevertheless."

CHAPTER ELEVEN

The Drexler Farm

"Mary, you can't be serious."

"I've never been more serious in my life. I want to go back to Pennsylvania. Please, Herman, let's go home."

"What do you mean, let's go home? I thought this was our home. Mary, we've worked hard to make this farm go. And we are just about there. You know this. We were talking about it just last week."

"And last week Jimmy was still alive," Mary said.

"I think Jimmy would want us to stay here."

"Why? So you can be killed the way he was?"

"Jimmy's death was an accident, Mary, you know that. He wanted to save his horse, and he ran into that barn."

"Do you think I don't know that the barn didn't catch on fire by accident? Someone set that fire. Someone who wants to force us to leave."

"Maybe."

"No maybe about it, Herman. I know that you and the other men found a kerosene can."

"All right. I won't lie to you."

"Don't you see, Herman? If they tried once, they'll try again. And it might be you they kill."

"Mary, I can't just run out on the others like that. When we had that meeting over at Puddle's place, I gave my word I would stick it out."

"Please, Herman, take me home."

"All right. But, what are we going to do with all our stuff?"

"We'll take it with us," Mary said. "We'll load it up, take it into town, and ship it back home."

Herman nodded. "All right, Mary. If that's what you want."

The Drexlers had just finished loading their wagon when Chris Logan dropped by. "What are you doing? Where are you going?"

Herman helped Mary up onto the seat, then climbed up beside her and picked up the reins. "Back to Pennsylvania, Chris. We're pulling out."

"But you can't just up and leave, Herman. I thought we were all going to stick together."

"We tried that."

"Look, I just came by to tell you that we're goin' to build a new barn for you. We've already talked about it. And we're goin' to replace your horses and your milk cow, too."

"What about my boy?" Drexler asked. "Can you bring him back?"

Logan looked down. "I'm sorry about Jimmy, Herman. We're all sorry about Jimmy."

"I appreciate the offer of building the barn back and replacing my horses and cow. But Mary and I have made up our minds. We're goin' back to Pennsylvania.

"I hate to hear that, Herman. You've been a very good neighbor and important to all of us. Look, consider this. If we all stick together, just as we discussed at the meeting, we'll get through this. If we stick together, Garneau can't win."

"Yeah." Drexler snapped the reins against the back of the team. "Yes, he can." The team strained forward to pull the load.

Neither Drexler nor his wife said a thing during the forty-five minute drive into town. Then Mary spoke. "Before we go to the land office, can we stop at the cemetery? I want to tell Jimmy good-bye."

"All right."

Drexler stopped the wagon and they walked out to Jimmy's gravesite, the mound of fresh dirt still visible.

"I hate leaving before we even have a headstone for him," Drexler said.

"We don't need a headstone. We'll keep him in our hearts," Mary said.

The two stood there for a long moment, Drexler's arm around her as he pulled her close to him.

"Well, let's go see how much we can get for our farm," Drexler said, as they started back toward the wagon.

* * *

In the pastor's study at back of his church, Reverend Owen stood at the window watching Herman and Mary Drexler. He saw them walk up to the gravesite, stand there for a moment, then go back to the wagon. He had already heard they were leaving and said a prayer for them. "Lord, bring them peace in this time of their great sorrow."

"Three hundred dollars?" Drexler said, shocked at what he heard. "That's the offer?"

"That's the offer," Perkins said.

"But I don't understand. His first offer was for one thousand dollars."

"You should have taken the offer when it was first made," Perkins said. "Then you were in a position of control. You had land that he wanted. Now you are in a position of weakness. You need to sell your land, and you want someone to buy it."

"But three hundred dollars will barely pay our way back if we ship furniture," Drexler complained.

"Take it, Herman, please," Mary said. "I want to get out of here."

Drexler sighed. "All right, I'll take it. I don't want to, but I'll take it."

Smiling, Perkins counted out the money, then presented the deed for Drexler to sign over the property to Lucien Garneau.

From the land office, they drove to the depot, bought tickets, and made arrangements for the furniture to be shipped.

"What are you going to do with the horses?" Wilson asked.

"They aren't mine," Drexler said. "My horses were killed in the fire. I rented these from the livery."

"Well, you won't have time to turn 'em back in. If you want, you can just leave them here. I'll take care of them for you."

"Thanks. Oh, and you don't even have to unhook 'em from the wagon. I traded Zeke the wagon for the use of the team."

The sound of a whistle came from the west.

"That's your train," Wilson said. "It's right on time."

Long Trek

"Three hundred dollars, Colonel," Templeton said. "That's all it cost you. We got Drexler. The others will come around."

"How are you going to do that? You can't burn everyone's barn," Garneau said.

"We don't have to burn everyone's barn. We don't have to burn any more barns. But we may have to show a little strength. And I know just where to start."

"Where?"

"With Humboldt Puddle. From everything I've been able to learn, he's their leader. If we can convince him to leave, right on the heels of Drexler leaving, the rest of them will fold like a house of cards. Daniels, Babcock, and now Drexler. I'm tellin' you, getting Puddle's land will do it for us."

"All right," Garneau said. "Do whatever you have to do to get Puddle to sell out to us."

Carro de Bancada Ranch

Humboldt Puddle had his wagon up on a stand, and the wheel removed. He was packing the wheel hub with grease when he saw a rider coming toward him. Wiping his hands as clean as he could, he reached into the bed of the wagon and turned the rifle so the barrel was pointing toward the approaching rider.

It wasn't that he was an unfriendly man. Under normal conditions, he would welcome a stranger, offer them water, maybe even invite them to take a meal with him. Since his wife had died of the fever, he actually enjoyed company every now and then. But these weren't normal conditions. Garneau was increasing the pressure on everyone to sell their land. Drexlers had sold and left right after they buried their son.

"That's far enough, mister," Puddle said when the man came within thirty feet of him. That wasn't a distance he had chosen arbitrarily. He knew from that distance he couldn't miss, even if he had to fire from the hip.

"Well now, that's not very friendly, is it, Mr. Puddle?"

"I'm not exactly in the mood to be friendly. What do you want?"

"My name is Templeton, Mr. Puddle. Deekus Templeton. I would like to talk to you. You are an important man in these parts, one all the other ranchers here in the valley look up to."

"I wouldn't say that."

Templeton smiled. "No, you wouldn't say that because you are a modest man."

"What do you want to talk about?"

"I work for Colonel Garneau, Mr. Puddle."

"The Frenchman," Puddle said, making it almost a swear word.

"He is from France, that's true. But now he is an American."

"He'll never be an American."

"I'm sorry you feel that way, Mr. Puddle." Templeton started to dismount.

"I don't believe I asked you to get down, Mr. Templeton," Puddle said.

"Well, that's not very neighborly of you."

"Neither is burning a man's barn. Especially when his boy gets killed trying to save the horses."

"Are you accusing me of that, Mr. Puddle? Because that was just a real tragedy, his boy getting killed like that. And I don't appreciate being blamed for it."

"Who said I was blamin' anyone?" Puddle replied. "All I did was say that wasn't a very neighborly thing to do. What do you want, Templeton?"

"As you may know, Colonel Garneau is trying to expand his land holdings, and he has made offers to buy many of the smaller ranches in the area. At a generous price, I might add. I'm sure you have heard by now that he bought the Drexler place."

"Yeah, I heard. I also heard what he paid for the place. And if you call that a generous price, then you and I have totally different ideas as to what is generous."

"Well, of course, if Drexler had sold his place to Colonel Garneau when the offer was first made, I think ever'one would have called it generous. But he waited too long. He waited until he had no choice but to sell the place. As it was, he was real happy to sell, even though he didn't make as much as he would have, if he had listened to reason when the offer was first made. I mean what with losin' his boy like he done, well, he was just real glad to get enough money to leave here and start over again."

"How could he possibly be happy with getting about one fourth what it was actually worth?" Puddle asked.

"Yes, well, that was a case of Drexler wanting to get on with his life, you understand." Templeton smiled a mirthless smile. "It created what you might call a buyers' market."

"What are you doin' here, Templeton?"

"Colonel Garneau wants to buy your place."

"It ain't for sale."

"He is prepared to give you forty thousand dollars for it."

"Forty thousand? That's considerably more than the place is worth. Why would he be willing to pay so much?"

"Because Colonel Garneau is a very generous man."

"I can't see him being that generous."

"Well, let's put it this way. The colonel feels that if you sell out, you being sort of a leader and all, well, the other smaller landowners will also sell out."

"So, I'm to be the Judas goat. Is that it?"

Templeton laughed. "Yes, you might put it that way. How old are you, Mr. Puddle?"

"What does my age have to do with anything?"

"You look to be a man at least in your fifties. Is that right?"

"I'm fifty-eight years old."

"A man your age . . . workin' on a ranch can't be that easy for you. But if you was to take the forty thousand dollars Colonel Garneau is willin' to give you, why, you could go to some place like Denver and live just real comfortable for the rest of your life. What do you say?"

"I say I'm not interested, and I'll thank you to get off my place."

The smile left Templeton's face, and he stared hard at the rancher. "Puddle, you are going to leave this land, and how you do it is up to you. You can do it easy, with money in your pocket, or you can wind up leaving it like Drexler did, with barely enough money to get to someplace else."

Puddle had never left his position behind the wagon and had not exposed the fact that he was armed. He lifted the rifle, holding it cradled across his folded left arm. "Get off my land."

"You're not plannin' on shootin' me, are you?" Templeton asked. "Because let me tell you, that's an awesome thing, shootin' a man. Most men don't have the stomach for it."

"Is that a fact?" Puddle replied calmly.

"Yes, sir, that is a fact. Chances are if I was to make a move toward my gun now, you'd hesitate just a second before you pulled the trigger. I mean, thinkin' about killin' 'n all." Templeton smiled. "And that second is all I'd need."

Puddle pulled the hammer back on his rifle, then matched Templeton's smile. "Try me," he invited calmly. "I was with BerDan's Sharpshooters at Gettysburg. I killed fourteen men in one afternoon, Mr. Templeton."

Templeton said nothing, but the smile on his face faded.

"Now, like I said, Templeton. Get off my place."

Templeton stared at him for a moment longer, then turned and galloped away.

Puddle watched until he was sure the man wouldn't be coming back, then he put the rifle down and returned to the task of packing the wheel hub with grease.

CHAPTER TWELVE

Long Trek

"He turned down an offer of forty thousand dollars?" Garneau said in response to Templeton's report. "Why, that's"—he did the math in his head—"two hundred thousand francs." He still could not comprehend the value of American money without first converting it into francs.

"He's a stubborn man," Templeton said.

"I thought you said you could convince him to sell."

"Yes, well, I thought if we could get Puddle to sell, most likely the others would come around. But maybe we are going about this backwards. Maybe if all his neighbors sell, and he is left absolutely alone, he'll have a change of heart."

"Didn't you say that as long as Puddle hangs on, the others will?"

"Babcock is gone, Daniels and Drexler both sold

out. I'm certain we'll find someone else we can convince to sell to us. I'll do a little more probing."

In the bunkhouse, the Long Trek cowboys were playing a game of draw poker for matchsticks.

"I bet one," Hoyt Miller said, sliding a matchstick toward the center of the table. "You know, Templeton's in there talking to the colonel again. I swear, I don't what that feller's job is, but he sure don't spend much time here. And what time he is here, he is mostly talkin' to Garneau."

Several men working at Long Trek were legitimate cowboys, men who had been punching cows at the ranch back when Munger owned the place. In addition to them, a few others had come over when the ranch where they worked was assimilated into Long Trek.

In addition to the cowboys who worked, there were ten men who had no apparent job. They had made it known they weren't cowhands, and would take no part in any of the work required to keep the ranch going. The fact that they were doing no work didn't mean they weren't getting paid. They were not only getting paid, they were getting paid more than the cowboys. And, because they weren't working, they managed to spend a lot of time in town.

"What I would like to know," Miller continued, "is just what the hell are all them other men good for? Why does the colonel keep hiring men like that? Has anyone figured that out?"

"I hear tell they are to protect the herd from cattle rustlers," Gately said.

"Cattle rustlers? What cattle rustlers?" Anderson asked. "I ain't seen no cattle rustlin'. You'd think if there was rustlin' goin' on those of us who actually work out on the range would know about it, wouldn't you?"

"Yes, well, I've tried to tell the boss that I don't think there's any real rustling goin' on," Calloway said. "But he just says I don't know what's goin' on."

"Well, I'm with Andy. I've yet to see the first cattle rustler, so I don't have an idea in hell what he's got all those extra folks for."

"Well, you know that feller, John Noble?" Elmer Gately replied.

"Yeah, I know 'im," Miller said. "Fact is, he's one of the men I'm talkin' about. I ain't never seen him do a lick of work."

"No, and you ain't goin' to, neither. I asked him once what he was doin' here, and he said he had been hired as a bodyguard. Him and Curtis and Nixon."

"Bodyguards?" Anderson said. "Who the hell are they guardin'?"

"They're guardin' Colonel Garneau," Gately replied. "I mean, him bein' one of them lords or dukes or somethin' fancy like that. I expect back in France where he come from, people that's royalty like he is always has to have guards around 'em."

"Well, I don't like it," Miller said. "I've heard folks talk. Did you know there's some folks that think Colonel Garneau is the one that burned Drexler's barn?"

"Only he didn't do it," Calloway said. "I know he didn't do it, because the night that barn got burned down and the Drexler boy got hisself killed, I drove Colonel Garneau into town, 'n he stayed there all night long. He didn't have nothin' to do with it, and I know it, 'cause I picked him up the next mornin' and brung him back home."

"That don't mean that Templeton, or Nixon, or one of them boys that the colonel has hired, didn't have nothin' to do with it," Miller said. "Have you seen the way them boys all wear their guns? They wear 'em like they know how to use 'em. And I ain't one for wantin' to find out whether or not it's all for show."

"I can tell you true," Gately said, "they ain't wearin' them guns for show."

The cowboys watched Templeton come out of the main house and call Noble, Nixon, and Curtis over to him. The four men then saddled their horses and rode off.

"Where do you think they're goin' now?" Anderson asked.

"More 'n likely they're goin' into town to get drunk and visit the whores," Miller said.

Gately laughed. "Well, what else do they have to do?"

"Burn barns, I reckon," Anderson said.

"They ain't headin' toward town," Miller said.

"Where are they headin'?"

"Toward the Butrum place."

* * *

Marvin Butrum wasn't a rancher. Like Drexler had been, Butrum was a farmer trying to make a living for himself, his wife, and two children on half a section of land, 320 acres. Most of his land was sowed in wheat, but he was also raising corn. The crops were coming along so well that he and his wife Emma were already making plans to add another room to their house. In addition to their cash crops of wheat and corn, they also had a rather sizeable garden. With produce from their garden, meat from pigs and chickens, and milk and butter from their cow, they were totally self-sufficient.

At the moment, Butrum was in the machine shed, thinking about how much better off he was in Colorado than he had been back in Arkansas where he had sharecropped a cotton farm. He was sharpening a plough shear when a shadow fell across him. "What are you doing out here, Clara? I thought your mama had you working inside," he said without looking up.

"Mr. Butrum, I wonder if we might have a little talk?"

Looking up in surprise, Butrum saw a man standing in the door of the machine shed. He recognized him immediately as the man Garneau had hired to run the farmers and small ranchers out of the area.

"What are you doing here, Templeton?"

"Now, Mr. Butrum, that isn't very nice of you. I call you *Mister* Butrum, and you don't have the courtesy to call me *Mister* Templeton? Oh, I've brought a few of my associates with me." Templeton stepped away from the door, and Butrum saw three mounted men. All three had their pistol holsters prominently displayed.

"I want you to meet Oliver Nixon, Pete Curtis, and John Noble. I've never worked with three finer men."

"What do you want?" Butrum asked. The presence of four armed men made him uneasy.

"We want to do a little business with you, Mr. Butrum."

"I know what kind of business you want to do. And I've told you before, I'm not interested in selling my farm."

"Colonel Garneau is willing to pay you fifteen hundred dollars. That's a fair price."

"I can earn that in two years. Why would I be interested in selling my place? Especially this year."

"Oh, I don't know. Crop failures, maybe? No drinking water, famine, fire, flood. There are all sorts of reasons a person might want to leave a farm."

"Yeah, well none of that is my concern." Butrum pointed to his well. "I've got a well full of water, and this year I expect I'll have the best crop since I moved out here from Arkansas."

"You may have a well full of water, but it's no good if the water is bad. And your water is bad."

"My water is bad? What are you talking about? Why, I've got the sweetest water in the entire county, if not the state."

"You may have *had* the sweetest water, but that was before a pig stumbled into your well and died."

"Why, no such thing. How would a pig stumble into my well?"

Templeton smiled, than reached down to pat the neck of his horse. "That's a good question. And now that I think about it, the pig didn't stumble. He was thrown in."

"What? Good Lord man, help me get him out."

"All right, we'll help you, though it might be too late. It's already too late to save your wheat crop."

"To late to save my wheat crop? What are you talking about?" Butrum stepped out of the machine shed, then looked toward his wheat field where he saw smoke billowing into the sky.

"My God! The wheat is burning!"

"Yes, it does appear to be, doesn't it?" Templeton said.

"Emma! Get out here, fast!" Butrum called. He ran back into the machine shed where he grabbed several grain sacks.

"What is it?" Emma asked, stepping onto the back porch, but one look toward the field, and seeing all the smoke roiling into the sky answered the question for her.

Then she saw Templeton and the other three men. "Who are these men?"

"Don't worry about them. We've got to dunk these toe sacks into the well to get 'em wet so we can use 'em to fight the fire."

"Don't just sit there on your horses," Emma said. "Come help us!"

"We've come to make your man an offer on the

farm," Templeton said. "We will give you fifteen hundred dollars."

"I told you, it's not for sale!" Butrum said as he lowered the bound sacks down into the well. Emma went over to help him, and when the bags came up, they were not only wet, they were red.

"What is this? This is blood!" Emma said in shock.

"Yes, they threw a pig in the water," Butrum said.

"They did what?"

"We'll talk about it later. Come on, Emma. Help me. If we don't get the fire put out, we'll lose our whole crop!"

Carrying the wet bags out to the field, Butrum started to fight the fire, but he had no more than started, when he knew it was a lost cause. It wasn't a small accidental fire that could be fought. It was a full-fledged conflagration that spread all the way across the field.

"Oh, Marvin!" Emma said, the expression in her voice saying it all.

Butrum put his arm around her, and they stood there, helpless, as the fire consumed an entire year's work and income.

Back at the main house, nine-year-old Clara was standing on the back porch, looking at the smoke roiling into the sky. She wasn't sure what it was, but from the reaction of her mama and daddy, she was sure it wasn't good. Looking toward the garden, she saw several men pulling up plants and tossing them aside.

She ran out to the garden. "What are you doing? Mama and Daddy won't like you pulling up plants like that. You aren't supposed to be in the garden."

"Why, we're just having a good time," one of the men said. "You want to come help? It's lots of fun."

"No!" Clara said. "I'm going to tell Mama and Daddy on you, and you will be in trouble!"

The man laughed. "Yes, you go tell your mama and daddy."

Clara ran out to the burning wheat field where her mother and father were standing together, watching the fire. "Mama, Daddy, those men are pulling up our garden!" Clara shouted, pointing back toward the house.

"Those sons of bitches," Butrum said angrily, starting back toward the house.

"Marvin, no!" Emma shouted as she ran after him. "There are four of them. And they are armed!"

By the time Butrum made it back to the house, the garden was completely destroyed. He saw a couple men playing with five-year-old Mickey. One of them had a ball, and he was pretending to throw it, then jerking it back, and Mickey was laughing.

"Mickey, go back inside the house," Butrum ordered.

Mickey started to turn, then he held his hand out. "Give me my ball."

"Sure thing, kid. Here is your ball," Nixon said.

Taking the ball, Mickey smiled, then ran into the house.

"You leave my children alone," Butrum said angrily.

"Yeah, well, we were just playing with him. He's a good kid," Templeton said. "It's a shame about your wheat, Butrum. I take it you didn't get there in time to save it?"

Butrum glared at Templeton, but knew he was absolutely powerless to do anything.

"All right," Butrum said. "You win. I'll take the fifteen hundred dollars."

"You'll take fifteen hundred dollars? What fifteen hundred dollars would that be?" Templeton asked.

"What fifteen hundred dollars? You know damn well what fifteen hundred dollars! I'm talking about the fifteen hundred dollars you just offered for my farm."

"Oh, but that was when you had water and a crop," Templeton said easily. "Surely you don't think it's worth that now?"

"What is it worth now?" Butrum asked.

"Five hundred dollars."

"Five hundred dollars? Are you crazy?"

"It's only worth five hundred dollars now, while you still have a house."

"You are out of your mind if you think . . ."

Emma saw one of the other men moving toward the house. "Marvin, take it," she pleaded. "For God's sake, take it!"

"All right," Butrum said. "All right, I'll take it."

"That's very smart of you, Mr. Butrum," Templeton said. "I will come back tomorrow. If you have your wagon loaded, I'll give you the five hundred dollars."

CHAPTER THIRTEEN

Long Trek

Lucien Garneau poured brandy into a snifter, whirled it around, and lifted it to enjoy its "nose." He didn't offer any to Templeton.

"Tell me, Monsieur Templeton, how many *paysans* have you convinced to move?"

"Four, so far. And in every case you were able to buy the land for much less than the property was worth."

"What about those men who were killed in town the other day? I'm told they had papers on them, recruiting them to come work for me."

"Yes," Templeton said. "They were coming to join us when they got themselves killed."

"They were killed by the keeper of a *création potable*. A drinking establishment," he translated. "Monsieur Templeton, if the quality of your recruitment is such that they can't even deal with the manager of a saloon, how can I have confidence in those we have gathered?"

"Louis Longmont isn't your average saloon keeper," Templeton said. "And he wasn't alone. Smoke Jensen was with him."

"Smoke Jensen, ah yes. Am I right in assuming it is he who is my greatest adversary?"

"Yeah, he is," Templeton said. "But I don't think he will be for much longer. I've hired a couple men to solve that little problem for us. Permanently."

Two attempts had been made on Smoke Jensen, one unauthorized attempt by three men coming to Long Trek, but who had not yet been hired, and the other by Jake Willard, who Templeton had promised a thousand dollars if he killed Jensen.

Neither attempt had been successful, so Templeton decided to try again. He was discussing the problem with two men, Crenshaw and Harding.

"I don't know as I'd want to go up ag'in Jensen, even if there is the two of us," Crenshaw said.

"That's the beauty of my plan," Templeton said. "You won't actually be facing him at all. If you use the plan I've got worked out for you, you'll shoot him from an ambuscade, and he'll never even see you."

"Ha! What you're sayin' is, we'll dry gulch him, right?" Crenshaw asked.

"Yes."

"That don't hardly seem fair, do it?" Harding asked.

"Do you have a problem with that, Harding?" Templeton asked.

Harding giggled. "Hell, no! That's 'bout the best idea I ever heard."

"Then we are in agreement," Templeton said.

"Damn right, we're in agreement," Crenshaw replied.

Two days later, Crenshaw and Harding tied their horses off to one side of a line shack at the extreme edge of Smoke's Sugarloaf Ranch.

"Shouldn't we take the horses around back?" Crenshaw asked. "If we leave them tied out here, Jensen will see them, won't he?"

"We want him to see them," Harding explained. "When he sees a couple strange horses tied up at his own line shack, he'll come to investigate. We'll be waiting inside, and when he gets close enough, we'll shoot him right out of the saddle."

"Yeah," Crenshaw said. "How much did Templeton say he would give us?"

"Five hundred dollars," Harding said. "That's two hundred and fifty dollars apiece, which is damn near a year's wages if you're punchin' cows."

The two men went into the line shack and had a look around.

"Damn, I ain't never seen a line shack this clean before. This looks more like a house downtown than it does a line shack," Crenshaw said.

"There's somethin' tacked on to cabinet there. A note." Harding went over to read it.

"What's it say?"

"It says, 'Stranger, you are welcome to use this shack as shelter for a few days. You'll find the makin's of coffee in the cabinet, also a few cans of beans and peaches. Use what you need, but leave some for others if you can. And when you leave, please leave the shack as clean as you found it. Jensen.'"

Crenshaw chuckled. "Well now, that's just real nice of him, ain't it? You almost hate to kill a real nice man like that."

"Let's open us a can of peaches. I like peaches," Harding said.

"Yeah, good idea." Crenshaw took down two cans of peaches and, using his knife, opened both of them.

For the next few minutes, they ate the peaches out of the can, then Crenshaw tossed the can into the corner, spilling juice onto the floor. "Ha! How's that for leaving it clean?" he joked.

"Quiet! There he is," Harding said, holding his hand out.

Crenshaw walked over to the window and saw a single rider approaching. Both gunmen jacked a round into the chambers of their rifles and waited.

Smoke liked to ride around his ranch. He justified it by saying it was good to have a look for several reasons—to make certain no calves were in trouble anywhere, to make certain no cows were stuck in a mud wallow, and to check that there was an adequate flow of water. But the truth was, it was something he enjoyed doing. He had not inherited the ranch. He had built it himself, and was proud of it.

While making a routine ride around his ranch, he saw two horses tied alongside the line shack. Knowing none of his cowboys were there, he wondered who it might be. It was more a thing of curiosity than concern. He didn't mind the occasional itinerant using the shack for shelter, as long as it wasn't abused.

He rode over to the shack for a visit, to let them know they were welcome, and to see if they needed help of any kind. A hundred yards from the cabin, he saw a couple flashes of light in the window, and heard the report of rifle shots.

His horse went down and Smoke went with it, hitting the ground hard. The horse fell on his leg and he was pinned beneath it. He needed to be in position to defend himself, and stretched to recover his pistol that had fallen out of the holster when he hit the ground, but it had slid just beyond his grasp.

As he stretched, he saw two men leave the cabin, mount the horses he had seen tied alongside, then come riding toward him, slowly, confidently, and arrogantly.

"Well now, Crenshaw, what do you think about this? Here is the great Smoke Jensen caught like a rat in a trap."

"You know what I think, Harding?" Crenshaw said. "I don't think he looks like a rat at all. I think he looks more like a little, helpless mouse. Squeak for us, won't you, mouse?"

Both gunmen laughed.

Crenshaw was the larger of the two. He had a flat nose, no doubt the result of it having been badly broken at one time. Harding had one eyelid that drooped so it looked as if that eye was half closed all the time.

"Nah, now that I look at him, he ain't a mouse or a

rat," Crenshaw said. "You know what we got here? We got us a goat, that's what we got. A goat, all staked out like bear bait. And you know what happens to bear bait, don't you? Most often, bear bait gets itself kilt."

Neither of the two men had dismounted, and both looked down at Smoke, their drawn pistols pointed at him.

"You got 'ny last words, before we kill you, Mister Smoke Jensen?" Crenshaw asked.

"I might be interested in knowing why you are going to kill me."

"He wants a reason why we are goin' to kill him. What do you think, Harding? Do you think we ought to give him a reason?"

"Ha!" Harding exclaimed. "We can give him five hundred reasons."

"Yeah," Crenshaw agreed as a broad smile spread across his face. "Yeah. We got five hundred reasons to kill you, and each one of 'em is worth a dollar."

"So, you are getting five hundred dollars to kill me?" Smoke asked.

"Yeah, we are. Does that bother you?"

"Well, yes, it bothers me. I thought I would be worth a lot more than five hundred dollars."

Crenshaw laughed. "He thought he was worth more than five hundred dollars. You're a funny man, Jensen. Did you know that? Yes, sir, you're a real funny man."

"Why are you men doing it so cheaply?"

"Why? 'Cause it's easy money, that's why. Killin' you is goin' to be about the easiest thing either one of us ever done."

"What if I pay you a thousand dollars to let me go?" Smoke asked.

"I don't trust you. How do I know you'll give us a thousand dollars if we don't kill you?"

"How do you know the person who has hired you to kill me will pay off?" Smoke countered.

"Ha! If he don't pay what he owes, we'll kill him," Crenshaw said.

"Well, if I don't pay off, you can kill me," Smoke said. "That way you'll still get the five hundred from whoever it is that's paying you."

"He may have a point, Crenshaw," Harding said.

"No, he don't have a point," Crenshaw insisted. "Ain't you ever heard about him? Once he gets a gun in his hand there can't no ordinary man, or any two men, handle him. Let's just kill 'im now and get it over with."

Smoke was not bargaining for his life, he was playing for time. As he was keeping the conversation going, he was also working his rifle out of its saddle sheath and, much more difficult, out from under the horse.

"Enough talk," Crenshaw said. "Say good-bye, Jensen."

The gunmen raised their pistols to complete the job.

At that exact moment, Smoke gave a yell and managed to yank his rifle free. He had no time to aim. All he could do was jack a round into the chamber and fire. His bullet hit Crenshaw in the chest. In a reflexive action, Crenshaw pulled the trigger, shooting his own horse. His horse spun around, causing Harding to jerk his horse out of the way.

Smoke jacked another round into his rifle and fired a second time, sending a bullet right into the middle of Harding's forehead. Both of his would-be assailants were down. He kept a wary eye on them as, finally, he was able to free himself from beneath his horse.

Still cautious, Smoke got to his feet and, picking up his pistol, walked over to have a closer look at the two men who had shot at him. It didn't take much of an examination to confirm they were dead.

"Oh, yes. I think you wanted me to say good-bye." Smoke stared down at them for a moment longer. "Good-bye."

Sally was beginning to wonder what was holding Smoke up. She wasn't worried. He was on his own ranch, just a lot later coming back to the house than normal. On the other hand, she knew if he found something that needed to be taken care of, he would do it. She was about to put it out of her mind, when she saw him in the distance. Right away, she noticed he wasn't riding the same horse he had left with. He was also leading a second horse.

Dismounting, he opened and closed the gate, then came riding up the road toward the house.

Sally hurried out on the porch to meet him. "Smoke! What happened?"

"Let's go inside. You make me some lemonade and I'll tell you all about it.

A few minutes later, Sally refilled Smoke's glass. He had told her the entire story, from the opening shots that killed his horse, to the end, when he had killed Crenshaw and Harding.

"You say they were talking about being paid five hundred dollars for killing you?" Sally asked.

"That's what they said."

"Do you believe them?"

"I don't think they would have attacked me for no reason at all."

"Who do you think was going to pay the money? Do you think it was Garneau?"

"I don't know." Smoke said. "They never said who was paying them."

"It had to be him. You know it was."

Smoke shook his head. "Not necessarily, Sally. I've made a lot of enemies in my day. It could have been any one of them."

"It could have been someone else," Sally agreed. "But you are going to have to convince me it wasn't Garneau. Please, Smoke, be careful."

"I'd better get a wagon hitched up, and get those two men downtown to the undertaker."

"I'm coming with you," Sally said.

"Why on earth would you want to ride into town with two bodies?"

"I won't be riding with two bodies. I'll be riding with my husband."

Smoke dropped Sally off in front of the mercantile, then he drove on to the sheriff's office, stopped, and went inside.

"Hello, Smoke," Sheriff Carson said. "What brings you to town?"

"Hello, Monte. I've got a delivery to make over to Tom Nunnley's shop. I thought you might want to take a look at them first."

Sheriff Carson put his hat on, then walked out front with Smoke. Smoke's load had already drawn a handful of people to look on in morbid curiosity.

"You do it?"

"Yes. They ambushed me on my own ranch. Killed my horse."

"You don't have to justify it to me, Smoke. If you are the one who killed them, they damn sure needed killin'. Who are they? Do you know?"

Smoke shook his head. "I'd never seen them before in my life, but I did hear them call each other by name. This one is Crenshaw, this one is Harding," Smoke said, pointing out each one. "I have no idea what their first names are."

"I don't recognize the names," Sheriff Carson said. "More 'n likely they were just a couple low characters wanting to make a name for themselves by killing Smoke Jensen."

"I'd better get them over to the undertaker," Smoke said.

CHAPTER FOURTEEN

From the *Big Rock Journal:*

Quick Finding in Inquiry

JUSTIFIABLE HOMICIDE

Crenshaw and Harding, first names unknown, lay in wait in order to, by stealth, kill Mr. Kirby Jensen, well known rancher and resident of Eagle County. This scurrilous attack took place on Sugarloaf Ranch, Jensen's own property.

While successful in killing Mr. Jensen's horse, they were unsuccessful in killing him. When the two villains approached Jensen to complete their nefarious scheme, Mr. Jensen was able to energize two shots, the balls taking immediate effect, sending the iniquitous pair to the One whose final judgment we must, one day, all face.

"Is this how you were going to take care of Jensen?" Garneau asked Templeton after reading the article in the paper.

"I will take care of Jensen. Don't worry. Right now I'm more interested in moving out those people who are keeping you from expanding."

"You have succeeded with four," Garneau said. "That means seven remain."

"Yes, but we don't have to move seven. Right now it all boils down to Humboldt Puddle," Templeton said. "He's the leader of all the small land owners in the valley, and if we can convince him to leave, the others will leave as well."

"I believe you tried talking to him once before, but without success."

"Yes. That time I used the carrot," Templeton said. "This time I will use the stick."

"I do not understand."

"I just mean this time I will be more—let us say, persuasive."

"I understand he is an *obstiné* man. Obstinate," Garneau translated.

Templeton chuckled. "Yeah, he's hardheaded all right. But, like I said, if we can get rid of him, the rest of them will leave."

"Then by all means, get rid of him."

"It isn't going to be easy."

"I don't pay you because it is easy."

"What I'm saying is, we may have to get rid of him permanent, if you know what I mean."

Garneau lifted the goblet to his mouth and took a

swallow of brandy. He didn't speak and Templeton took that as his approval.

"All right, I'll get right on it," Templeton said.

"Hey, Gately," Miller said. "There goes Templeton with Nixon, Curtis, and Noble again."

"Yeah, I see 'em. Ken Conn is with them, this time."

"Where do you think they're goin'?"

"I don't know, and I don't want to know. I'm beginnin' to think the less we know about what Garneau is doin' around here, the better off we're goin' to be.

Miller nodded. "Yeah, you may be right."

Templeton led the four men to within half a mile of Carro de Bancada, Humboldt Puddle's ranch.

"Are we going to do the same thing we did with Butrum?" Nixon asked. "Poison his well, tear up his garden?"

"I doubt Puddle even has a garden, and his well isn't an open well. Besides which, we aren't goin' to waste time trying to talk him into selling out," Templeton said.

"Well, what are we goin' to do?"

"You're goin' to kill 'im," Templeton said in a matter of fact manner.

"Kill 'im?" Noble asked.

"Do you have a problem with that?"

"I don't have a problem. But for killin', I get a little more money."

"Don't worry, I'll get all of you a bonus," Templeton said.

"What kind of bonus?"

"A hundred dollars apiece."

Curtis smiled. "Then what are we waiting around here for? Come on, boys, what do you say we do some killin'."

Templeton watched the four men ride off, then he returned to Long Trek.

Humboldt Puddle was at the pump, pumping water, when a bullet whizzed by his head so close he could hear it pop. He knew immediately what it was.

Dropping the water bucket, Puddle ran quickly to the wagon, where he grabbed his rifle and levered in a round. Then, looking toward his apple orchard, he saw a man on horseback pointing at him with a pistol. Puddle raised his rifle, fired, and saw the man tumble from his horse.

Puddle made a big mistake. Unaware there were more than one person, he started toward the fallen man and felt a blow to his stomach. Looking down in surprise, he saw that he had been shot. Moving as quickly as he could to a fencerow, he lay down and looked back toward the apple orchard to see if he could locate any others.

Smoke was at the southern end of his ranch when he heard the shooting. It wasn't the shooting of a hunter, or someone taking target practice. To Smoke, who had been in more gunfights than he wanted to remember, there was a distinct sound to gunfire, a tone and tint that told him those were the gunshots of men in desperate battle.

Smoke urged his horse into a gallop, the gunshots growing louder as he approached. He could see gun smoke floating over the scene, and as he rode closer he saw his neighbor Humboldt Puddle lying behind a fence, besieged by an unknown number of gunmen.

Smoke didn't know the reason for the gunfight, but he did know his neighbor and could see he was outgunned. That was all Smoke needed to see. Out of range at the moment, he fired at the assailants, just to let them know Puddle was no longer alone. The gunmen, seeing Smoke approach, turned their attention toward him.

That was their mistake. Three mounted gunman rode toward him, firing at him. Smoke fired twice, and two of the saddles were emptied.

The other rider turned and galloped away.

Smoke didn't give chase, instead hurried to check on his neighbor. Puddle sat on the ground, leaning back against the fence of his corral. The rifle he had been using was on the ground beside him, and he was holding his hands over his belly. Smoke could see blood spilling through his fingers.

"Mr. Puddle!"

"Hello, neighbor," Puddle said, managing a weak smile. "I got one of them. Thanks for givin' a hand."

"Who were they? Did you recognize them?"

"No, I never got a close enough look to see. But I

don't need to. I know who they are. They work for the Frenchman, just as sure as a gun is iron."

Smoke looked at Puddle's wound and shook his head. "I'd better get your wagon hooked up so we can take you in to see Doc Urban."

"Don't waste your time, Smoke. You and I both know there ain't nothin' a doctor can do for this." Puddle pulled his hand away from his wound, and the cupped blood flowed more profusely.

He looked down at his wound. "That sure is a dandy of a wound, ain't it?" He chuckled. "You know what we used say about wounds like this during the war?"

"What's that?" Smoke asked, knowing Puddle wanted to talk.

"We used to say a deep belly wound was God's way of tellin' you to slow down." Puddle laughed at his own joke, but the laughter deteriorated into a spell of spasmodic coughing.

He reached up and grabbed Smoke by the arm, leaving a bloody handprint on his shirtsleeve. "Smoke, I need you to promise me something."

"Whatever it is, I'll do it if I can," Smoke said.

"Go into my kitchen. In the cupboard under the butter dome, you'll find an envelope. It's got my will in it, and the address of my nephew, Malcolm Puddle. He lives in New York. He's my brother's son and the only relative I got. I aim to leave this place to him. Will you promise me you'll get that to him?"

"I promise."

"I'll be gone, so there won't be much I got to say about it one way or the other. But I'm hopin' Malcolm will consider hangin' on to the place. And I'm hopin' that if he does, maybe you'll give him a hand."

"You can count on it."

"Do you reckon that once I get to the other side, I'll run into them fellas I kilt durin' the war?" Puddle asked. "Far as I know, they was good men, all of 'em. They just happened to be wearin' a different color uniform than I was, is all. I'd like to run into 'em 'n tell 'em there wasn't nothin' personal in it. I hope they ain't holdin' no grudge against me."

"I'm sure they aren't," Smoke said.

But Puddle didn't hear his response, because he was dead.

Big Rock

Smoke drove Puddle's wagon into town, with his own horse tied on behind. There were four bodies in the wagon. Humboldt Puddle was behind the driver's seat, completely covered with a blanket. The other three were sprawled out in the back, uncovered. The arrival in town of a wagon loaded with bodies created quite a stir so that by the time Smoke turned onto Center Street, at least two dozen people were following. Nobody spoke to him until he pulled up in front of the hardware store and undertaker shop. There, he set the brake on the wagon, then tied off the team.

"Smoke, that's Humboldt's wagon, ain't it?" one of the citizens asked.

"Yes."

"Is Humboldt the one under the blanket?"

"Yes." Smoke answered no more questions as he

walked around the hardware store, to the back door that opened to the mortuary.

Tom Nunnley looked up as Smoke stepped inside. "I saw you coming, so I'm getting my tools ready. Who do you have for me?"

"Humboldt Puddle and three others," Smoke said.

"Four? You have four bodies?"

Smoke nodded.

"All right. Let's go have a look."

Smoke led Nunnley out to the street where several more had gathered.

"Who are these men? Do you know?" Nunnley asked.

"I don't have the slightest idea. But I'm sure they worked for Garneau, so he'll probably know."

"Yes, but the question is, will the Frenchman pay for their burying?"

"If he won't, the city will pay," Sheriff Carson said, coming over to join them. "Did you kill 'em, Smoke?"

"I killed two of them. Humboldt killed one of them before they killed him."

"Do me a favor, will you, Tom? Hold off on buryin' these three until I can find out who they are."

"All right," Nunnley said. "I tell you what I'll do. I'll get 'em in a pine box, then I'll stand 'em up out front here. Someone in town may know who they are."

CHAPTER FIFTEEN

Long Trek

"Puddle is dead," Ken Conn said.

"How do you know?" Templeton asked.

"I seen 'im when Jensen brung him into town. He had Nixon, Curtis, and Noble too."

"All right. Thanks." Templeton walked over to his horse and pulled a bottle of whiskey from his saddlebag. "Here. You've earned it."

"Yeah," Conn said. "I was the only one to get away alive. Who would've thought Jensen was goin' to show up?"

Templeton went into the big house to report to Garneau. "Puddle's dead."

"Good. You're sure it can't be traced back to me?"

"I don't know."

"You don't know? What do you mean you don't know?"

"Three of our men were killed—Nixon, Curtis,

and Noble. Sheriff might be able to trace them back to you."

"How? What is there to connect them to me?"

"Well, nothing, I guess. Unless you claim the bodies."

"Why would I do that?"

"No reason, I guess."

"Monsieur Templeton, I have led men in time of war, I have lost men in time of war. As a leader, you cannot dwell upon the individuals under your command. You command an army. You do not command individuals. Losses are to be expected in battle, and when they occur, you simply move on. Those three men . . ."

"Nixon, Cur—"

Garneau raised his hand to stop Templeton. "I don't care to hear their names again. They accomplished their purpose. That is all I need to know."

Templeton chuckled. "Yes, sir, if you look at it like that, I guess you have a point."

"I shall go into town and meet with Monsieur Perkins. It would appear that Carro de Bancada has come on the market, and I intend to buy it."

"Do you want me to ride into town with you, Colonel?"

"You may if you wish."

Big Rock

"Oh," Don Pratt said when Smoke handed him Puddle's will. "I'm afraid there is an assessment due on this ranch, and this will can't be probated until the taxes are paid." The probate clerk was slightly flushed.

"How much is the assessment?"

"Two hundred dollars," the clerk said.

"All right. I'll pay it."

"If you pay it, ownership of the property will pass to you."

"I don't want ownership to pass to me. I want it to pass to Mr. Puddle's nephew, Malcolm Puddle."

"Then Malcolm Puddle will have to pay the assessment."

"Can I pay it in his name?"

"If you have his power of attorney."

"All right. I'll get his power of attorney."

"I don't think you'll have time to do that," the probate clerk said. "The money has to be paid by the end of next week. There isn't time for him to mail you his power of attorney."

"Let me see what I can do," Smoke said. "If I can't get his power of attorney here on time, I'll pay the assessment and take possession of the land, then figure out how to transfer it to him."

"Very well, but remember, you have only eight days. No, six, actually. The last day of the month is on Sunday, which means the taxes will have to be paid by Friday."

One block away from the courthouse where Smoke was attempting to probate the will, Lucien Garneau and Templeton dismounted in front of the land office, then went inside.

"Yes, sir, Colonel, how is my most valued client this afternoon?" Perkins asked by way of greeting.

"Monsieur Perkins, I understand Monsieur Puddle met with a tragic accident today," Garneau said. "Carro de Bancada may be available for purchase and if it is, I wish to buy it."

"Oh, heavens," Perkins said. "I haven't heard anything about an accident. What happened?"

"From what I understand, a group of outlaws may have come by his place in an attempt to rob him. Monsieur Puddle fought them bravely, but was killed in defense of his land."

"He killed three of 'em before they got him," Templeton added.

"That's a shame. Puddle was a good man," Perkins said.

"And he was my neighbor," Garneau said. "After I buy his land, I shall put a plaque on the property in his honor."

"Well, I'm sure he would appreciate that," Perkins said as he got out his land chart book. Opening the book he went through the pages until he came to Humboldt Puddle's land. He examined it for a moment, then shook his head.

"Well, it's not going to be easy, Colonel. I'm afraid he owned the land outright," Perkins said. "There's no chance of acquiring it just by paying off the mortgage, though you might be able to buy it from whoever inherits the land."

"And who would that be? Do you know?"

Perkins shook his head. "No, I don't. For all I know

he may have died intestate, in which case the land will revert to the county. If it does, it will be auctioned off, so you will have a chance to buy it then."

"I don't want to have to deal with an auction. I want to buy it now."

"Well, as I said, that's not . . . wait a minute. Here's something," Perkins said as he examined the land charts.

"What?"

"You may remember how we were able to acquire the Babcock land by paying the taxes?"

"Yes. Will we be able to do the same thing with Puddle's ranch?"

"Perhaps. I see here that he hasn't yet paid the assessment for water improvement. That means there is an unsatisfied lien against the land. And, just as you did with Babcock, if you pay the assessment you can take possession of the land."

"Where do I pay that?"

"Well, you would pay it at the assessor's office, but if I were you, I would just go across the street to the law office and see Robert Dempster. He could make certain everything is properly done so the land is transferred to you."

"*Merci*, Monsieur Perkins," Garneau said. "I will do so." He turned and left the land office.

"Ha!" Templeton said when he caught up with Garneau out front. "Once you get Puddle's property, it'll be easy to get everyone else to come around. Puddle was their leader."

"We will not count our chickens until the eggs have *éclos*."

"Until the eggs what?"

"Hatched."

"No problem," Attorney Dan Norton said to Smoke. "If Malcolm Puddle has a certified witness on hand, he can send you the power of attorney by telegraph. That will suffice for thirty days, which will give him time to send a certified power of attorney by mail."

"Thanks, Dan."

"It's a shame about Mr. Puddle getting killed. I didn't know him that well, but from what I did know of him, he was a decent man who tended to mind his own business."

"That was Mr. Puddle, all right," Smoke said. "Well, I'd better get the telegram sent off."

Brooklyn, New York

Malcolm was in the transit office checking the items to be shipped against the invoice. It was a very detailed procedure, and he had to be very accurate. If he made a mistake, he was liable for any differences between the invoice and the actual shipment. He was good at it, but he disliked the tedium. It was to escape the tedium he'd decided to become a professional prizefighter. But the people who fought in the middleweight division made very little money, so Malcolm had to keep his job, boring though it was.

He was just finishing with one shipment and about to start another when a Western Union messenger came into the office. "Is there a Mr. Malcolm Puddle here?"

"I'm Malcolm Puddle."

"Telegram, Mr. Puddle." The messenger handed over the envelope, then waited for his tip. "Thank you, sir," he said, when Malcolm gave him a quarter.

Malcolm opened the envelope and removed the telegram.

REGRET UNCLE HUMBOLDT PUDDLE KILLED STOP
YOU INHERIT RANCH BIG ROCK COLORADO STOP
TELEGRAPH TEMPORARY POWER OF ATTORNEY TO
ME STOP I WILL PAY $200 TAX STOP MAIL CERTIFIED
POA BY ONE MONTH STOP PLEASE ADVISE BY RETURN
TELEGRAM STOP KIRBY JENSEN

"I don't know who this Kirby Jensen person is," Malcolm said to David Blanton, his lawyer. "I haven't heard from my uncle in a long time, and I don't know if he really is dead or alive. What should I do?"

"First, let's find out if your uncle really is dead, and if such a will exists," Blanton said. "We can do that by telegraphing the court in Eagle County. We can also check on this man, Kirby Jensen, who sent you the telegram."

"How soon do you think we'll hear back?" Malcolm asked.

"Oh, I expect we'll have a response within the hour," Blanton said. "Why don't we go over to the telegraph office and send off a telegram? We can wait for the reply in Ned's Bar."

They stopped at Western Union, and Blanton sent the telegram.

"We'll be in Ned's Bar when the answer comes back," Blanton told the telegrapher.

"Very good, sir."

They left the telegraph office, bought beer in the bar, then found an empty table.

"I hear it took Toby Gleason two months before he could talk again," Blanton said with a chuckle. "He swears you hit him with a club."

"I would have, if I could have found one," Malcolm said.

Blanton chuckled. "I don't blame you. He's a big, powerful man. So is Costaconti. People are still talking about how you handled them."

"Being big and strong means nothing, if you don't know how to fight," Malcolm said. "And clearly, neither of them know how to fight. They've always depended on their strength to get their way."

"About your inheritance," Blanton started.

"If there *is* an inheritance," Malcolm said.

"Yes, if there is. Will you be going to Colorado?"

Malcolm smiled. "Yeah, I think I will."

A few minutes later, a Western Union messenger came into the bar and began looking around. Seeing him, Malcolm called out. "Are you looking for me?"

The messenger smiled. "Yes, sir, Mr. Puddle." He brought the telegram over and Malcolm tipped him, then opened the envelope.

HUMBOLDT PUDDLE DEAD STOP ESTATE LEFT TO
MALCOLM PUDDLE STOP TAX DUE STOP KIRBY JENSEN
UPSTANDING CITIZEN STOP MONTE CARSON SHERIFF
EAGLE COUNTY

Malcolm showed the telegram to Blanton. "What do you think?"

"I think the whole thing is legitimate," Blanton replied.

Malcolm smiled and stuck his hand across the table. "How would you like to shake hands with a genuine rancher?"

"What do you know about ranching?" Blanton asked.

"That's where you raise cows, isn't it?"

Blanton chuckled. "I assume so."

"You think they raise cows to milk? Or for meat?"

Blanton laughed out loud. "If I were you, I wouldn't ask that question once you get out there."

CHAPTER SIXTEEN

Big Rock

Smoke was in Longmont's Saloon, having a beer with Louis, when Sheriff Carson came in.

"What have you got, Monte?" Smoke asked.

Sheriff Carson joined them at the table. "We've identified the three men who were killed out at Puddle's place." Carson pulled out three wanted flyers and showed them to Smoke, one at a time.

$1,000 REWARD

to be paid for

OLIVER NIXON

WANTED *for* MURDER

The other two wanted posters were exactly like the first, except the names were Pete Curtis, and John Noble.

"But there was nothing noble about either of

them, I can tell you that," Sheriff Carson said. "Back in Nebraska John Noble killed an entire family, the mother and father and their two little ones. Anyway, it looks like you have just earned yourself three thousand dollars."

"I only got two of them. Mr. Puddle got the other one."

"Yeah, well, Puddle is dead, so you may as well take the money."

"I tell you what. Puddle left everything to his nephew. Suppose we give the money to him. That is, if we can find him and he comes out here."

"All right. Sounds fine to me." Sheriff Carson looked at the woodcuts of the three outlaws and shook his head. "What in the world were they doing at Carro de Bancada in the first place?"

"According to Mr. Puddle, they were working for Lucien Garneau."

"I wouldn't doubt it," Carson said. "But even if we can prove they worked for him, it doesn't necessarily connect the murder to him. They could have been acting on their own. Every one of them has a record, and like I said, Noble once killed an entire ranch family."

"A real nice guy," Smoke said sarcastically.

"I know Puddle didn't get along with Garneau. It could be he just assumed the men who attacked him were working for the Frenchman. Seems more likely they were just planning to rob him."

"Rob him of what?" Longmont said. "I knew Puddle. He never had more than one beer when he came in here. He was always watching his money."

"I don't know. Maybe they wanted his horses. He did have a pretty good string of horses," Sheriff Carson said. "Where are the horses now, by the way? Are they still at Puddle's ranch?"

"Yes, I sent one of my men over to keep an eye on them."

"Pearlie or Cal?"

Smoke shook his head. "Neither one. They're both in Denver running my processing plant."

"Ha! Knowing those two boys, I don't expect either one of them is very happy about that."

"There's no doubt they'd rather be back at Sugarloaf," Smoke said. "But they are good men and do what needs to be done without much protest."

"You're right about that. They are both good men. Tell me, Smoke, what do you think is going to happen to Puddle's ranch now?"

"I don't know," Smoke answered. "I guess that will be up to Humboldt's nephew."

"I wonder what kind of man he is?"

"If he's anything like his uncle, he'll be a good man," Smoke said.

Sheriff Carson nodded. "You've got a point there, my friend."

At that moment, the Western Union messenger came into the saloon, and seeing him, Smoke called out, "I'm over here, Eddie."

Smiling, Eddie brought the telegram to him. Smoke tipped him, then read the message.

BY THIS MESSAGE MALCOLM PUDDLE TRANSFERS
POA TO KIRBY JENSEN LIMITED TO PAYING TAXES

ON CARRO DE BANCADA RANCH IN NAME OF
MALCOLM PUDDLE STOP NOTARIZED POA TO
FOLLOW STOP MALCOLM PUDDLE

"Good," Smoke said. "I'm going to the clerk's office now to pay the taxes so the will can be probated."

He left the saloon and stepped into the clerk's office a few minutes later, recognizing the very large man standing at the counter. Dempster wasn't a lawyer for whom Smoke had a lot of respect.

Smoke addressed the probate clerk. "Mr. Pratt, I'm here to probate Humboldt Puddle's will. I have Malcolm Puddle's power of attorney to pay the taxes."

"You are too late, Mr. Jensen," Dempster said. "I am here to pay the assessment on that property. Once I do, I will assume ownership."

"Once you do? You mean you haven't paid the taxes yet?"

"I'm filling out the forms now."

"Then it isn't too late."

"Oh, but I'm afraid it is. I got here before you."

"How are you going to fill out those forms?" Smoke asked.

"What do you mean, how am I going to fill out the forms? I'm just going to do it."

"No, I mean, how are you going to write with a broken hand?" Smoke asked calmly.

"What? Are you threatening me?"

"I wouldn't call it a threat." Smoke smiled at Dempster, but there was absolutely no humor in his smile. "I would say it is more along the line of a promise."

"I will have you arrested and put in jail for this!" Dempster said. "And Pratt will be my witness."

"Witness to what?" Pratt asked. "I haven't seen anything."

"You heard him threaten me."

"Like I said, Mr. Dempster, I haven't seen anything."

"What's it going to be, Dempster? Are you going to walk out of here with no bones broken? Or do we give Pratt here something to see so he won't testify for you?"

"You! You!" Dempster sputtered. "I won't stand for this. Do you hear me? I simply won't stand for it!"

Smoke looked over at Pratt. "Has he given you the two hundred dollars yet?"

"No, he hasn't."

Smoke took two hundred dollars from his pocket and gave it to the clerk. "Here's the money. I'd say that puts me in front of him, wouldn't you?"

Pratt smiled and nodded. "Yes, sir. I would say that it does."

Smoke turned toward Dempster. "Are you still here?" Dempster glared at him, but said nothing before he turned and left the clerk's office.

Seven days after Malcolm Puddle boarded the train in New York, it rolled into Big Rock, Colorado. He sat at the window on the left side of the car, taking in the town that was to be his new home. He took in every building and sign as the train rolled by—Earl's Blacksmith Shop, GOOD WORK DONE FAST; Dunnigan's

Meat Market, OUR MEAT IS FRESH AND CLEAN; the *Big Rock Journal*, EAGLE COUNTY'S LEADING NEWSPAPER; Longmont's Saloon, BEER, WINE, WHISKEY; Murchison's Saddle and Leather Goods store, CUSTOM LEATHER WORK; Delmonico's Restaurant, FINE DINING; Nancy's Bakery, PIES OUR SPECIALTY; and White's Apothecary, FINEST POTIONS AND SYRUPS.

The train stopped, and Malcolm saw the Western Union office and the Denver and Pacific depot building. The depot was constructed of red brick, and had a small white sign hanging from the end.

BIG ROCK, COLORADO

ELEVATION: 8,675 FEET

Reaching into the overhead rack, Malcolm retrieved his bowler hat and a leather case in which he had his important papers, including the notarized limited power of attorney. He was wearing a tan suit, a dark brown vest, and a yellow, four-in-hand tie. He stepped down onto the platform, listening to the sounds the train made behind him; from the popping sounds of cooling bearings and journals to the rhythmic venting of steam from the actuating cylinder. He decided the first order of business would be to retrieve his luggage, then locate a hotel, and finally look up Dan Norton, the Big Rock lawyer with whom his lawyer had been in contact.

The arrival and departure of trains was always an event of great interest in Big Rock, and it generally drew people who had no other reason to meet the train than to give vent to that interest. Two such characters were Curly Roper and Slim Taylor, cowboys who worked at the Long Trek Ranch. They'd ridden into town just after lunch, and had spent most of the afternoon drinking—first in Longmont's Saloon. When they got a bit rowdy, Louis nicely asked them to leave. Nobody who knew him ever made the error of mistaking his gentlemanly request for weakness, for to do so could be a fatal miscalculation. They spent the rest of the afternoon in the Brown Dirt Cowboy, where rowdiness was more or less expected.

Fairly well liquored up, they were at the depot watching the arriving and departing passengers.

"Hey, Slim, take a look at that little feller that just got off the train," Curly said. "He's all slicked up like some kind of Eastern dude, ain't he? Look at that hat he's wearin'. What kind of hat would you call that?"

"I don't know what you call it, but it sure ain't no sombrero," Slim said.

"I think I'm going to go over there and wear me that hat." Curly started toward the man.

Seeing the man coming toward him, Malcolm smiled. "Excuse me, sir, but would you happen to know where I might find a Mr. Dan Norton? I believe he is an attorney."

"He's a what?"

"A lawyer. I have secured his services."

Curly chuckled. "Have you now?" He pointed to the hat. "Tell me, what do you call that thing you've got on your head?"

"Why, it is a hat, sir. Specifically, it is a bowler."

Malcolm took off his hat and held it out. "Would you like to examine it?"

"Yeah," Curly said with a little laugh. "Yeah, that's what I want to do. I want to examine it." He took the hat, looked at it for a moment, then took his hat off and put the bowler hat on.

Malcolm cringed a bit. He was very fastidious in his personal hygiene, and the man looked as if he hadn't washed his hair in months. Malcolm could almost feel the head lice. "I don't mind you looking at it, but I would rather you not put it on."

"Well, that's too bad, dude, because I'm already wearing it, and there's nothing you can do about it."

"Actually, there is," Malcolm said calmly. "But I would rather not have an altercation on my first day in town. Especially as I intend to settle here."

"Do you now?" Curly asked. "And just what will you be doing here? Working in some fancy restaurant? We've only got one of those, that's Delmonico's, and they ain't hirin'."

"Please, sir. My hat?"

"Why don't you take it off of me, dude?" Curly challenged.

"I'd really rather not. As I said, I have no wish to get involved in an altercation on my first day in town."

"Alterca. . . . alter. . . . alter what? What is that?"

"Altercation. You might call it a fight. I really don't want to get into a fight, my first day here."

Curly laughed. "Yeah, I'll just bet you don't. But, dude, if you want this hat back, the only way you are goin' to get it is if you take it off my head." He sported a challenging grin. "Go ahead, take it off me."

"All right," Malcolm said. "But remember, you invited this."

Malcolm reached for the hat with his left hand. and just as he knew he would, Curly brought both hands up to block him. That left his stomach open, and Malcolm drove his right fist into it, glad this finger had been only jammed, and not broken, in an earlier fight.

Curly doubled over with a loud and involuntary expulsion of breath, bringing his head down in a deep bow. It was a perfect set up, and Malcolm wanted to hit him a second time, but he eschewed the opportunity and chose, instead, to pluck the hat from Curly's head. He examined it closely for any signs of vermin before he put it back on his own head.

A few feet away, Slim had been watching, amused by the way Curly was playing the Eastern dude. When he saw a punch double Curly over, he was shocked and angered. He started for his gun.

"I wouldn't, if I were you," a calm but authoritative voice said. The warning was punctuated with the deadly sound of a .45 pistol being cocked.

Slim looked around to see Sheriff Carson holding a pistol leveled toward him.

"I wasn't actual goin' to shoot the little man, Sheriff," Slim said. "I was just goin' to keep him from hittin' Curly any more. Me 'n Curly was just going to roust him around a bit, is all."

"It looks to me like you and Curly are the ones who got rousted. What are you doing down here at the depot, anyway? Are you going somewhere? Are you seeing anybody off or meeting anyone?" Sheriff Carson asked.

"No, it ain't nothin' like that. We just like to watch the trains come 'n go, is all. Lots of people come down here to do that."

"Everyone else who comes down to watch the trains does just that. They watch the trains. They don't harass the passengers. Now, if you and Curly don't want to spend the night in my jail, I suggest you get on back to the Long Trek."

"We got the day off so we could spend time in town," Slim complained.

"You've spent all the time in town you're going to. Now get going, the both of you."

"What about this fella, Sheriff?" Slim said, pointing to Malcolm. "Maybe you didn't see what he done, but he hit Curly for no reason at all."

"That's not quite the truth. I was watching everything, and I wouldn't say it was for no reason at all, Sheriff. This fella here"—the town citizen pointed to Curly—"took the little fella's hat and wasn't goin' to give it back. That's when the little fella hit him."

"Little fella?" Sheriff Carson asked.

The citizen chuckled. "Well, yeah, I guess he looks little. But he sure don't hit like no little man, does he? He pure doubled that bigger fella over."

"See? Like he said, he doubled me over," Curly said. "Are you goin' to arrest him?"

"Arrest him? Why should I arrest him? I may give him a medal," Sheriff Carson replied. "Now you and Slim get on out of town like I told you. Otherwise, I meant it when I said you would spend the night in jail."

Grumbling, the two cowboys left the depot, with Curly still holding his hand over his stomach.

Sheriff Carson chuckled, then walked over to Malcolm. "I saw Curly start to bother you and I figured I would come over here and put a stop to it, but you seem able to take care of yourself."

"I appreciate your assistance, nonetheless, Sheriff. Especially as it looked as if the other gentleman was about to withdraw his pistol. As you can see, I am not armed, so I would have been greatly disadvantaged."

"Yes, sir, I reckon you would be. If you want some advice, you probably should start wearing a pistol."

"Why? I don't know anything about guns. I've never even fired one. I'll just try not to get into any situation that is beyond being able to take care of it with my fists."

"That's just it," Sheriff Carson said. "These cowboys don't have a lot of sense, but they do have a lot of pride. Getting whipped by someone who looks . . . and dresses . . . the way you do isn't going to go down very well with them. I'm afraid you will always have someone like Curly or Slim to deal with."

"Do you think it would help matters if I change the way I dress?"

Sheriff Carson smiled. "Some Western duds would help, that's for certain."

"Then I shall do that as soon as I see Mr. Norton."

"Norton. Dan Norton?"

"Yes, sir. I believe he is an attorney here."

"He is, and a good one. Do you have an appointment with him?"

"In a manner of speaking, I do. At least, I have been in communication with him by telegraph. Could you tell me where I might find him?"

"I certainly can." Sheriff Carson pointed south, across the track. "This is Front Street and the street that runs south away from it is Tanner Street. Go down Tanner Street one block until you get to Center Street. Turn left on Center, go by the BR Hotel and the stagecoach office, cross Ranney Street, and you'll see the Dempster law office."

"Dempster? I think I'm supposed to see a Mr. Norton."

"I know. I just told you about Dempster's office so you wouldn't get confused. Mr. Norton's law office is in the building after Dempster's. It's the McCoy Building. You can't miss it. It's the biggest office in town. He's on the top floor.

"Thank you."

"Oh, and a word of caution?"

"Yes, sir?"

"It looks to me like you are pretty handy with your fists. I'd be a bit more careful in using them if I were you. You might wind up hitting someone with your fists, and, like Slim was about to, he might respond with a gun."

"Thank you, Sheriff, for the warning. And for coming to my assistance."

CHAPTER SEVENTEEN

Malcolm followed Sheriff Carson's directions, and a few minutes later was standing in front of a two-story redbrick building. An outside stairway climbed up the left side of the building and hanging from an arm that protruded from the side of the building was a sign. Painted on the sign were a clinched hand with one finger pointing up the stairs and the words *Dan S. Norton, Atty. at law.*

Malcolm climbed the stairs, then knocked on the door at the top. It was opened by a man who wasn't any taller than he was. Like Malcolm, he was wearing a suit, and he had freckles and thinning hair.

"Mr. Norton?"

"Yes?"

"Mr. Norton, my name is Malcolm Puddle. I believe you and I have communicated."

A big smile spread across Norton's face and he stepped back from the door, then made a sweeping, inviting motion with his arm. "Indeed we have, Mr. Puddle, indeed we have. Come in, sir, please come in."

Inside the office, Malcolm was offered a seat. Then Norton went over to a bar where he picked up a decanter of whiskey. "May I offer you a drink?"

"I don't drink whiskey, but when we have completed our business, I would be glad to buy you a beer."

"It's a deal," Norton said, sitting down across the desk from Malcolm. "Now, Mr. Puddle, what can I do for you?"

"First, I would like to make certain my uncle's will has been probated, and that I am, indeed, the heir to his ranch. The Carro de Bancada I believe it is called."

"I assure you, Mr. Puddle, that you are the heir to your uncle's ranch, and the deed to the Carro de Bancada has already been transferred to your name. For it to be validated, however, you will have to show the tax clerk that Smoke did have your power of attorney to pay the taxes in your name."

"I beg your pardon. Smoke? I gave no authority to anyone named Smoke."

"I'm sorry. In all our communications with you, we referred to him as Kirby. Kirby Jensen, and indeed, that is his real name. But everyone who knows him calls him Smoke. Even his wife."

"I appreciate him doing that for me, and I should like to see him so I can repay the money. I've got the money right here. Two hundred dollars, I believe it was?"

Norton smiled broadly. "Yes, but you don't need to worry about reimbursing Smoke. That's already been taken care of."

"I beg your pardon? How was it taken care of?"

Norton opened the middle drawer of his desk and pulled out an envelope. "It has not only been taken care of, but you have eight hundred dollars left over."

"What? Mr. Norton, I assure you, sir, I have no idea what you are talking about. I have sent no money here, either by wire or post."

Norton chuckled, then held up his hand. "Perhaps you had better let me explain. It seems that your uncle killed one of the men who went to the ranch to kill him. That man was a known outlaw, and there was a one thousand dollar reward posted for him, dead or alive. Since your uncle was unable to collect, I convinced the sheriff to allow me to hold the money in escrow for you."

Norton counted out eight one-hundred dollar bills.

Malcolm smiled. "Oh, wow, I certainly didn't expect this. And you say Mr. Jensen has already been paid back?"

"Yes. I'll tell you what kind of man Smoke is. Three of the attackers were killed at Carro de Bancada. Smoke killed two and could have claimed all three, since nobody was there to dispute him. But he said your uncle had killed one, and, by rights, the money should go to you."

"I can't wait to meet Mr. Jensen."

"You will. He will be your neighbor, and I'm sure that, as a neighborly thing, he and Sally will invite you over for a meal. You haven't lived until you've tasted her cooking. Come, we'll go see the clerk now, show him the power of attorney, and everything will be all squared away."

"Thank you. You have been most helpful. I do hope to pay for your services."

"We'll work something out," Norton said. "I'm not going to try and get all my money up front. I hope to make you a client, so I can bleed you for a long time."

"What?"

Norton laughed. "I'm teasing, my boy. I'm merely teasing."

Malcolm laughed. "Oh, by the way, what does the name mean?"

"Smoke?"

"Well, that too, but I imagine Mr. Jensen will tell me that in due time. No, I'm talking about my uncle's . . . I mean, *my* ranch. If I'm going to be a ranch owner, I should at least know what Carro de Bancada means."

"It means saddle," Norton said.

They came to a big building on the corner of Center and Sikes Streets.

"Here's the courthouse," Norton said. "The clerk is inside."

Don Pratt looked up when the two men went inside. "Hello, Mr. Norton."

"Hello, Don. This is Malcolm Puddle."

Pratt smiled. "I had a feeling you would show up in person."

"I have a notarized copy of the power of attorney to validate the one I sent by wire."

"All right. Let me see it, and I'll sign off on this, then turn the deed over to you."

"What are you going to do with the ranch, Mr. Puddle?" Norton asked.

"I haven't decided yet. Why do you ask?"

"You will, no doubt, be visited by Lucien Garneau or his agent, offering to buy you out."

"What is the land worth?"

"It's twenty-five hundred and sixty acres, and the last land transaction I dealt with was five dollars an acre. Though in your case it might be worth a little more because your uncle did a lot of work on the land. For example he dug a canal from Frying Pan Creek to provide water. in addition to the land, your uncle has three hundred and twenty-five head of prime Herefords. They are worth at least thirty-five dollars a head." Norton did some figuring. "With land, cattle, and improvements to include house, barn, machine shed, and smokehouse, I would say the Carro de Bancada is worth somewhere in the neighborhood of twenty-five thousand dollars.

"Wow," Malcolm said. "That's a lot of money."

"Garneau is a shrewd businessman so, no doubt, if he makes an offer, he probably won't offer that much."

"If he seriously wants it, he will," Malcolm said.

He finished his business about the ranch and stopped next at Goldstein's Mercantile.

"Yes, sir, may I help you?" Gary Goldstein asked, greeting him as he stepped through the door and into the store.

"I need some"—Malcolm recalled Sheriff Carson's description of the apparel—"western dudes."

"I beg your pardon?" Goldstein asked with a puzzled expression on his face.

"Oh, I think that is duds," Malcolm corrected. "I need some western duds."

"Very good, sir. Do you have anything specific in mind?"

"Look at me," Malcolm said, taking in his clothing with a wave of his hand. "Would you agree these make me stand out?"

Goldstein laughed. "Yes, sir, I have to say that your clothes, elegant looking though they are, do make you stand out."

"Well, what I have in mind, specifically, is clothes that don't make me stand out."

"Leave that to me, I'll take care of it for you."

Half an hour later, Malcolm left the mercantile wearing boots, blue denims, a white cotton shirt, and a white Stetson hat. He was carrying a bag in which he had three more outfits just like the clothes he was wearing, plus the clothes he had been wearing when he went into the store.

When he returned to the Dunn Hotel, he was met by the sheriff and another man as soon as he stepped into the lobby.

"Mr. Puddle?" Sheriff Carson called him out with a smile. "I almost didn't recognize you."

"Do these clothes make me fit in?" Malcolm asked with a smile.

"Well, I don't know that you entirely fit in, but the

clothes do help," Sheriff Carson said. "You said you wanted to meet Smoke Jensen. Here he is."

"Mr. Jensen," Malcolm said with a big smile and an extended hand. "How nice to meet you, and to thank you in person for what you have done."

"The name is Smoke. Your uncle was a good friend."

"I can certainly see that he made friends," Malcolm said. "And for that I am most grateful."

"I see that you have taken a room here at the hotel," Smoke said. "But if you would like to ride out to your ranch, I'll be glad to take you there."

"Ride out? What would I ride? I don't have a horse."

"Yes, you do. I brought your uncle's riding horse into town. It's put up over at the livery."

"Thank you. That was very thoughtful of you. Uh, does my uncle have any employees? The reason I ask is because I was told there are three hundred and twenty-five cattle there and I'm concerned they haven't been looked after."

"No, there aren't any full-time employees there," Smoke said. "The cattle pretty much look after themselves until roundup time, or until you take them to market. Then Mr. Puddle would put on a couple hands."

"I see. Yes, I would like to ride out to the ranch."

"All right. I'll take you out to see it, then I want you to come over to my house for dinner tonight. You can even spend the night with us, and get an early start tomorrow to have a close look at Carro de Bancada."

"Carro de Bancada," Malcolm said. "Ha! I'm a

landowner. And not just a landowner. I actually own a ranch. I can't wait to tell all my friends back in Brooklyn."

"Are those my cattle?" Malcolm asked, looking out over a field they were riding by. Several cattle were grazing.

"No, those cows belong to the Frenchman."

"The Frenchman?"

"That's what everyone calls him. He likes to call himself Colonel. Colonel Lucien Garneau."

"He is the one who wants to buy the ranch, isn't he? Mr. Norton told me about him."

"I expect he will make an offer," Smoke said. "He's bought out several ranchers already."

"I take it Uncle Humboldt wasn't interested in selling to him?"

"No, he wasn't. Well, there it is," Smoke said. "That's the gate into your place."

It had taken Smoke and Malcolm a little over half an hour of leisurely riding to reach the ranch. The gate Smoke pointed to made an arch over the road. A sign hung from the top of the arch, reading CARRO DE BANCADA. Positioned on top of the arch was a saddle, complete with hanging stirrups.

From the arch the road ran about a quarter mile up to the house, which was a rather modest, single story dwelling. Smoke identified the three other buildings as a barn, a machine shed, and a smokehouse.

"I know you have at least three or four cured

hams in there, and a couple sides of bacon. And you've got a milk cow and a garden that's coming along fine."

"That's good to know," Malcolm said. "I guess I'll have to learn to cook."

"Nothing to it," Smoke said. "You just light a fire, then heat things up."

They dismounted in front of the house.

"Where was my uncle killed?"

"He was over there, behind the corral fence," Smoke said. "He put up quite a fight. There were four who came for him, and he held them off for quite a while."

"Who were they?"

"Your uncle was certain they were working for the Frenchman, but of course, Garneau has denied any connection to it. Since there's no way of connecting the men to him, the official word is they were outlaws come to rob your uncle."

"Do you believe that?"

"I don't know," Smoke admitted. "One of them, a man named Noble, had a record of doing just that— hitting remote ranches, killing everyone there, and then robbing them. It's possible, I guess."

"But you think it was the Frenchman, don't you?"

"Your uncle thought that," Smoke said without being anymore specific in his reply. "What do you say we go on over to Sugarloaf now? I'm getting hungry, and my wife sure can cook."

CHAPTER EIGHTEEN

Welcome to Sugarloaf," Sally said after Smoke took Malcolm to the ranch and made the introduction. "Tell me, Mr. Puddle, what do you think of Colorado, so far?"

"Please, call me Malcolm. I love Colorado so far. The mountains are quite impressive and beautiful."

"They are a bit overwhelming, aren't they? I remember my impression of them the first time I came here."

"You mean you aren't from Colorado?"

Sally laughed. "Heavens no. I'm not sure anyone is actually from Colorado. But once I got here I became so attached this is truly my home now, and Boston seems just like a place I have visited. Of course, I've visited New York as well, so I know what a tremendous difference it is for you."

"Monte told me about Malcolm's welcoming committee at the depot," Smoke said.

"Welcoming committee?" Sally asked.

"A couple of the Frenchman's cowboys decided to roust him. One of them took his hat and dared him to take it back."

"Oh, that's awful."

Smoke laughed. "Not so awful. Malcolm took it back." Smoke looked back at Malcolm. "Monte said you pack quite a punch."

"I was a professional fighter for a while," Malcolm said.

"Ha! I thought it might be something like that. It's good to be able to take care of yourself, but be careful where and how you use that skill. No matter how good you are with your fists, they're no match for a gun. And I'm sure you have noticed just about everyone out here carries a gun."

"Yes, I have noticed. But I'm not good with a gun." Malcolm chuckled. "The truth is, I've never even fired one."

"We'll take care of that soon enough." Smoke turned to Sally. "Have we got anything to feed our guest?"

"Smoke, have I ever turned anyone away?" Sally replied.

Smoke smiled. "No, you haven't. And, shamelessly, I have taken advantage of that."

"Shamelessly," Sally said, returning Smoke's smile.

"What's for supper?"

"How about fried ham? And I'll fry some potatoes and scramble some eggs in with them."

"And biscuits?" Smoke asked.

"Of course."

"Sounds good."

Long Trek

Templeton knocked on the door of the big house and heard Garneau call from inside.

"*Entrez.*"

Templeton went inside. He saw that Garneau had a large piece of paper spread out on the dining room table.

"Come, I want you to see this," Garneau invited. A very detailed map had been drawn on newsprint he had gotten from the *Big Rock Journal.*

"I wondered what you wanted with that big piece of paper," Templeton said.

"Here," Garneau said, pointing at the map, "is Sugarloaf. And here is Long Trek. Here is Carro de Bancada."

"Yeah, Puddle's nephew has come to take it. But I'll bet you can buy him out cheap. He's some Eastern dude who doesn't know a thing about ranching."

"That may be true," Garneau said. "But one thing I learned at St. Cyr is a good officer is always prepared for any contingency. Suppose he doesn't want to sell to me?"

"I don't think it would take much to convince him to sell."

"I am told he has befriended Smoke Jensen."

"Yeah, that's what I've heard as well," Templeton said.

"Smoke Jensen is a formidable adversary. After all, he killed Willard, the three men who came to join us, the two men you set to ambush him, and Nixon, Curtis, and Noble."

"He is just one man."

"Just one man who has already dispatched nine men. Also, he is quite obviously a leader. What if he gathers the other *paysans* into an organized resistance?

"What would he have if he did do that? They are nothing but a bunch of pig farmers and small ranchers who couldn't fight their way out of a paper bag."

"I studied your Civil War while I was at St. Cyr. Most of both armies were made up of farmers, ranchers, merchants, and mechanics. As Euripides once said, 'Ten men wisely led will beat a hundred without a head.' I wouldn't dismiss them so readily."

"All right. So what should we do?"

"We are going to form an army," Garneau said. "Turn out every man. I will speak with them."

Dressed in the uniform of a French colonel of cavalry, Garneau stood before every man who worked for him, cowboys and the gunmen Templeton had recruited. "Starting today, I am doubling the salary of everyone who works for me."

The men cheered and patted each on the shoulders.

Garneau let them express their joy for a moment, then he held his hands up to call for quiet. "You will earn that money."

The cheering stopped, and the men looked at him in curiosity.

"You may be wondering about the clothes I am wearing. This"—he took himself in with a small sweep of his hand, "is the uniform of a colonel of cavalry. I fought, honorably, in the Franco-Prussian War, and I am quite comfortable with command. You may look at me as your commanding officer because, starting today, we are going to become an army."

"We're goin' to become what?" Curly Roper asked.

"An army," Garneau said. "And an army demands discipline. Let us begin by lining up in formation. Capitaine Templeton, you will be my second in command."

"Yes, sir," Templeton said with a big smile.

"Briggs, Mathis, Carr, you three will be my sergeants. The rest of you men will take your orders from them, as they will take their orders from me."

"Why are you doin' this, Colonel?" Hoyt Miller asked.

"Because, Mr. Miller, I am trying to build something here, something grand and unique. I am building a cattle empire, and like any empire, we have made enemies and, no doubt, we will make more enemies in the future. In addition, this is not the kind of empire that can survive merely by staying in place. We must grow, and the only way we can grow is if we convince the small ranchers in the valley to sell out to me. Quite frankly, gentlemen, we must convince them to sell at a price that is right for me. That is going to take some persuasion, the kind of persuasion that must be backed by use of arms, if necessary."

"Colonel, it sounds to me like you are talking about a war, here," Miller said. "I didn't sign on to go to war. If I wanted to do that, I'd join the army and go fight the Injuns."

"Miller, do you know how much a private makes in the army?" Templeton asked.

"I ain't got no idea," Miller replied.

"Sir," Garneau said.

"What?" Miller asked.

"When you speak to Capitaine Templeton, or to me, you will say sir."

"Thank you, Colonel," Templeton said. "Miller, for your information, a private in the army makes thirteen dollars a month. Most cowboys work for twenty dollars a month and found. Because of the colonel's generous raise today, you will be getting sixty dollars a month. You don't have to pay for where you sleep at night, and you don't have to pay for your food. That means you have sixty dollars you can use any way you want."

"I'm going to be spending my money on the girls at the Brown Dirt," someone said, and the others laughed.

"You'll be making four and a half times more money working for the Long Trek than you would make in the army. Do you really want to go join the army?"

"No, I guess not."

Over the next several days, the ranch was alive with the sound of repeated gunfire, the echoes rolling back from the nearby mountains to double the intensity. Someone not aware of what it was, might have thought a battle was taking place, when in fact, it was nothing of the sort. Templeton stood beside Garneau as they watched their "army" train. The Frenchman had organized his men into three squads of nine, plus the "sergeants" he had put in command of each squad. Briggs, Mathis, and Carr were skilled gunmen, and they were conducting shooting exercises for the other men.

"How do you think they are doing?" Garneau asked.

"Some are doing better than others," Templeton replied.

"Yes, that is always the case when any army is trained."

"Colonel, I have a suggestion. That is, if you care to hear it."

"I would be a poor commander indeed if I refused to listen to a suggestion from my second in command."

"Jensen has two men who work for him, and one of them is almost as good with a gun as Jensen is. Fact is, he used to be a gunman himself. The other one isn't quite as good, but he is good enough that, if they joined Jensen, it could cause us some trouble. I think we should take care of them before we start anything."

"Who are these men?"

"Pearlie, and Cal Wood."

"Why haven't I heard of them? I've been here for over six months and I've never heard of either one of them. Shouldn't I have heard of them by now?"

"They've spent near on to a year now in Denver. It seems Jensen has started a slaughterhouse there, and Pearlie and Cal Wood are running it."

"If they are in Denver, then they are of no concern to us," Garneau said.

Templeton shook his head. "No, sir, that's not quite true. If they ever get the idea Jensen is in trouble, they'll be back here faster than a duck can jump on a June bug."

"How do you propose to take care of them?"

"I think we should send someone to Denver," Templeton said.

"Who do you suggest? If they are as good as you say they are I don't think any of our men would be a match for them, except possibly Mathis, Briggs, or Carr. And I don't want to send them right now. They are too valuable in training the others."

"If we put out a reward on Jensen's men, we won't have to send any of our men. Someone out there will do it for us."

"How much of a reward do you think I should post?"

"A thousand dollars ought to do it."

"And how am I to do this? I can't very well go to the newspaper office and have them print up reward posters for me."

"You won't need to," Templeton said. "All we have to do is put out the word. It'll spread all over, believe me."

"Very well. Put out the word that I will pay one thousand dollars to anyone who kills Cal Wood and Pearlie . . . Pearlie what? What is his last name?"

"I don't know."

"I can't put out a reward on someone if I don't know who we are looking for, can I?"

"Let me ask you this, Colonel. How many men do you think are named Pearlie?"

Garneau laughed.

"If you've got no objection to it, I'll start puttin' out the word."

"By all means, put out the word."

CHAPTER NINETEEN

Sugarloaf

Long Trek wasn't the only place where training was taking place.

It was going on at Sugarloaf as well, though there were only three people participating in the exercise, compared to the thirty-two men undergoing military instruction at Long Trek. Smoke and Sally were the trainers. Malcolm Puddle was the one being trained.

Smoke handed Malcolm a loaded pistol, then pointed to one of several tin cans sitting on a fence. "See if you can hit that can."

Malcolm raised the pistol then closed one eye and squinted down the barrel.

"No, don't raise your pistol to eye level and try to aim it," Smoke said. "In a fight, you won't have time to do that."

"How am I supposed to aim, if I don't sight down the barrel?" Malcolm asked.

"Do it kinesthetically," Sally suggested.

"I beg your pardon. Do it how?"

"You are a boxer, right?"

"Yes."

"When you throw a punch, do you raise your fist to your eyes and aim it?"

Malcolm laughed. "No."

"What do you do?"

"Well, I just sort of feel where the . . . oh! I think I see what you are talking about. You're saying I should just sense where I'm shooting."

"Yes."

"But that's not the same thing as hitting someone with your fists."

Smoke laughed. "Sure it is. It turns out that I've been shooting kinesthetically all along, but I didn't know it until Sally told me that's what I was doing."

"But can you really hit something that way?"

"Watch." Sally nodded at Smoke, and he turned his back. She picked up two bottles and gave one to Malcolm, while keeping the other. Then, silently, she indicated to Malcolm he should toss the bottle into the air. They launched both bottles at the same time.

"Now, Smoke," Sally said calmly.

Faster than Malcolm would have believed possible, Smoke whirled around, drawing his pistol as he did so. He shot twice, the bang of the two shots so close together the young man would have thought he fired only once, had not both bottles been broken.

"Wow, kinesthetically," Malcolm said.

"Does that answer your question as to whether you can actually hit anything that way?" Sally asked.

"Lord," Malcolm said. "If everyone out here can shoot like that, I would be an idiot to actually get into a gunfight with anyone."

"Trust me, not everyone can shoot like my Smoke," Sally said proudly.

"Try it," Smoke said.

Malcolm fired, but the tin cans stayed in place.

"It's not hard." Sally fired from her waist, knocking one of the tin cans off the fence.

"I thought you said everyone couldn't shoot like that."

"Sally's just showing off," Smoke said. "But she's a better shot than ninety-nine percent of the people you will meet out here."

"I thought you said you were from Boston."

"I am."

"Well, I know you didn't learn to shoot like that in Boston."

"I didn't. I came out here to teach school. I didn't learn to shoot like that until Smoke taught me."

"You taught her?"

"I did."

Malcolm smiled. "You must be a good teacher. Maybe there is hope for me." He fired again, and missed again.

"Maybe," Smoke teased. "But don't count on it."

"Smoke!" Sally scolded. "Don't talk like that. You know I couldn't hit anything when you first started teaching me. And I'm not the only one. Look at Matt. He's as good as you."

"Maybe better," Smoke said.

"Who is Matt?"

"Matt Jensen is a young man Smoke raised," Sally said without any further explanation.

Malcolm fired again, continuing to fire until the pistol was out of bullets.

"Here," Smoke said. "Reload and fire again."

"Are you sure I'm not just wasting your ammunition?"

"It's not exactly a waste. Even though you aren't hitting anything yet, you are getting a feel for the gun. And that is important."

Malcolm emptied the pistol two more times, then after reloading, he hit one of the cans with his first shot. "I hit it!" he yelled excitedly.

"Can you do it again?"

"I don't know. That may have just been luck."

"No," Smoke said. "It wasn't luck. Look at the can, then feel the pistol lining up with it."

"Kinesthetically," Malcolm said.

"Kinesthetically," Smoke agreed.

Malcolm stared at the can, then "felt" the pistol lining up with it, and pulled the trigger. The can flew off the post.

"Wow!" Malcolm said. "I can't believe it!"

He shot four more times, hitting two more cans. The next time he reloaded, he hit five out of six cans.

"I'm beginning to get the feel for this now," he said.

"Don't lose the feel. We'll do some more shooting tomorrow," Smoke said. "But now, I promised Sally we would go into town. Johnny McVey is giving a piano concert at the Reasoner Theater."

"Who is Johnny McVey?"

"He's one of the bartenders at Longmont's," Smoke said, as if that statement needed no further explanation.

Smoke, Sally, and Malcolm rode into town, then stopped in front of Lambert's, a restaurant, which proudly boasted it was the home of tossed rolls.

"What is a tossed roll?" Malcolm asked.

"You'll see," Sally said with a grin as they dismounted.

"Who wants a hot roll?" someone shouted as soon as they stepped in through the door.

"Here!"

Malcolm saw someone throw a roll, and it sailed across the room, caught by someone at one of the tables. No sooner had the three of them taken their table, than three rolls came flying toward them. Throughout the meal the rolls were tossed around, and there was a great deal of shouting and laughing.

"What do you think of the place?" Smoke asked.

"It's . . . interesting," Malcolm said.

"We have three restaurants in town, and since we have a population of less than five hundred there's no way all three could survive unless each of them carved out their own niche," Sally said. "This one is sort of a participatory restaurant, with tossed rolls and all the interplay between the waiters and the customers. The City Pig specializes in barbeque beef, pork, and chicken. But my personal favorite is Delmonico's."

"Delmonico's? There is a restaurant by that name in New York."

Smoke chuckled. "And in half the towns of the West, all of them trying to emulate their New York namesake."

"And while our Delmonico's isn't as large or as grand as the one on fifty-six Beaver Street, it does feature the finest cuisine in town . . . if not in the entire valley," Sally said.

After dinner they rode together to the Reasoner Theater to attend the concert.

"Smoke, did you say the pianist tonight is a bartender?"

"Yes. He tends bar for Louis Longmont."

"Is he a good pianist?"

"I've never heard him play, but Louis has. He is the one who set up the concert. Louis wouldn't do that unless he thought McVey was good enough."

"Good evening Monsieur and Madame Jensen."

"Mr. Garneau," Smoke replied.

"The gentleman with you?"

"This is your neighbor, Malcolm Puddle," Smoke said.

"Monsieur Puddle, please allow me to express my

sympathy to you for the loss of your uncle. It was a tragic thing."

"Yes, it was," Malcolm said.

"I would like to call on you sometime soon, neighbor to neighbor," Garneau said.

Malcolm nodded.

"Come, before all the good seats are taken," Sally said.

"Good evening to you, sir," Malcolm said with a nod of his head as he joined Smoke and Sally.

Inside, the theater was illuminated only enough to allow the audience to find their seats. The stage was bare except for the piano, and it was held in a spotlight from a carbon arc lamp.

Two hundred people filled the Reasoner Theater to hear the bartender give his first concert. The audience applauded as Johnny McVey walked out onto the stage. He looked nothing like the man who dispensed drinks in Louis Longmont's establishment. He was wearing a white shirt and black bow tie, a formal black jacket with tails, striped pants, and a black cummerbund. He approached the piano bench, flipped the tails back from his swallow-coat, and took his seat at the piano.

The auditorium grew quiet as McVey sat before the keyboard for a long moment as if composing himself. Then he began to play Beethoven's Piano Sonata no. 26 in E-flat major ("Les Adieux"), and the music spilled out into the theater, caressing the collective soul of the audience.

Sally reached over to put her hand in Smoke's, and

as he looked toward her he saw tears in her eyes as she was reacting to the beauty of the music.

Smoke thought of the incongruity of the moment. There on stage was a man whose skilled hands upon the keyboard were filling the theater with beautiful music. And yet, but a short time ago, those same hands were holding a double-barrel shotgun and threatening to kill, if necessary, three men.

But, it was easy enough to put that image out of his head so, like Sally, he could enjoy the music.

The next day, the *Big Rock Journal* carried a story of the concert performed by Johnny McVey on the night before.

Wonderful Concert

JOHNNY MCVEY DISPLAYS
HIS VIRTUOSITY ON THE PIANO

To the patrons of Longmont's Saloon, Johnny McVey may appear to be nothing more than a bartender. And though he is a bartender par excellence, last night he proved to the citizens of Big Rock that he is much more.

Johnny McVey is a pianist of the first order. Performing on stage in the Reasoner Theater last night, he held the audience spellbound. It was a magical display, and with his skill he managed to resurrect the genius of the composer so that, to the listening audience, Johnny McVey and Ludwig Beethoven were one and the same.

Citizens of Big Rock know the Reasoner Theater is the scene for good entertainment, from the classical music prowess of Mr. McVey, to the elocutions of learned men and women, to the presentation of the latest plays, performed by traveling troupes of actors. Every citizen owes a degree of debt to Mr. James Reasoner for having the foresight to build his theater in Big Rock.

CHAPTER TWENTY

Denver

Jack Emerson was at Nippy Jones' Saloon, having a drink with Bud Lane, when Lane told him something he had just learned. "I know someone who will pay a thousand dollars to anyone who can do a certain job for him."

Emerson frowned. "A thousand dollars? That's a lot of money."

"I reckon it is, but I ain't about to try and collect it. In the first place, it's blood money."

"What do you mean, blood money?"

"Just what I'm asayin'. They's two men here in Denver this feller wants dead."

"Who is it? And who is wantin' 'em dead?"

"The two men the feller is wantin' kilt is named Pearlie and Cal. They're workin' over at the abattoir, runnin' it for Smoke Jensen. And as far as who it is that's awantin' 'em kilt, it's Deekus Templeton."

"Deekus Templeton?"

"Yes."

"Do you know him?"

"Yeah, I know him." Lane looked around the saloon to make certain he couldn't be overheard before he made the next comment. "Me 'n him pulled a job together once. We held up a stagecoach up in Wyoming. Got twenty-five hundred dollars."

"Can this Templeton be trusted to pay off?"

"Well yeah, I reckon he can, but Jack, don't tell me you're actually thinkin' about doin' it."

"A thousand dollars is a lot of money. If I could be sure this Templeton person would actually pay off . . ."

"Well, I'll tell you this. I know where to find him. I expect you could persuade him to pay off . . . if you know what I mean."

"Yeah," Emerson said with a smile. "Yeah, I know what you mean."

Armed with the information about the reward money being paid to anyone who killed a couple men named Pearlie and Cal Wood, Emerson contacted Nelson Battle.

"Who wants 'em dead, and why?" Battle asked.

"I'm told it's a man named Deekus Templeton who wants 'em dead. I don't know why, and I don't care. All I know is, he's payin' a thousand dollars for it."

"A thousand dollars? That's good money," Battle said.

"You're damn right it's good money."

"Do you know this man, Templeton? Can he be trusted?"

"I don't know him, but I know Bud Lane, and I trust him. He knows Templeton, and says he will pay off."

"These two men we're supposed to kill. Do you know how to find 'em?" Battle asked.

"Not hard to find 'em. They're right in Denver, runnin' the Jensen abattoir."

"How are we going to do it? You got 'ny ideas?" Battle asked.

"Oh, yeah. I've got it all planned out," Emerson said. "We're going to go see 'em and let on like we are cattlemen. We want to run some of our cows through there. We'll invite them out to supper, then, when they don't suspect anything, we'll kill 'em."

"Yeah," Battle said. "That sounds like a good idea. It'll be the easiest five hunnert dollars I ever made."

The abattoir was easy to find. It was adjacent to a big railroad marshalling yard and at least five thousand cattle were penned up outside the buildings that made up the complex. One building was where the cows were led in, one at a time, then maneuvered down a narrow chute until they reached a place where they could go no farther. A powerfully built shirtless man stood on a platform just above the animal. Once the animal was in place, he used a sledgehammer to strike it a mighty blow between the eyes. Almost instantly a tackle and pulley arrangement lifted the dead steer up, and it travelled down an overhead steam-operated conveyor track as men removed the hide, head, and feet. By the time the steer reached the end of the conveyor track the denuded carcass had already been split into two halves. Those halves were then sent into the next building where they were packed in ice, awaiting shipment by refrigerated cars to markets back east.

In front of the building, Emerson approached a man in a long white coat spotted with blood. "I'm looking for two men, Pearlie and Cal. Could you tell me where I might find them?"

"Pearlie and Cal? You'll find them both back there," the man said, pointing to two who were standing at the back of the building, watching the operation.

Emerson and Battle walked toward them.

"I thought this Pearlie feller was supposed to be a gunman," Battle said. "There ain't neither one of 'em even wearin' a gun."

Emerson smiled. "We'll try and keep 'em that way."

"We've been here for over six months now. How long do we have to stay here and watch over this business?" Cal asked.

"Smoke said we wouldn't be here forever. Just until the operation is goin' smooth. Then he'll hire someone to manage it," Pearlie replied. "He wants us here until everything is going well, and I figure we owe him that much. Don't you?"

"Yeah, I guess so. But I don't mind tellin' you, this place is beginnin' to give me the willies," Cal said.

"What do you mean, give you the willies?"

"Well, think about it, Pearlie. What have we done our whole lives but take care of cows? We feed 'em, we make sure they have water, we keep the wolves and big cats away from 'em. We protect them.

"And now what are we doing? We're leadin' 'em down a long chute to slaughter. And because we've took care of 'em for their entire lives, they trust us. They go along, thinkin' ever'thing is goin' to be just fine, then, *bam!*" Cal hit himself in the forehead with the heel of his palm. "We kill 'em! It just don't seem right to me, is all. It's like we're double-crossing them or something. I can see it in their eyes."

"Cal, you eat steak, don't you? Roast beef?"

"Well, yeah, I eat it."

"Where do you think it comes from?"

"I know it comes from cows . . ."

"Cows that we have taken care of for all their lives," Pearlie said.

"Yeah," Cal said. "Well, if you put it like that, I guess you're right. But it still gives me the willies, killin' 'em like that. I mean, when they are so trustin' an' all."

"I wonder what these men want." Pearlie said, looking toward the two men who were approaching. "Yes, sir, can we help you gentlemen?"

"We were told you two men are in charge here."

"That's right."

"We're cattlemen from up in Wyoming. Always before, we've shipped our cattle back to the eastern markets while they're still on the hoof. But I've been told the best way to do it now, is to get them processed here first."

"Yes, sir, that is the absolute truth of it. Doin' it this way brings you about a ten percent higher profit," Pearlie said.

"My name is Emerson, this is Battle. I wonder if we could buy you two gentlemen supper tonight and talk about bringing our cattle here?"

"You don't have to buy our supper just to do business with us," Pearlie said.

"But you are welcome to," Cal added quickly.

"Great!" Emerson said. "Suppose we meet you at Little Man's Restaurant at nine o'clock tonight."

"Nine o'clock?" Cal said. "Ain't that awful late to be eatin' supper?"

"Unfortunately that's the earliest we can do it," Emerson said. "I'm afraid we have some other business to take care of, first."

"Are you sure you want to meet at Little Man's?" Pearlie asked. "That's way on the other side of the marshalling yard. I know a lot of the yard workers take their breakfast and lunch there, but I've never known anyone to eat supper there. I'm not sure it's even open for supper."

"Oh yes, it's open. We've eaten there several times since we came down here. They set a fine supper table," Emerson said.

"All right," Pearlie said. "Little Man's at nine o'clock. We'll see you then.

Because they were staying in Denver for an extended period of time, Pearlie and Cal had rented a small house. That evening both men took a bath then got dressed in what Cal called their "business" suits.

"This is another thing I don't like about bein' here," Cal said as he pulled his shirt collar away from his neck. "We have to get all dressed up like some sort of dandy. Why couldn't we just wear regular clothes?"

"These are regular clothes for businessmen," Pearlie said.

"Yeah, well, I ain't a business man. I'm a cowboy. And what I want to know is, why this business of eating supper so late? Who eats supper when it's so dark you can't see ten feet in front of you?"

Pearlie chuckled. "I think the high toned people eat their supper real late, only they don't call it supper, they call it dinner."

"Ha. Dinner is what you have in the middle of the day," Cal said.

"You ready to go?" Pearlie asked.

"Ready. I've starving to death here, and you ask me if I'm ready to go eat."

The two men reached the front door, then Pearlie stopped and stretched out his hand to stop Cal. "Hold it."

"What?"

"I don't know. I've got a funny feeling about this."

"I've got a funny feeling too, only it's a big hollow space in the pit of my stomach. It's called being hungry."

"Wait a minute." Pearlie started back toward his bedroom.

"Where are you going?"

"To get my gun. I think you should get yours too."

"Why?"

"Just do it, Cal. I told you, I've got a funny feeling. I can't explain it, but I don't like it. I don't like it one bit."

"All right. You're the old man here. If you got a feeling, who am I to argue with you?"

The two men returned to their respective rooms, then met a moment later at the front door, both of them armed.

Little Man's was about a half mile from their cabin, on the other side of a large, crisscrossing network of tracks. It wasn't convenient to ride horses over this ground. The elevated tracks, the rails, and even the gravel and ballast could injure a horse in the middle of the night. They started across the marshalling yard, their feet making crunching sounds as they walked across the ballast and coal clinkers strewn about. In addition to the sound of their footfalls, they could hear the switch engines in the yard, making up freight trains for dispatch.

"Damn, it's dark out here," Cal said.

"Yeah, it is."

"Pearlie? You know that funny feeling you had?"

"Yes."

"Well, I've got it too. What do you say we just turn around and go back toward town?"

"I thought you were hungry."

"I am hungry. But we can stop at the first café we see."

The sound of one of the switch engines grew louder as it approached. Passing them, the headlamp threw a beam ahead, and in the beam they could see, for just a moment, the little building that housed Little Man's Restaurant. Then the train came between them and the building, so until all the cars passed, they could see nothing.

"Did you see the restaurant building?" Cal asked.

"Yeah, I saw it."

"Did it look like it had any lights on?"

"No, it didn't."

"There is something funny about this, Pearlie, like you said. And I don't like it. I don't like it at all."

The train cleared then, and no sooner had the train cleared, than a couple muzzle flashes lit up the night. One bullet hit a rail, sending up sparks, then ricocheted off into the night, screaming as it did so. A second bullet popped by Pearlie's ear, coming so close he felt the air pressure of its passing.

"Get down!" Pearlie shouted, and he and Cal leaped over to the opposite side of the railroad track, getting down behind the berm.

"Who is shooting at us?" Cal asked.

"I have a pretty good idea who," Pearlie said. "What I don't know is why."

From a distant part of the yard, they could hear another switch engine, working the cars.

"Emerson, is that you?" Pearlie asked.

"Oh, you figured that out, did you?"

"What do you want? Are you planning on robbing us? Just how much money do you think people like us would be carrying, anyway?"

"Oh, it isn't what you are carrying," Emerson replied. "It's what you are worth to us dead—a thousand dollars."

"What are you talking about? Neither of us is worth a cent. There's no paper out on us. You aren't going to collect a cent from the law."

"It ain't the law that's payin'," Emerson said.

"What? Who is paying?"

"What does that matter to you? You'll be dead."

"What makes you think we'll be dead?"

"Because Battle and I are going to kill you." Emerson laughed. "I'll just bet you didn't bring your pistols with you, did you? I mean, going to a nice business supper and all. Why would you?"

Pearlie was quiet for a long moment, then, almost hesitantly, he said. "Uh, yeah, we did. We brought our guns."

Emerson laughed again. "I'm sure you did. I'll tell you what. Just to show you what kind of men we are, we'll kill both of you real quick. You won't feel a thing."

A second train came by then, and once again Pearlie and Cal were separated from Emerson and Battle by the passing of a long line of freight cars.

"Cal," Pearlie said, standing up. "Let's jump on this train."

Cal stood as well, and running alongside the moving cars until they matched its speed, Pearlie jumped in through the open side door of one of the boxcars. Then reaching down to grab Cal's hand, he pulled him in.

"Thanks," Cal said, breathing hard from the exertion.

* * *

Battle, come on!" Emerson said. "I just seen 'em jump onto this train!"

Moving quickly, Emerson and Battle jumped onto the train and climbed to the top. That way, they would be able to see when Pearlie and Cal jumped off the train. They squatted down and waited as the train proceeded some distance, then stopped, preparatory to backing the assembled cars onto a sidetrack.

"Let's get out here," Pearlie said, and he and Cal jumped down from the train.

"Where do you reckon they are?" Cal asked.

"Half a mile away by now," Pearlie answered.

No sooner had Pearlie spoken, than Cal let out a sharp exclamation of pain. Concurrent with Cal's shout was the sound of a gunshot.

"Where are you hit?" Pearlie yelled.

"In the arm."

There was a second gunshot and Pearlie saw the muzzle flash coming from the top of one of the boxcars. When the flash receded, he saw two men standing there.

"There they are!" Cal shouted, having spotted them at the same time.

"Yeah, I see 'em." Pearlie fired twice, and had the satisfaction of seeing both men tumble from the top of the car. Gun at the ready, he ran to them. It was his hope they would still be alive so he could learn who had put a reward on Cal and him, and even more important, why?

He didn't get the opportunity to ask those questions, though. When he reached them, both were dead.

Pearlie ran back to Cal. "You were hit. How bad is it?"

"I think it was more of a crease than anything. I've felt around and I don't feel a hole in my arm. Are they dead?"

"Yeah, both of 'em."

"Who do you think wanted us dead? And why?" Cal asked.

"Cal, my friend, I don't have the slightest idea."

CHAPTER TWENTY-ONE

Sugarloaf

Smoke was currying his horse when Eddie, the young Western Union messenger, rode up. He didn't see the rancher and headed directly for the house.

Smoke called out to him. "Eddie, are you looking for me?"

"Yes, sir, Mr. Jensen, I am. I have a telegram for you."

Smoke washed his hands in a basin, dried them, then walked out to retrieve the telegram.

"It's from Pearlie," Eddie said.

"I hope there's no problem at the plant." Smoke gave Eddie a quarter, then read the message.

ME AND CAL ATTACKED BY TWO HIRED KILLERS
LAST NIGHT STOP CAL WOUNDED SLIGHTLY STOP
KILLERS DEAD STOP NOT KNOWN WHO HIRED
THEM STOP PEARLIE

"Johnny wants to know if you want to send a message back," Eddie said.

"Yes, I do. Come on in. I'll get it ready."

"Yes, sir," Eddie replied. He followed Smoke into the house.

Sally had just baked a batch of cookies and they were cooling on the table. "What is it about men? Do you have some sort of secret sense that tells you when there are cookies available?"

"Oh, no ma'am. Nothin' like that," Eddie said.

Sally chuckled. "Help yourself."

"Thank you," Eddie replied, grabbing one of the cookies. It was still so hot he had to toss it from hand to hand for a second until it was cooled.

Smoke sat down at the table to compose the return telegram.

"Smoke, what is it?" Sally asked, concerned by the expression on his face.

"Someone tried to kill Pearlie and Cal last night. Cal is hurt."

"Oh, Smoke! No! How badly?"

"It's hard to tell. Pearlie says it isn't bad, but he would probably say that anyway, just to keep us from worrying about it."

"What if the men try again?"

"They won't."

Sally frowned. "How do you know they won't?"

"Because, according to Pearlie, they are dead."

"Oh, well, thank goodness for that. At least Cal and Pearlie are out of danger."

"Maybe not," Smoke replied. "According to the

telegram, someone was paying the men to kill them. Whoever that was is likely to try again."

"But why, for heaven's sake? Who would want to kill Pearlie and Cal?"

"That's what I'd like to know. I'm going to bring them both back home."

"Who will run the abattoir operation for you?"

"Mr. Evans is about ready to take over. I'll just have to trust that he's ready."

Smoke wrote the message. *Turn operation over to Lloyd Evans. Return home now. Smoke.*

"Here you go, Eddie." He gave him the message, money to send it, plus a tip.

"Thanks, Mr. Jensen. I'll see that it gets sent right away."

Palmilla, New Mexico Territory

In a sane world, a world where size and strength meant something, Jeremiah Priest would be someone you would pass on the street with hardly a second glance. He was a small man, barely five feet four inches, very thin, with a prominent Adam's apple, a nose that seemed too large for his face, thinning blond hair, and pale blue eyes.

But the world Priest occupied wasn't sane. He was a shootist, a gunman whose draw was greased lightning and whose marksmanship was deadly accurate. Once people heard his name and associated the unimpressive looking man to the reputation he had acquired, even the biggest and strongest man quaked in his boots.

Priest stepped out of the sunshine and into the Pair of Aces Saloon. It was quite busy, but he found a quiet place by the end of the bar. He ordered a beer, then nursed it as he studied the dark haired, dark eyed man at the other end of the bar. A full mustache curved around his mouth like the horns on a Texas steer. He was leaning against the bar with his fingers wrapped around a shot glass.

The man was Coleman Wesley, a bounty hunter who made a good living by chasing down wanted criminals. He turned them over to the law belly down across the saddle as often as they were upright. Wesley was deadly fast with a gun, and in all the outlaw camps and hideouts, his name was brought up as someone whose path you never wanted to cross.

So far, Wesley hadn't noticed the gunman, and probably wouldn't have recognized him if he had. But he would know the name. Jeremiah Priest was a man who hired his gun out for money . . . a great deal of money.

"Mr. Wesley," Priest called.

Wesley didn't look around.

"Wesley! I'm talking to you!" Priest called again. His voice was loud and authoritative, and everyone in the saloon recognized the challenge in its timbre. For a moment, all conversations ceased. Then the drinkers, seeing that Coleman Wesley had been challenged by a little pipsqueak of a man, laughed.

Wesley looked up from his whiskey. "What do you want, little man?"

"I want to kill you," Priest said easily.

There was a universal gasp of surprise. Nobody recognized Priest, but nearly all knew Wesley, and they wondered who would be foolish enough to brace him.

"And why would you want to kill me?" Wesley asked without the slightest hint of apprehension.

"Because I'm being paid to," Priest replied as if that explained everything.

"Who is paying you?"

"Why do you want to know?"

Wesley tossed his drink down. "Because after I kill you, I'm going to kill whoever hired you."

"Don't worry about it. You aren't going to kill me."

For the first time, Wesley began to show a little emotion. Who was this little man who had challenged him with so little regard as to the bounty hunter's reputation?

Everyone moved away from the bar. Even the bartender left his position behind the bar and joined the others gathered against the back wall, as far away as they could get within the confines of the saloon.

The long moment of absolute silence was broken only by the loud tick-tock of the Regulator clock that hung from the wall, just above the piano. Several glanced toward it to fix in their minds the exact time they watched Wesley kill the insolent stranger.

Two men came in through the batwing doors.

"So I told Johnson, you've done bought back the

same horse you sold last month," one of them said, and both laughed.

They started toward the bar but stopped when they saw that the bar was completely empty except for the two men who were staring at each other. Everyone else in the saloon was standing as far back from the bar as they could. Nobody was sitting at a table, and nobody was talking.

The new customers looked at each other. "What the hell is going on?" one asked.

"I don't know," the other hissed. "But I'm not goin' to get in the way."

They joined the other saloon patrons standing against the back wall.

"Mister, if you walk out of this saloon right now, I'll let you live." Wesley smiled, though it wasn't a smile of humor. "You can tell everyone you know that you once braced Coleman Wesley and lived."

"Now, why would I want to do that?" Priest wiped the foam from his lips with the back of his hand.

"I didn't figure you'd take my offer, but I thought I'd give you one last chance."

Priest set his beer mug down, then stepped away from the bar. He flipped his duster back so his gun was exposed. He was wearing it low, and kicked out, the way a man wears a gun when he knows how to use it. "Are you through talkin', Wesley? Because if you are, I reckon it's about time you and me got this thing settled."

"All right. It's your call." Wesley stepped away from

the bar as well, and like Priest, wore his gun low and kicked out.

"What might your name be, mister?" Wesley asked. "We'll need it for the undertaker to carve into your headstone."

The gunman smiled at him. "The name is Priest. Jeremiah Priest."

Again, there was a gasp from those in the saloon. While few knew what the notorious gunman looked like, many had heard of him. A recent newspaper article had called him "the deadliest gunman in the West."

Wesley's face, which had been coldly impassive, suddenly grew animated. His skin whitened and a line of perspiration beads broke out on his upper lip.

The bounty hunter had been in shoot-outs before and he was fast. Maybe fast enough, especially if he had the edge of drawing first. Without another word he made his move, pulling his pistol in the blink of an eye.

But Priest, whether reacting to Wesley's draw or anticipating it, had his own pistol out just a split-second faster, pulling the hammer back and firing in one fluid motion. In the close confines of the barroom, the gunshot sounded like a clap of thunder.

Wesley didn't even get a shot off. The bullet from Priest's pistol hit him in the middle of the chest, slamming him back against the bar before he fell. His unfired pistol clattered to the floor.

* * *

The hearing lasted less than an hour. There was no shortage of witnesses willing to testify, enjoying their proximity to such an event. All testified that it was a fair fight. Some even said they believed Wesley started his draw first. No charges were filed, as it was a case of justifiable homicide, justifiable by reason of self-defense.

CHAPTER TWENTY-TWO

Carro de Bancada

Malcolm was pumping water when two men came riding up toward him. He recognized one of them as Garneau, but he had never seen the other one. Although their presence made him a bit nervous, especially as he wasn't wearing his pistol, he smiled at them in order to maintain his composure. "Hello, gentlemen," he said by way of greeting. "Colonel Garneau." He looked at the other rider. "And I'm sorry, sir, but I've never had the pleasure of meeting you."

"The name is Templeton. Deekus Templeton," the other rider said in a gruff voice."

"Well, climb down from your horses. I'm about to make some lemonade. Why don't you come in out of the sun?"

Garneau and Templeton followed Malcolm into the house. It still reflected Humboldt Puddle's personality . . . the unit flag of the First Sharpshooter Regiment, to which Puddle belonged, framed photographs of his parents, who were Malcolm's grandparents, and antlers and game heads he had taken in hunts all hung on the walls. A dining table and chairs Humboldt had built with his own hands still sat in the kitchen.

Malcolm had squeezed the lemon and mixed it with sugar earlier. He added cool water, stirred it, and the lemonade was done. He poured three glasses, then gave a glass to each of his visitors.

"Merci," Garneau said, taking the glass.

"*Vous êtes les bienvenus*," Malcolm replied.

"*Parlez-vous français?*"

"Yes, I speak French. I found that in my old job as shipping clerk, and in dealing with shipments to foreign countries, learning other languages was beneficial to my work."

"I'm impressed," Garneau said. "Did you enjoy the work you were doing? Working as a shipping clerk?"

"Not particularly." Malcolm took another swallow of his lemonade and studied the two men over the rim of his glass. He knew it wasn't just a neighborly visit, and he was pretty sure he knew what they wanted, but he decided to wait and let them bring up the subject.

He didn't have long to wait.

"Monsieur Puddle, how would you like to return to New York with enough money that you could live quite comfortably for several years? You wouldn't have to return to a job that, by your own admission, you don't particularly like."

"And how would I do that?"

"By selling your ranch to me," Garneau said.

Malcolm figured that was what the Frenchman's trip was all about, so he wasn't surprised. He was interested, though, in finding out how much money Garneau was willing to offer him. He remembered Mr. Norton telling him his land and stock were worth about twenty-five thousand dollars. "How much would you offer?"

"Thirty-five thousand dollars," Garneau said without hesitation.

Malcolm spit out the drink of lemonade he'd just taken. "Thirty-five thousand dollars?" he repeated.

"It is a very generous offer," Garneau said.

"It is more than generous," Malcolm replied.

Garneau smiled. "Then, may I conclude that you accept the offer?"

Malcolm thought about it for a moment, remembering Smoke had told him the other ranchers were holding out because his Uncle Humboldt had held out. But, he also knew some of the ranchers who had sold or had been forced off their land wound up getting much less than their properties were worth.

Malcolm looked at Garneau and realized buying Carro de Bancada would give him entrée to the remaining ranchers. "Did you offer my uncle this much money?"

"The offer I made to your uncle was quite generous," Garneau replied.

"And he refused?"

"Yes. He believed he had some obligation to his

neighbors. You, of course, having but recently arrived in the valley, have no such obligation. And, because the amount I am offering you is generous, very generous, I'm sure you are intelligent enough to accept."

"Give me twenty-four hours to consider it," Malcolm replied.

"Twenty-four hours? Why would you need twenty-four hours? Do you not understand that what I have just offered you is much more than this miserable piece of land is worth?"

Malcolm shook his head. "Anything of value is worth exactly what someone is willing to pay for it. The fact that you are offering me thirty-five thousand dollars means this land is worth thirty-five thousand. If it is worth that to you, it is worth that to me."

"Don't be foolish," Garneau said. "If you think by holding out on me I will raise the offer, you are sadly mistaken. Others have made the same mistake, only to ultimately sell to me for much less than my original offer."

"As I said, give me twenty-four hours to consider it," Malcolm repeated.

"Very well. I will give you until exactly this time tomorrow. If you have not made a decision by then, the offer will be withdrawn. Do you understand the consequences of that, Mr. Puddle? It means that you will be losing thirty-five thousand dollars."

Malcolm smiled. "No, I would be losing only ten thousand. I can easily get twenty-five thousand from anyone. And that is twenty-five thousand dollars more than I had last month."

Garneau had taken only a couple swallows from his

lemonade, and he slammed the glass down angrily. "Twenty-four hours, Mr. Puddle. Not one minute longer."

"I understand."

"I'm not sure that you do." Garneau stood up and Templeton followed suit.

Malcolm walked to the front door with them, then watched as they returned to their horses. Templeton had not spoken a word since he first introduced himself. As he mounted his horse, he kept his eyes on the young ranch owner, staring at him with a malevolent intensity.

Malcolm found it disconcerting. He waited until the men left his ranch before he saddled his horse and rode over to report the visit to Smoke.

Long Trek

"I can't believe Puddle would turn that offer down," Garneau said angrily. "Why would he?"

"Maybe he wants to be the hero," Templeton suggested. "His uncle wouldn't sell out, so Malcolm Puddle decides he won't sell out either."

"I have to confess I hadn't counted on that. I was sure he would sell out if I offered him enough."

"We've made a mistake in thinking Malcolm Puddle was the key here," Templeton said.

"What do you mean?"

"There is no way Puddle would turn that money down if he didn't have someone behind him. And that someone is Smoke Jensen. He's your real enemy, not Malcolm Puddle. I think it's time we quit fooling around and get to the center of it. Take care of Smoke Jensen, and you won't have any problems."

"And by take care of, you mean?"

"Kill him," Templeton said.

"We have tried that, remember?"

"We haven't tried it with the right people. To kill someone like Smoke Jensen, we are going to have to hire someone who is even better than he is."

"And just who would that be, I ask you?"

"Jeremiah Priest." Templeton showed Garneau a copy of the *Big Rock Journal*. "You may read about him here."

BY DISPATCH TO THE *JOURNAL*

Deadly Encounter in Palmilla, New Mexico Territory

On the 5th instant, two men known for their skill with the pistol faced each other in a deadly confrontation in the Pair of Aces Saloon. It is not known what precipitated the engagement, but those who witnessed the fight say never have two pistols been so rapidly drawn, for only one to be so effectively engaged.

As in all encounters there must be one who prevails, and one who fails. He who prevailed was Jeremiah Priest, and indeed, Mr. Priest walks among us today. The other participant in this deadly pas de deux was Coleman Wesley, a well-known bounty hunter. Mr. Wesley paid for his unfortunate encounter with Priest by forfeiture of his life,

he being but a split second slower than his
adversary.

It is being said by those who witnessed the
event, that nobody in the country could
match Priest for the quickness of his draw,
and the accuracy of his marksmanship.

Garneau read the article, then looked back up at
Templeton. "And you think this man"—he glanced at
the article again to be sure of his name—"Jeremiah
Priest, can take the measure of Jensen?"

"Yes."

"Then, by all means, make arrangements for him
to come."

"He won't come cheap," Templeton said.

"How much?"

"For someone like Priest? Ten thousand dollars."

"Ten thousand dollars?" Garneau said, the words
exploding from his mouth.

"You were going to pay more than that to Puddle
for his ranch. Without Jensen behind him, you can
probably get it for a couple hundred dollars.

"But still, ten thousand dollars for one man is a lot
of money."

"Colonel, you are relatively new here, so you don't
know all there is to know about Smoke Jensen. You
are going to have to find someone who is good—very
good—to take care of the man. Someone like Jeremiah Priest. And that is going to cost you." Templeton smiled. "But the beauty of it is this; you won't
have to have to pay him one red cent unless he actually completes the job."

"Yes, that's true, isn't it?"

"It is."

"Very well, Monsieur. Find this man, Priest, and secure his services."

Sugarloaf

Smoke was in the tack shed looking over the saddles and harness to determine if he needed to buy any new equipment, when he saw Malcolm come riding up. He stepped to the open door and called out to him. "Malcolm, I'm out here."

Malcolm turned his horse and rode over to the tack shed.

Smoke chuckled. "You did that like a real Westerner."

"Did what?" Malcolm asked as he dismounted.

"The way you rode over here instead of walked." Smoke laughed again. "I once had an old cowboy tell me if God had wanted man to walk, He would have given us four legs."

Malcolm laughed as well.

"What's up?" Smoke asked. "Not that I'm not happy to have you visit, but I expect this is more than a social call."

"It's not exactly a social call. I had a couple visitors today."

"Let me guess. Garneau and Templeton?"

"Yes. They offered to buy me out."

"What was the offer?"

"Thirty-five thousand dollars."

"Thirty-five thousand?" Smoke whistled. "That's a lot of money."

"Yes, sir, it is. Especially considering my whole place, stock included, is worth somewhere around twenty-five thousand."

"What did you tell him?"

"I told him to give me twenty-four hours before I had to give him an answer."

"I see."

"Smoke, like you said, thirty-five thousand dollars is a lot of money."

"Yes, it is. And I don't think anyone would hold it against you, if you sold out to him."

"I would," Malcolm said. "I would hold it against me."

Smoke didn't answer.

"I mean, I should hold out, shouldn't I? Aren't the other farmers and ranchers sort of depending on me to hold out?"

"Malcolm, I can't make up your mind for you," Smoke said. "You have to make up your own mind."

"I . . . I just want to know that I am doing the right thing."

"Whatever you do will be the right thing," Smoke said.

Malcolm chuckled and shook his head. "That's no help."

"Malcolm, let me put it this way. If you decide to sell out and go back to New York, I won't hold any hard feelings toward you. This isn't your world. You were drawn into it through no fault of your own."

"That's true. And with thirty-five thousand dollars

in cash, I could buy a small business in New York. Maybe meet a nice girl, get married, and have a family."

"That's right," Smoke agreed.

"What if I decided to stay here?"

"It could get rough."

"I know."

Smoke smiled. "But you wouldn't have to face it alone. The other ranchers and farmers will be with you"—he paused for a moment—"and so will I."

"All right!" Malcolm said, letting out a loud breath of relief. "That's what I wanted to hear. Tomorrow, when Garneau comes to see me, I'll tell him, *Je vous remercie, mais la réponse est non. Je ne vendrai pas.*"

"What?" Smoke asked, laughing.

"Thank you, but the answer is no. I will not sell," Malcolm translated.

"I'll be there when you tell him. I want to see his face."

CHAPTER TWENTY-THREE

Carro de Bancada

Malcolm had invited his neighbors over for a "get acquainted" potluck dinner. As they arrived, he asked that they park their buggies, buckboards, spring wagons, and horses in the barn so they were out of sight. Smoke put his horse and wagon with the rest. He had come to stand with the young rancher against Garneau.

"I know you may wonder why I asked you to keep your horses and conveyances out of sight," Malcolm said when everyone was gathered in the keeping room. "Yesterday, Lucien Garneau made me an offer for my land. It was a very generous offer. And today he's coming to hear my response to his offer."

The expression on the faces of Malcolm's neighbors indicated their disappointment.

"I am going to tell him no," Malcolm said quickly, before anyone could say anything.

"You're a good man, Malcolm Puddle," Woodward said.

"When he arrives, I want him to be surprised to see you all here. I want him to know the resolve we all have, to keep our land."

"You're damn right!" Keefer said and he and the others applauded.

The meal was served then and, after the meal, the women began cleaning up while the men gathered once more in the keeping room. Cigars were lit and brandy was passed around as they discussed the situation.

"I've heard talk of Garneau putting together an army over at his place," Speer said.

"Why would he do that?" Logan asked.

"For intimidation," Woodward said. "But if we don't allow ourselves to be intimidated, it will fail."

"Here he comes." Smoke chuckled. "And he's not alone."

"Oh, he probably has Mr. Templeton with him," Malcolm said.

"Yes," Smoke replied. "Templeton and four others."

"Four others? You mean there are six of them?"

"Yes. Apparently, he wasn't prepared to take no for an answer."

"That's not the only thing he isn't prepared for," Malcolm said. "I don't expect he is prepared to see all of us here."

"Chris," Woodward said. "Tell the ladies and the children to stay in the back of the house."

"All right," Logan said.

The men waited until they heard footsteps on the front porch, followed by a knock on the door.

"Come in, Colonel Garneau," Malcolm called. "The door is unlocked."

The door opened and Garneau, Templeton, and the four other men went into the house.

"Monsieur Puddle, your twenty-four hours are up," Garneau said. "What is your . . . ?" His voice trailed off in shock to see so many men gathered in the room, one of who was Smoke Jensen.

"What is this?" Garneau asked.

"Oh, it is too bad you weren't here earlier, Colonel Garneau. You could have eaten with us. All my neighbors came over to welcome me. They brought food, and we had a fine meal."

"I . . . uh . . . came to hear your response to my offer."

"Yes, well, as I said yesterday, Colonel, your offer was most generous. But, now that I have met all my neighbors, I feel I would be doing them a disservice if I ran out on them. Again, I thank you for the generous offer, but I must decline."

"You are making a big mistake, Monsieur Puddle. When next we do business, and we will do business again, you will find my offer to be much less generous."

"Oh, I don't see much possibility of our ever doing business, Mr. Garneau," Malcolm said, purposely not using the military title. "By the way, please don't visit again, uninvited and unannounced. It does make for an awkward situation."

Nobody said a word until Garneau and those with

him rode away. Then they broke out in laughter and self-congratulations.

"Did you see the expression on his face when he saw all of us here?" someone asked, and Keefer imitated it, opening his eyes and mouth wide as he looked around the room. His antics brought more laughter.

As the others made preparations to leave, Lucy Woodward came over to speak to Malcolm. He had noticed the pretty young woman when she first arrived, and was pleased she had come over to speak to him.

"I'm glad you are going to stay out here and not go back to New York," Lucy said.

"I'm glad too," Malcolm said. "There's nothing in New York for me." He made the pointed statement to let her know there were no women in his life.

"I don't know if anyone has told you, but every month there is a dance at the Dunn Hotel."

"Really? Well, that's very good to know." Malcolm smiled.

Lucy smiled back, nodded, and quickly followed her parents to their wagon.

Smoke and Sally had come in a spring wagon so they could meet Pearlie and Cal when their train came in. Leaving Puddle and the others, they drove straight to the depot.

"Hello, Smoke, Miz Sally," Phil Wilson greeted when they arrived. "Are you going somewhere or meeting someone?"

"We're meeting Pearlie and Cal," Smoke said. "They're coming home today."

"I'll bet those two boys will be happy to get back to

Sugarloaf," Wilson said. "You goin' to sit in the wagon or come into the depot?"

"I reckon we can come in." Smoke hopped down, tied off the team, then went around to help Sally down.

"I just made some coffee," Wilson said. "Come on in and share a cup with me."

They followed him inside the depot. A woman and a small girl, about four years old were waiting for the next train.

"We're goin' to see Nana," the little girl announced happily.

"Ellen Genoa, you don't need to tell everyone that," the little girl's mother said.

"Oh, but I'm glad you did tell me, Ellen Genoa," Sally said, smiling at the little girl. "Because I think that is very exciting."

"Mama, she's glad."

"That's because she is a very nice lady," Ellen's mother said.

Smoke and Sally went back into the office, where Phil Wilson filled three cups with coffee, then handed a cup to each of them. "Say, Smoke, what's going on out in the valley? I hear the Frenchman has already run Butrum and Drexler off their property. Is that right?"

"I'm afraid it is right."

"What is he going to do, just keep on until he runs ever'one out of the valley?"

"I don't think so. I think he's probably gone about as far as he's going to go. The other settlers are standing up to him."

"Look here, you don't think this is going to break

out into a range war, do you? I've been hearing reports the Frenchman has hired him a bunch of guns, and they are all out at his place now. He says it's to combat cattle rustling, but I haven't heard anyone complain about cattle thieves."

"The only thievery going on around here is Garneau's stealing of land."

"So, what's going to come of all this?"

"I'm not all that sure where it's going," Smoke replied. "I suppose we're just going to have to wait and find out."

At that moment, they heard the whistle of the inbound train and, shortly afterward, the chugging sound of the approaching engine. Sally and Smoke moved out onto the depot platform to greet their two arriving hands, though of course, they were much more than mere cattle hands. They were practically members of the family.

Cal was the first one down, jumping from the train even before it had come to a complete stop. Pearlie was right behind him. Seeing Smoke and Sally, they walked over to them quickly.

"Welcome home, boys," Sally said, greeting each of them with a hug. Smoke shook hands with each of them.

"How is the abattoir going?" Smoke asked.

"Smoke! You asked about that stupid processing plant before you ask about Cal's arm?" Sally scolded.

"My arm's fine, Miss Sally," Cal said, moving it around. "The bullet didn't do nothin' more 'n just sorta put a crease in it. Heck, I've been hurt worse gettin' hung up on barbed wire."

"The plant's going great," Pearlie said. "And you made a smart decision, turning it over to Beans. He's a good man."

"Turning it over to who?" Smoke asked, puzzled by Pearlie's comment.

"Lloyd Evans. Ever'one calls him Beans," Pearlie said. "And he knows that business from top to bottom. He used to work with de Mores, when he had his plant up in Dakota Territory."

"Say," Cal said. "As long as we're in town, why don't we go over to Lambert's and have somethin' to eat. One of his rolls would be real good about now."

"Tell me, Cal, is there ever a time when one of Mr. Lambert's rolls wouldn't be good? Or Miss Sally's? Or anybody's rolls for that matter?"

"No," Cal replied seriously. "I can't think of such a time."

With their luggage thrown into the back of the spring wagon, they walked across the street to Lambert's. Several of the patrons greeted them when they went inside. Those who knew Pearlie and Cal had been gone for a while welcomed them home.

"Here you go, Cal! Welcome home!" Lambert shouted from across the room, throwing a roll even as he greeted him.

Cal caught the roll easily, and had it half eaten by the time they took their seats at a table.

"Hey, Smoke, who is that fella over there in the corner?" Pearlie asked. "He's starin' at us, and it don't look none too friendly."

In the corner of the restaurant, a well-dressed man was sitting alone.

"That, Pearlie, is Mr. Lucien Garneau, though he likes to call himself Colonel Garneau.

"Is he a colonel?"

"Certainly not in the U.S. Army," Smoke said. "Whether or not he was ever a colonel in the French Army, we have only his word for it. And so far he has not proven himself to be a man whose word I'm inclined to take."

"Does he live here, now?"

"Yes, he bought Long Trek. And since he bought Long Trek he has bought four more spreads."

"What's he tryin' to do, own the whole valley?"

Smoke nodded. "Apparently, that is exactly what he has in mind."

Garneau didn't know who the two men with Jensen were. He thought perhaps they were men the rancher had hired as personal bodyguards. How good would bodyguards be if a concerted effort was made to kill somebody? Garneau didn't know, but he was fully committed to that effort.

Templeton had said Smoke Jensen would have to be killed for the Frenchman to accomplish his objective. But that was just one reason to kill him. Garneau wanted him dead simply because he didn't like the man.

He wondered how Templeton was doing in his task of recruiting Jeremiah Priest.

CHAPTER TWENTY-FOUR

When Deekus Templeton stepped off the train in Palmilla, New Mexico Territory, he headed for the nearest saloon. It had been his experience a person could find out more by visiting a saloon than he could by reading a month's worth of local newspapers.

"A beer," he ordered. When it was delivered, he paid for it with a dollar bill.

"Beer only costs a nickel," the bartender said. "Ain't you got no change?"

"If I get the right information, I don't need any change," Templeton said.

The bartender squinted his eyes. "What kind of information?"

"I'm looking for a man named Jeremiah Priest."

The bartender opened the cash drawer, pulled out ninety-five cents, and slid it across the bar. "I've never heard of him."

"Sure you have. He killed a man in this town. It was in the paper."

"I never read the paper," the bartender said. "And

if you want to stay alive, you won't be readin' it, either. Jeremiah Priest ain't the kind of man you want to be askin' questions about."

"I thought you said you didn't know him."

"Mister, finish your beer and go somewhere else to ask your questions."

"You've got the wrong idea," Templeton said. "Priest is a friend of mine. I'm just trying to find him, that's all."

"Well, try somewhere else."

Templeton finished his beer, then took the bartender's advice. He visited another saloon, and was in the third saloon when he finally found someone who would talk to him. Templeton offered him two dollars if the man would tell him where he could find Priest.

"What do you want with him?" asked the man who identified himself as Dagan.

"What I want with him is my business," Templeton replied. "Like I said, if you can tell me where he is, I'll give you two dollars."

"The reason I asked," Dagan said, "is 'cause if you're plannin' on goin' up against him, you're goin' to get yourself kilt and I won't get my money. You give me the two dollars now, and I'll tell you where to find him."

"All right," Templeton said. "Here's the two dollars."

Dagan took the two bills, examined them for a moment, then slipped them in his pocket. "You see that fella back in the corner. The one with two women?"

"Yes, what about him? Does he know where to find Priest?"

"Ha. Mister, you don't know it, but you are lookin' at Priest."

"Wait a minute. Are you telling me that little runt of a man is Jeremiah Priest? There must be some mistake. The Priest I'm looking for is a . . ." he hesitated before saying the word *killer*.

"If you're lookin' for the man who kilt Coleman Wesley, that there is him," Dagan said. "And if you think there ain't nothin' to that little fella, well that's what Wesley thought. Don't let the way he looks fool you."

"Thanks." Templeton started toward the table, then stepped over to the bar. "What are Priest and the two women drinking?"

"Mr. Priest don't drink nothin' but beer. The women drink their special whiskey."

Templeton knew he meant the women were drinking tea. They had to. They drank with men all day long. If they were actually drinking whiskey, they would be passed out drunk by midday. "Let me have a beer and two of their drinks."

"If you're wantin' Mr. Priest's autograph, he don't give it," the bartender said.

"I'm not after his autograph."

The bartender poured the drinks and Templeton took them to the corner of the room where Priest sat. He put the women's drinks down on a separate table, then laid a five-dollar bill alongside each glass. "If you ladies would have drinks here, and give me a moment with Mr. Priest, I would appreciate it. I'll only be a moment and you can come right back."

The two women smiled broadly at the unexpected largesse.

One of the bar girls patted Priest's hand. "Honey, we'll be back as soon as this gentleman is finished."

"Yeah? Well, he may be finished a hell of a lot sooner than he thinks." Priest turned to Templeton. "What do you mean, running my ladies off?"

"I didn't run them off. They'll be right back. I just need a moment of your time." Templeton put one hundred dollars on the table in front of Priest.

"You're not plannin' on buyin' me with a hunnert dollars, are you?" Priest asked.

"Not at all," Templeton said. "For that money, all I want is a few moments of your time."

Priest picked up the money and put it in his pocket. "All right, you got a couple minutes. For what?"

"I want to make you a business proposition."

"What kind of business proposition?"

"Your kind of business."

Big Rock

Pearlie and Cal had gotten back just in time for the monthly dance at the Dunn Hotel. Neither man had a particular woman friend. Cal explained as they finished up the day's work, "This way we get to dance with all the ladies, and nobody gets their feelings hurt because we aren't dancin' with them."

By evening, the entire town was aware of the impending dance. A platform, built just for the occasion, had been brought out of storage and placed in the front of the ballroom for the musicians and they could be heard all along Front Street. The floor was cleared of all tables and chairs, and the room gaily decorated with bunting and flowers. Children began to gather around the glowing, yellow windows on the ground floor of the hotel and peered inside.

Buggies, spring wagons, buckboards, and horses began arriving from out in the county, and soon every hitching rail on Front Street, and even down Sikes Street all the way to Center Street, were full. Men and women who lived in the town walked along the boardwalks toward the hotel, the women in colorful ginghams, the men in clean, blue denims and brightly decorated vests.

As always, there were more men than women at the dance, but most of the ladies, even those who were married, made themselves available so everyone could have a good time.

"Pearlie, Cal! Where have you boys been?" Hoyt Miller asked as the two cowhands entered the hotel.

Pearlie told him about the abattoir in Denver. "What about you, Elmer, and Andy? What have you been doing since Mr. Munger died?"

"You mean you haven't heard? A man named Colonel Garneau bought the Long Trek, and we're still workin' there."

"What about Homer Nance? He still the foreman there?" Cal asked.

Miller looked down. "No, he got fired."

"Fired? What for? Nance was one of the best foremen in all of Eagle county," Cal said.

"Yeah, that's what I thought, too. Don't nobody

know for sure why he got fired. There's some strange things goin' on at Long Trek."

Somebody called to Miller and, excusing himself, he left.

Another young man approached them. "Are you Cal and Pearlie?"

"Yes," Pearlie answered.

The young man extended his hand. "Smoke told me about you two. He thinks very highly of you. I'm Malcolm Puddle."

"Oh, yes," Pearlie replied with a smile. "You're Mr. Puddle's nephew. You own Carro de Bancada now, don't you?"

"Yes."

"Well, it's good to meet you, Mr. Puddle."

Malcolm shook his head. "Mr. Puddle was my uncle. I'm Malcolm."

"Then it's good to meet you, Malcolm," Pearlie said.

As the ballroom continued to fill, the excitement grew. A very pretty young woman came up to Malcolm. "I see you came to the dance."

"I wouldn't have missed it for the world," Malcolm replied. "Oh, uh, Lucy Woodward, this is Pearlie and Cal." Malcolm looked a little embarrassed. "I didn't find out which one of you is Pearlie and which is Cal."

"This is Pearlie and this is Cal," Lucy said, identifying them.

"Oh." Malcolm laughed. "Here I was going to introduce you, and you wound up introducing me."

"Dancers, form your squares!" the caller shouted through his megaphone.

"Who's that callin'?" Pearlie asked. "How come Sheriff Carson ain't callin'?"

"The band brought their own caller," Lucy answered, as she held her arm out toward Malcolm, who took it.

Pearlie and Cal joined the cowboys advancing toward the unattached girls, and when a couple girls accepted their invitation to dance, they made up the final two sets for Malcolm and Lucy's square.

The music started and the caller began to shout, dancing around on the platform as he called, bowing and whirling as if he had a girl and was in one of the squares himself. The dancers moved and swirled to his commands.

Lucy danced with Pearlie and Cal during the evening, but most of the time she danced with Malcolm. It was apparent to all who paid any attention that there was a growing attraction between them.

"Folks, me 'n the band is goin' to take us about a fifteen minute break," the caller shouted through the megaphone. "So why don't you just visit with one another or enjoy some of that fine punch the ladies put together for us tonight?"

"And that the cowboys have improved!" someone shouted from the floor and everyone laughed. All were aware of the "doctoring" the cowboys had done by adding whiskey to the fruit drink.

It was then two new men came in. Unlike everyone else at the dance, they were wearing guns.

"Who are those two?" Pearlie asked as he stood with a group of cowboys. "And what are they doing wearing guns at a dance?"

"You don't want to mess with them two boys, Pearlie," Miller said. "That's Manning and Gilchrist. They are part of Colonel Garneau's army."

"Colonel Garneau's army? What do you mean, *army*?"

"I mean army," Miller said. "Colonel Garneau has done recruited him a bunch of gunmen, and he's trainin' 'em all like an army."

"Why?"

"I don't know. He says it's because of cattle rustlin', but I'll be honest with you, Pearlie, I ain't aware of any rustlin' goin' on at all."

Across the room, Lucy and Malcolm were enjoying some of the nondoctored punch.

"Malcolm, my mother asked me to invite you to dinner tomorrow. Do you like chicken and dumplings?"

"I don't know that I've ever had chicken and dumplings."

"You haven't? Why, how can you have never had chicken and dumplings?"

Malcolm laughed. "I'm from New York. It's just not something I've ever eaten."

"I think you will love it. I don't know anyone who doesn't. Will you come?"

"Lucy, I would come if your mother was serving nothing but cauliflower. And I really don't like cauliflower."

Lucy laughed.

"Hey, you pretty thing," someone said. "My name's Earl Manning and this here fella is Billy Gilchrist. What is your name?"

"As you can see, I'm talking to this gentleman," Lucy replied. "It is very rude of you to interrupt."

"Gentleman? Are you talking about this little pipsqueak?"

"Malcolm, it's a little close in here," Lucy said. "Do you suppose we could go outside for a little air?"

"Yes, of course." Malcolm offered his arm to Lucy and they started toward the door.

Manning stepped in front of them. "I tell you what, honey. Why don't I just take care of this little feller for you, then it'll just be me 'n you?"

From where he stood, Pearlie watched. "Uh-oh. It looks like our new friend is in trouble."

Pearlie and Cal started toward the couple just as Manning grabbed Malcolm by the shoulder and spun him around. The armed man made a sweeping swing with his fist, but Malcolm ducked under it easily and landed a right uppercut on the point of Manning's chin, knocking him down.

"Damn you!" Gilchrist said, stepping in from Malcolm's side and sending a straight jab toward his head.

The young rancher leaned back and watched the punch slip by him without effect. Dancing back, he answered with a hard left to Gilchrist's stomach, doubling him over. Malcolm followed that with a right cross to the jaw, and Gilchrist went down to join Manning.

"We'd better get their guns," Pearlie said, reaching to pull Manning's gun from its holster. "I don't expect they're goin' to be any too happy when they come to."

Following Pearlie's example, Cal took Gilchrist's gun.

The excitement had gathered a crowd. Malcolm, embarrassed by the scene, apologized. "I'm sorry folks. It wasn't my intention to create a disturbance."

"It wasn't your fault, mister. Most of us seen what happened," one in the crowd said.

Manning was the first one to come to, and he leaped to his feet with an angry shout. "I'm goin' to blow your head off!" He reached for his pistol, only to find his holster empty. "What the hell?"

"Are you looking for this?" Pearlie asked, showing Manning his pistol.

"What are you doin' with my gun?"

"Right now, I'm holding it on you. And I'm going to keep it on you until Sheriff Carson gets here."

"I'm here, Pearlie," Sheriff Carson said. "Mr. Miller came for me."

The sheriff pulled Gilchrist up from the floor and turned to Manning. "Come on, boys. I think you two need to spend the night in the jail."

Hamburg, Germany

While in Geneva, Inspector Laurent had learned that Mouchette had exchanged nearly all the stolen francs for U.S. dollars and he was certain the man was going to America. But some of the stolen money had been exchanged for German marks. Putting two and two together, Laurent had come to the conclusion Mouchette had probably left from Hamburg.

He walked into the port authority office on the Elbe River and introduced himself to the director, then told him who he was looking for.

"*Nein*, no passenger named Mouchette has departed from this port, *Herr* Inspector."

"What about a man named Antoine Dubois?"

"No, nobody named Antoine Dubois."

"Have any Frenchmen departed from this port in the last six months?"

"I must examine all the records. I am afraid that will take a few days," the director replied.

"Please do so, Monsieur Director," Laurent said. "It is very important we find this man. He may also have passed himself off as Belgian or Swiss."

"I will do what I can, Herr Inspector."

"*Merci*."

Two days later Laurent was called back to the director's office where he received a stack of papers listing the names of all French, Swiss, and Belgian passengers. He thanked the port director profusely for the information.

Laurent took the papers back to France so he could investigate all five hundred names.

Long Trek

"I will do it for ten thousand dollars," Priest said. "But I want five thousand dollars up front."

"Why should I do that?" Garneau asked. "What if I pay you five thousand dollars, and Jensen kills you? I'll be out five thousand dollars, and Jensen will still be a problem."

"That's a chance we are both taking," Priest said. "All you stand to lose is money. I would be losing my life. But you won't lose any money, and I won't lose my life. I will kill Jensen."

"Are you really that good?"

"I'm really that good."

"I would like to see some sort of demonstration."

"What do you want me to do? Shoot at a target?"

"No. Target shooting is for children. I would like to see a demonstration as to how you act in a kill or be killed situation."

"How are you going to see that?"

"I will arrange it, if you are willing to participate."

"How are you going to arrange it?"

"Oh, it's quite simple, really. Over the last few months, I have collected some of the most skilled gunmen in the West. I will offer a thousand dollars to any of them who can kill you in a fair fight."

"Wait a minute. Are you saying you are going to pay someone to kill me?"

"Yes. That is, I'm going to pay someone to *try* to kill you. Does that prospect frighten you?"

"No."

"Very good. Monsieur Templeton, would you visit with some of our . . . soldiers . . . make the offer, and see if anyone is willing to accept the challenge?"

"All right." Templeton left the house to carry out Garneau's instructions.

"Are you serious, Garneau? You want me to kill one of your own men, just so you can test me?"

"I'm quite serious," Garneau replied. "Unless, of course, you find it . . . distasteful."

"Distasteful? No, I don't find it distasteful. A little

weird, maybe. But not distasteful. But I do have a condition."

"And what would that condition be?"

"If I kill the man who decides to take the challenge, I want the thousand dollars you are promising him."

"But of course. You will get ten thousand dollars if you kill Jensen."

Priest shook his head. "No, you don't understand. I want the thousand dollars you are promising the other man, in addition to the ten thousand dollars. And I want it paid the moment I kill him."

"All right," Garneau agreed. "If that is what it will take for you to give me a demonstration, I'll do that."

At that moment, Templeton came back into the house. "Colonel, I've got a man who says he'll do it."

"Very good," Garneau said. "Who is it?"

"It's Strode."

"Strode, yes, an excellent choice," Garneau said.

"Strode? Vince Strode?" Priest said.

"Yes," Garneau replied. "Do you know Vince Strode?"

"I know him," Priest answered. "He's a friend of mine. Me 'n him wintered together a year or so back."

"You're friends, and he has agreed to try to kill you?"

Priest laughed. "We used to wonder which one of us would kill the other if it ever came down to it. I reckon we're about to find out."

"If neither of you are bothered by the fact that you are friends."

"There's a thousand dollars riding on it. For a thousand dollars, I'd shoot my own brother."

Since gathering his army, Garneau had decided to house the gunmen in an additional barracks away from his working cowboys in the bunkhouse. At the moment, Strode was in the barracks oiling the barrel and frame of his pistol. He had already checked the loads in the cylinder.

"Strode, are you sure you want to do this?" Ken Conn asked.

"Yeah, why not? A thousand dollars is a thousand dollars." Strode spun the cylinder, then put the pistol in his holster. He drew it a couple times, and smiled. "Besides, I always did think I was faster than that little pissant."

"Strode, I don't know," Conn said. "They say Priest has killed twenty men."

Strode chuckled. "I ain't exactly a virgin, you know. I didn't get into this game yesterday. Tell you what. After I kill the feller, what do you say you an' me go into town, have us a good meal, get a few drinks at the Brown Dirt, and then a couple women?"

"Strode, you know I ain't got enough money to do all them things."

"Don't worry. I'll pay for all of it. I'll have the thousand dollars by then. And I need somebody that'll be pullin' for me, when I go up ag'in Priest."

"Hell, Strode, you're my friend," Conn said. "You don't need to pay me to pull for you."

Templeton came back into the barracks then.

"Strode, did you mean what you said about facing Priest?"

"You're damn right, I meant it."

"Well, then you might want to get on outside. Priest is out there waiting on you."

Once again, Strode loosened the pistol in his holster, then looked over at Conn and smiled. "Only thing is, I get first pick of the woman tonight. "You got that? I get first pick."

"You got it, Strode," Conn said as he followed the gunman outside.

In addition to Jeremiah Priest, every other person on the ranch was standing around, waiting to see the show. Garneau and Templeton were sitting in chairs up on the front porch of the big house. Garneau held a drink in one hand and a fan in the other.

"Is that him?" Conn asked, pointing toward the small man standing about fifteen feet in front of the steps.

"That's him," Strode said.

"I've heard about him, but I ain't never seen him before. Hell, he ain't no bigger 'n a dog turd. There ain't a man on the place but couldn't slap him around."

"Yeah, well, his guns make him bigger."

"Hello, Strode. I ain't seen you in a while," Priest said. "When was it? Two years ago? Three maybe?"

"I think it might have been three years. How you been getting' along, Priest? Ever get rid of that disease you caught from that squaw?"

"Yeah, it took a while. How come you didn't catch nothin' from her?"

"Hell, Priest, I knowed she had been Frenchified. I thought it was a big joke on you."

"Takin' the mercury cure ain't much of joke," Priest said.

Strode laughed. "I thought it was funny. Bein' as it was between friends 'n all."

Garneau stood up and walked out to the edge of the porch. "Gentlemen, I want it clearly understood the two of you are entering into this . . . contest . . . of your own free will. I also want it clearly understood that I have not used coercion on either of you."

"I don't know what that word means, Colonel," Strode said. "But I was told if I kill Priest, you'll give me a thousand dollars. Is that right?"

"*Oui.* If you are willing to risk your life in this *affaire d'honneur*, I will give you one thousand dollars."

"All right then. That's why I'm here."

"And you will make the statement here, in front of all these witnesses, that you are entering into this competition, deadly though it may be, of your own free will?" Garneau said.

"Hell, yeah, I'll say that. What about you, Priest?" Strode asked. "Are you doin' this of your own free will? I mean, bein' as we're friends 'n all?"

"Yes," Priest replied.

"There you go, Colonel," Strode said. "You heard 'im. This ain't no more than a game between two friends."

"Very well. You may proceed," Garneau said.

Strode moved toward Priest, then stopped when he was about twenty feet away. Priest smiled at him. For a long moment the two men just stared at each other, and those who were watching the macabre dance of death, held their collective breath.

Out in the stable, a horse whickered.

Overhead, a circling crow called.

A freshening breeze ruffled leaves in the trees.

"Now!" Strode said as his hand flashed toward his pistol.

Priest's draw was so fast the men watching it were unable to see when the pistol actually appeared in his hand. They saw only a jump of his shoulder, concurrent with the sound of the gunshot.

Strode had not even cleared his holster, and when the bullet hit him in the chest, he let go of his pistol, and it dropped back into the holster. He staggered back two steps, then clamped his hand over the wound. Conn and the others who had gathered for the grisly show saw the blood streaming through Strode's fingers.

"I'll be damned," Strode said as he fell. "I had no idea the little pissant was that fast."

Conn ran over to him. "Strode!"

The gunman smiled up at him. "I reckon you'll be gettin' first choice of the women tonight, after all."

Conn watched Strode die. He was the closest thing to a friend Conn had. Suddenly, and unexpectedly, he grabbed Strode's gun from its holster and swung it toward Priest. "Damn you!" he shouted in anger.

Conn beat Strode, in that he was able to bring the gun up, but that was as far as he got. Priest, who had already holstered his pistol, drew and fired again. Conn was hit in the middle of the forehead, dead before he fell back on the ground.

"Damn!" someone said. "I ain't never seen nothin' like that in all my borned days!"

"I believe, Colonel, you had a question as to whether I would be up to the task you have chosen for me. Have I answered that question for you?" Priest asked.

"You have indeed."

"And it is my impression the one thousand dollars you were going to give to Strode is now mine."

"That is correct," Garneau replied.

"Very good." Priest turned to the others, all of whom were looking at him with eyes wide in wonder.

"Men, I am going into town to find a saloon. I will be buying drinks for anyone who comes with me."

The men who made up Garneau's army cheered loudly, though the cowboys were somewhat more reserved. It was Gately who quietly made the comment that brought the rest of them around. "Hell, boys. It wasn't one of us that got killed. I say we go into town and drink on the man's money."

"Yeah," Anderson said, and all started toward the corral to saddle their horses for the night on the town.

CHAPTER TWENTY-FIVE

Having been released from jail and paid their fine, Gilchrist and Manning had watched the shoot-out.

"Ten thousand dollars?" Gilchrist said. "Are you serious? Garneau is going to give Priest ten thousand dollars to kill Smoke Jensen?"

"That's what I've heard," Manning answered.

"Well, hell, what if somebody else kills him? Would he get the ten thousand?"

"I don't know why not," Manning said. "Garneau wants him dead. I don't think it really matters much who kills him."

"That's good to know."

"So are you coming with the rest of us to spend some of Priest's money?"

"I guess so. I mean, I liked Strode, and Priest killed him. So I may as well drink up some of his money."

"They're all goin' to the Brown Dirt. Come on, we can prob'ly catch up with 'em."

"All right," Gilchrist agreed.

Big Rock

"Mr. McVey, why are you tending bar when you can play the piano as well as you do?" Smoke was standing at the bar in Longmont's Saloon.

McVey was wiping glasses and putting them back under the bar. He smiled. "Because it is my time to tend bar. Besides, I have this habit I can't seem to break. I like to eat."

Smoke laughed. "You aren't telling me you can't make enough money as a pianist to make a living, are you?"

"I suppose I could, if I worked at it hard enough. My basic problem is that I'm too lazy."

Smoke laughed at his answer. "I don't believe that for a minute. Would you play something for us now?"

McVey looked toward Louis.

"Go ahead, Johnny. I'll run the bar for a while," Louis said.

"I won't be playing any cowboy ballads," McVey said.

"I don't want you to. You choose what you want to play."

"All right."

Gilchrist and Manning had reached town. As they rode past Longmont's Saloon, Gilchrist pulled up. Manning rode on for a short distance before he realized his partner had stopped. The gunman stopped as well, and looked back toward him. "What are you doing? They're all at the Brown Dirt."

"I think I'm going to step in here for a minute or two. You want to come with me?"

"No. Longmont's is too highfalutin a place for me. Besides, the free drinkin' is over at the Brown Dirt, not here."

"I'll be there in a few minutes," Gilchrist said.

"All right. But you better get there before all the money is drunk up."

"You go along. Like I said, I'll be there in a few minutes."

When Gilchrist stepped into the saloon he saw Smoke standing by the piano, his back to the entrance. The gunman smiled. He was about to earn ten thousand dollars.

He pulled his pistol, pointed at Smoke, and shouted, "Turn around, Jensen!"

Turning slowly, Smoke saw that Gilchrist had his pistol drawn, pointing it at him.

"You're worth ten thousand dollars to me, Jensen," Gilchrist said.

"You're mistaken," Smoke said easily. "There is no paper out on me."

"I ain't talking 'bout the law. I'm talkin' about a fella wants you dead, and he's willin' to pay ten thousand dollars for it."

"Do you really think you'll be able to collect that money?" Smoke asked. "Think about it. You've just admitted in front of all these witnesses that you are being paid to do this. If you kill me, you'll be arrested and hanged. Either that or you'll have to go on the run, and you'll never get the money."

"I'll take that chance." Gilchrist smiled. "I don't think I'll hang."

"No, you won't hang," Smoke said. "Because I'll kill you."

"Ha! Maybe you ain't noticed, but I've got my gun in my hand. Your gun is in the holster. When you get to hell, I got a couple friends that just went there—Strode and Conn. Tell 'em I said hello."

"You can tell them yourself," Smoke said, his voice as calm as if he were discussing the weather.

Gilchrist lifted his thumb up from the handle of his pistol, preparatory to pulling back the hammer, but his thumb never reached the hammer. Smoke drew and fired. His bullet slammed into the middle of Gilchrist's chest. The gunman looked down with an expression of surprise on his face. He looked back up at Smoke. "How? How the hell did you . . . ?" Gilchrist collapsed.

Mark Worley, who had joined the others in moving out of the way when the confrontation started, hurried over to him. The first thing he did was kick the pistol away, then he dropped down to one knee beside him. He put his hand on Gilchrist's neck. "He's dead."

"It's the damndest thing I ever seen," Andy Anderson told the others in the Brown Dirt. "Gilchrist was standing there with his gun in his hand, but Jensen drew his pistol and shot him before Gilchrist could even pull the trigger."

"That's impossible," Manning said.

"Yeah, well, I woulda thought so too if I hadn't seen it for myself. But I'm tellin' you the truth. Gilchrist had his gun in his hand and Jensen's gun was in his holster. But he pulled it and shot Gilchrist dead."

"I still say that's impossible," Manning said. "There ain't nobody that fast."

"I am," Priest said. "I can do that."

"I don't believe it," Manning said.

"Take your gun out of your holster and point it at me. When you see me start my draw, pull the trigger."

"Don't do it, Manning. Don't you 'member what happened out at the ranch? Conn was already pointing his gun at Priest, when Priest shot him."

"Oh. Yeah. Yeah, I do remember."

"Do you want to try it, Manning?" Priest asked.

"No. Uh, no. I take it back. I reckon you could do it."

"Glad to hear you say that. Priest smiled. "It means I don't have to kill you."

"Come on. Let's have a beer," Anderson said. "Priest is buyin'."

"Damn," Manning said as he wrapped his hands around a beer mug. "I was wonderin' why Gilchrist wanted to stop at Longmont's. I believe he had it in mind to make ten thousand dollars by killin' Jensen."

"That's exactly what he had in mind," Anderson said. "I heard 'im tell Jensen he was goin' to make ten thousand dollars by killin' 'im."

* * *

Sheriff Carson was at Longmont's having been summoned after the shooting. "And that's what you heard him say? That he was goin' to make ten thousand dollars by killin' Smoke?"

"We all heard it, Sheriff," Louis replied.

"I wonder what he meant by that. Smoke, do you think there's some old paper out on you?"

Smoke shook his head. "I used the name Bucky West when I was on the dodge. As far as I know, all that paper has been pulled back."

"Then what did he mean that killing you would be worth ten thousand dollars?"

"I'll tell you what I think it means," Hoyt Miller said.

"Miller, what are you doing in here?" one of the saloon patrons asked. "I was just over at the Brown Dirt. Seems like every hand the Frenchman has working for him is there. It's almost like a party."

"It is a party," Miller said. "Jeremiah Priest is buying everyone drinks."

"Jeremiah Priest?" Sheriff Carson said. "He's here?"

"He's one of Garneau's new hands."

"What do you mean, he's one of the Frenchman's new hands? Are you saying he's a cowboy?"

"No, I ain't sayin' that," Miller said. "Half the men Garneau has hired in the last month ain't never punched a cow in their lives. They don't do nothin' but practice target shootin'. That is, the ones that's still alive. Jensen kilt Gilchrist, and just before I come into town, Priest kilt Strode and Conn."

"What?" Sheriff Carson asked. "I haven't heard anything about that."

"It just happened," Miller said. "And truth is, there prob'ly wouldn't be nothin' you could do about it anyhow. It was a fair fight. All of us that was there seen it. Strode braced Priest, an' Priest kilt him."

"What were they fighting about?" Louis Longmont asked.

"They weren't fightin' at all."

"Wait a minute. Didn't you just say Priest and Strode faced each other, and Priest killed Strode?" Sheriff Carson asked.

"Yes."

"But they weren't fighting over anything?"

"Word I got is Garneau wanted to see how good Priest was, so he offered a thousand dollars to anyone who thought they could beat 'im in a gunfight. Strode tried and lost."

"You also mentioned a man named Conn," Smoke said.

"Yeah, well, turns out Conn and Strode were friends. When Strode got hisself kilt, Conn grabbed the gun and tried to kill Priest. Priest had already put his gun away, but he drew it and kilt Conn."

"Miller, you said you could tell us what it meant when Gilchrist said that killing Smoke was worth ten thousand dollars to him. But I got you off track," Sheriff Carson said. "You want to tell us what you meant?"

"The way I heard it, Garneau is going to give Priest ten thousand dollars if he kills Jensen."

"You actually heard Garneau say that, did you?"

Sheriff Carson asked. "Because if you did hear him say that, I'll go out to Long Trek and arrest him right now."

"Arrest him for what?" Miller said. "He ain't actually done nothin' yet."

"I would arrest him for solicitation of someone to commit murder," Sheriff Carson said. "But to make the charge stick, you would have to testify that you heard him do that."

Miller shook his head. "I can't do that."

"If he actually did solicit for murder, he'll go to prison, and he can't hurt you. Understand he is just as guilty if the murder isn't committed as he is if the murder is committed. So you don't have to be afraid to testify."

"That ain't it," Miller said. "I can't say nothin' about it, 'cause I didn't actual hear him say it. I just heard some of the other boys talkin' about it. Besides which, I ain't stayin' around no more. Nance had the right idea when he left. I shoulda left then too. I don't like some of the things Garneau is doin'."

Paris, France

Inspector Laurent had papers spread out on the desk before him, matching records with the five hundred names he had been given by the port authority in Hamburg. He'd matched up eighty-seven Swiss names with Swiss records. For every name on the passenger list, he found a corresponding name in the Swiss records, and saw nothing extraordinary. He had done the same thing with the one hundred and twelve Belgian names. That left him three hundred and one French names to go through.

The first name was Gaston Abadie. He listed himself as a mechanic and was traveling with his wife and two children. Laurent was sure Abadie wasn't Pierre Mouchette.

He went on to the next name.

CHAPTER TWENTY-SIX

Big Rock

"Hey, piano player. Play *Buckskin Joe*," Manning said to the piano player.

Gordon Beaver began to play the song.

In the Brown Dirt Cowboy Saloon, the atmosphere had changed with the onslaught of all the Long Trek riders. Although somewhat more animated than the patrons of Longmont's, the regulars were overshadowed by the men of Long Trek, who were exceptionally loud and boisterous. They were argumentative with the customers and with each other.

"Hey, piano player. Play *Buckskin Joe*, again," Manning shouted.

The piano player complied.

"That was very good," Manning said. "Play *Buckskin Joe* again."

Again the piano player complied.

"All right, how about *Buckskin Joe?*"

"For heaven's sake, I've played the song three times already," Gordon said.

"Play it again."

One more time, Gordon played the song.

"All right. Now, I want you to play *Buckskin Joe,*" Manning said.

"I have played it four times. I definitely will not play it again."

Manning pulled his knife, then walked over to the piano player and laid the sharp side of the instrument at the top of the piano player's ear, right where it was connected to his head. "Mister, you'll damn well play what I tell you to or I'll carve off this ear," he said menacingly. "Now, play *Buckskin Joe* like I told you to."

Shaking, with his face reflecting his fear, the piano player played *Buckskin Joe again.*

"Now, ain't that the prettiest thing you ever heard?" Manning said when the piano player was finished. "Play it again."

"Piano player, don't you dare play that song again," one of the other patrons said. "It's driving me crazy."

"Well now, ain't that just too bad?" Turning around, Manning saw the man who had called out had a pistol in his hand.

"Peterson, what are you doing? Put that gun away," Emmett Brown said.

"What am I doin'? I'm goin' to shoot that crazy piano player if he plays that song again. That's what I'm doin." The tone of Peterson's voice clearly showed his agitation. He cocked his pistol and aimed it at the piano player.

"And I'm going to cut your ear off, if you don't play it," Manning said, giggling. "That kind of leaves you in a pickle, don't it?" He demonstrated his willingness to do so by cutting into the ear just enough to make it bleed.

"Mr. Brown, what am I going to do?" Gordon called out to the saloon owner in fear.

"I don't know, Gordy. God help me, I don't know what to tell you to do," Brown said.

There was a gunshot, and Gordon jerked, causing more of his ear to be cut. He called out in pain, though also with some relief as he realized he hadn't been shot.

Peterson got a shocked expression on his face, then dropped his gun. Looking around he saw a small man, holding a smoking gun. "What . . . what did you do that for?"

"Me 'n my friends was enjoyin' the music," Priest said. "It looked like you was about to stop it."

Peterson staggered back against the bar, then slid down and died. The bar kept him in a sitting position.

Once more, Gordon began pounding away on the keys. Amy, one of the bar girls, came over to hold a towel against his ear to stop the bleeding.

"Hey, girlie. Sing the song he's playin'," Priest ordered.

"I'm not a singer."

"Sing it or I'll shoot the piano player," Priest said.

"Please! I don't know the words!"

"The words are here," Gordon said. "Sing it, Amy. Please, sing it."

"Gordy, you know I can't sing."

"It doesn't matter. Please, Amy," Gordon begged. "They will shoot me if you don't sing."

Amy cleared her throat, then began singing.

"He ties up one foot, the saddle puts on,
  With a swing and a jump he is mounted and gone.
  The first time I met him, 'twas early one spring,
  Riding a bronco, a high-headed thing.
  He tipped me a wink as he gaily did go,
  For he wished me to look at his bucking bronco.
  The next time I saw him, 'twas late in the fall,
  Swinging the girls at Tomlinson's ball:
  He laughed and he talked as we danced to and fro,
  —Promised never to ride on another bronco."

Just as the song finished, Sheriff Carson came into the saloon. "Brown, I heard a shot."

"I reckon you did, Sheriff. Peterson just got hisself kilt."

"Got himself killed? You mean he committed suicide?"

"No."

"Then you tell me how a man 'gets himself killed.'"

"By pointing a gun at me," Priest said.

Sheriff Carson looked over at the man who spoke. He was a small, thin man with a prominent Adam's apple and a big nose.

"Are you saying you killed him?"

"Yeah, I killed him. But it was in self-defense. Everyone in here will tell you he had a gun in his hand. Hell, look at 'im. He's still holdin' the gun."

Sheriff Carson looked over at Peterson's body, and, as Priest said, his fingers were still clinched around the handle of his gun.

"This has been a busy day for me and for Tom Nunnley." Sheriff Carson looked at Priest. "And for you. I understand you killed two men out at Long Trek."

Priest smiled. "News gets around fast, doesn't it?"

"Fast enough."

"I suppose you also heard that was self-defense. Both Strode and Conn drew on me."

"Like Mr. Peterson?"

Priest shook his head. "No sir, this one was different. You see, Mr. Peterson already had his gun out. He was threatening to shoot not only me, but the piano player."

Sheriff Carson frowned, then looked toward the piano. "Is that true, Beaver? Peterson was going to shoot you?"

"Tell him, piano player. Did he threaten to shoot you or not?"

Gordon was standing by the piano, holding a towel to his ear. Many red spots of blood were on the towel.

"That's true, Sheriff. He threatened to shoot me if I played *Buckskin Joe* one more time."

"One more time? What do you mean one more time? How many times had you played it?"

"I don't know," Gordy said. "Six or seven times, I suppose. I lost count."

"Good Lord, man. Why were you playing the same song so many times?"

"I-I play requests, Sheriff. You know that. What money I make is in tips. If the customers don't like what I'm playing, they won't give me tips."

"I see. What happened to your ear?"

Gordy looked over toward Manning, then toward Priest. "I cut it shaving."

"Are you sure there isn't more to it than that?"

Gordy shook his head. "No, that's all there is to it. I cut it shaving."

"Sheriff, are you through lookin' at the body?" Brown asked. "Because if you are, I'll get a couple men to carry it next door to the undertaker."

Sheriff Carson stared for another long moment at the piano player, then he studied Priest and the other Long Trek riders in the bar. If he pushed the issue too far, Priest and the others might turn on him. He wished Smoke had come with him. He wouldn't be nearly as anxious, if Smoke were there.

"Sheriff, the body? Can I have a couple men carry it out?" Brown repeated after the long, drawn out silence.

"Yeah," Sheriff Carson answered, and he turned and hurried out of the Brown Dirt.

"You two men, I'll give you five dollars apiece if you'll carry Peterson's body next door to the undertaker."

The two men nodded, then with one man at Petersons head and the other at his feet, they picked him up and carried him to the building next door.

Tom Nunnley already had three bodies laid out in the embalming room, when the two men came in with a fourth. "Lord Almighty, is there a war going on? This is the fourth gunshot victim I've seen today."

"Yeah, and a man named Priest kilt three of 'em," one of the two body bearers said.

The other man laughed. "You ought to give him a percentage of what you're makin'."

"Oh, my Lord, this is Clem Peterson," Nunnley said. "I just buried his wife last month. He's been actin' strange ever since. I guess I'm not all that surprised to see him."

It was nearly midnight when Chris Logan dismounted and walked over to look down at the dam on Frying Pan Creek. He was carrying three sticks of dynamite, tied and fused together, and he laid the dynamite on top of the wooden dam, rolled out a long piece of fuse, trimmed it, then lit it and backed away quickly.

He watched the fuse spark and sputter until it reached the sticks. There was a big explosion and the dam was destroyed. Once more, water began flowing through the natural channel of Frying Pan Creek.

Satisfied with his work, Logan mounted his horse to ride home. It had been his intention to pick up any bit of evidence that would suggest anything other than the natural failure of the dam, but as he rode off, a small, overlooked coil of fuse lay on the ground behind him.

Returning home he saw, with great satisfaction, that once again, water was flowing through his land.

When he went back into his house, he saw his wife sitting at the kitchen table, drinking coffee by the light of a single candle. Logan smiled at her. "We've got water again."

"Chris, please tell me you didn't do something to the dam," she said, the tone in her voice reflecting her concern.

"I can't tell you that, because that is exactly what I did do. That damn Frenchman had no right to dam up the creek, and you know it."

"What did you do?"

"I blew that damn dam to hell, that's what I did." Logan laughed. "Damn dam, that's funny."

"No, Chris, it's not funny. That was a dumb thing for you to do."

"Nobody saw me, Ethel."

"It doesn't make any difference whether they saw you are not. We are the only ones the dam had any effect on. How hard is it going to be for the French-man to figure out who did it? I'm afraid."

Logan put his hand on Ethel's shoulder. "Darlin', I was with Reno at Little Big Horn. I don't think I can ever be afraid again."

* * *

"Look there," Gately said the next morning, pointing to the spot where the dam had been. "The dam is gone."

Anderson, who was riding with him, dismounted and walked over to have a closer look. He saw several pieces of splintered wood lying about.

"It's not just gone. Someone took it down." He picked up a piece of wood and examined it more closely. "Like as not, it was dynamited."

Gately dismounted. "Let's toss these pieces into the stream," he said, picking one of them up and throwing it into the water."

"Why?"

"If Garneau finds out the dam was dynamited, it could get dangerous for someone. If he thinks the dam just failed due to water pressure, it would be much better."

"Yeah," Anderson said. "Yeah, I see what you mean." He joined Gately in tossing the shattered remnants of the dam into the water.

"What are you men doing?"

Startled, Gately looked around to see that Manning had ridden up on them.

"Nothing," Anderson said. "Just cleaning up a bit, is all."

"What happened to the dam?" Manning asked.

"I think the water pressure must have caused it to give way," Anderson said.

Manning dismounted and picked up one of the pieces for a closer examination. Shrugging, he started to toss it into the water, then he saw the small coil of fuse. Reaching down, he picked it up for a closer examination. "Water didn't do this. This dam was dynamited."

"Oh, I don't think so," Gately said.

"Really? What do you call this?" Manning held out the piece of fuse he had found.

"Damn, I didn't see that," Gately said.

CHAPTER TWENTY-SEVEN

Paris, France

Inspector Laurent was in General Moreau's office. "General, I believe I have found the man I have been looking for."

"You've found Mouchette?"

"Well, I haven't actually found him yet, but at least I am certain I have discovered the name he is now using."

Laurent placed some papers on General Moreau's desk. "He is Colonel the Marquis Lucien Garneau."

"Colonel the Marquis Lucien Garneau?" General Moreau replied with a puzzled expression on his face. He shook his head. "Inspector, I am aware of no such colonel."

Laurent smiled broadly. "Precisely so, *mon général.* But someone using that name booked passage from Hamburg, Germany to New York in America. And since there is no such person, I am certain it must be Mouchette."

General Moreau returned Laurent's smile and nodded. "Yes. Yes, I am sure this must be so." The smile left his face. "But if the *coquin* has escaped to America, I fear he has eluded us. America is a very large country."

"I would like to go to America to look for him."

General Moreau stroked his chin as he considered the request.

"General, this man not only stole two and a half million francs, he also murdered Sergeant Dubois," Laurent said, pushing his request. "And now, using a false name and rank, he is, no doubt, bringing discredit upon the French Republic. He must not get away with it."

"What makes you think you can find him in America?"

"Because, *mon général*, I have right on my side."

General Moreau nodded. "Very well, Inspector. Go to America with my blessings, and with the hope of all France that you find this criminal."

Laurent saluted. "I will find him, *mon général*."

Sugarloaf

"Pearlie?"

The cowhand was in the barn when he heard someone call out to him, and he went to the door. "Gately, what are you doing here?"

"I'm afraid there's goin' to be some trouble over at Logan's place."

"What kind of trouble?"

"Bad trouble. Garneau put up a dam on Frying Pan Creek to keep the water from flowing onto Logan's ranch. I think Logan must have blown the dam last night. One of Garneau's gunnies found out about it. I think Garneau plans to send some people over to teach Logan a lesson."

"Why are you tellin' me this, Gately? I thought you worked for Garneau."

"I did, but I don't work for him no more. Me 'n Andy has quit. I don't like the way the Frenchman does business."

"Thanks for tellin' me," Pearlie said. "I'll tell Smoke and see what he wants to do about it."

"I'm goin' with you," Malcolm said when Smoke, Pearlie, and Cal stopped by Carro de Bancada on their way to Logan's ranch.

"You don't need to go. We just stopped by to tell you what's happening," Smoke said.

"If I am the one who has talked all the others into staying, should I not subject myself to the same dangers I'm asking of them?"

"There's likely to be some shooting. You said yourself, you have no experience with guns."

"My father told me the story of Uncle Humboldt," Malcolm said. "He was a boy raised in Brooklyn, just as my father was. He had never even fired a gun until he went into the army during the war. At Gettysburg, my Uncle Humboldt was mentioned in the dispatches for what he did with a rifle."

Smoke chuckled. "Yes, I saw some examples of your uncle's marksmanship. He was very good with it. Very well, you can come along if you wish."

"Thank you. I'll just get my guns."

"Make sure you bring a rifle."

Concerned they might get to Logan's place too late, they were glad to see Logan, his wife, and his two sons working in the garden when they rode up. Logan looked up as the riders approached, at first with some apprehension, then with a smile when he recognized them.

"Well, Smoke, Malcolm, Pearlie, Cal. Welcome. What are you all doing here?"

"Chris, did you dynamite the dam on Frying Pan Creek last night?" Smoke asked.

The smile left Logan's face. "What if I did? I don't see where the Frenchman has the right to dam off a creek."

"Whoa. We're on your side, Chris," Malcolm said. "But the thing is, Garneau might be sending some men over here."

"Let 'im do it. If Crazy Horse and Sitting Bull didn't scare me, that peckerwood isn't going to. I'll stand up to him."

"You won't have to stand up to him alone," Smoke said. "We are going to be here with you. But it might be a good idea for Mrs. Logan and your two boys to leave. They can go to my place and stay with Sally for a while."

"Yeah," Logan said. "Now that you mention it, that might be a pretty good idea. Ethel, I'm going to get the buckboard hitched up. Take the boys over to the Jensen place."

"Chris, I . . ."

Logan took his wife's hands in his. "Ethel, you were a soldier's wife. You know how things are."

"But I'm not a soldier's wife anymore."

"Yes, you are. Once a soldier, always a soldier. And you're still my wife. Now, do like I tell you."

"All right."

"Mrs. Logan, go around by Cottonwood Pass Road," Smoke suggested. "That way there's little chance you'll run across any of Garneau's men."

Ethel nodded, then stood there with her sons until Logan brought the buckboard around a few minutes later. He kissed her, then helped her and the two boys into the buckboard.

"Stay with Sally until we come back," Smoke said.

Ethel nodded, then slapped the reins against the back of the team, and the buckboard left.

"Cal, why don't you ride out toward the south and keep an eye out. Let us know if you see anything," Smoke suggested.

"Will do," Cal agreed, and remounting, he left at a trot.

Logan watched his wife drive off for a long minute, then he turned back to Smoke and the others. "I lied."

"What?"

"When I said that Crazy Horse and Sitting Bull didn't scare me, I lied. They scared the hell out of me."

Smoke laughed. "Good."

"Good?"

"Yes, good. I don't want to be standing here, facing Garneau's men with a fool beside me."

Logan and the others laughed as well.

"Well, we may as well get ready for them," Smoke said. "Chris, this is your place, and you're an old army sergeant, do you have any ideas on disposition of the troops?"

"Yes. One of you should be in the hayloft over there. You'll have a good field of fire from the open door."

"I'll go there," Pearlie said.

"Another could be on top of the machine shop. Get on the other slope of the roof, just behind the peak."

"I'll do that," Malcolm said.

"Smoke, if you'd like, you can be down here on the ground, waiting just behind the cottonwood over there. I'll be by the watering trough. I can get down behind it quickly, if I need to."

The men heard the sound of an approaching horse, and looking in that direction, saw Cal coming back at a gallop.

"They're comin'," Cal said as he swung down from the saddle.

"How far, and how many?" Smoke asked.

"I'd say they're still a mile to a mile and a half away.
"I counted ten of 'em."

"That means they have us exactly doubled," Malcolm said.

"Is Garneau with them?"

"To tell the truth, Smoke, I don't know if he is or not. I've only seen him one time, and they were too far back to make out any actual features."

"No matter, we'll handle it all right. You get up into the hayloft with Pearlie. Malcolm, you may as well get yourself in position as well."

"Right," Malcolm said.

"Come on, Cal, let's get to our places," Pearlie said.

The three men left to climb into their perches, so that only Smoke and Logan remained behind.

"How do you think we should handle this, Smoke? Let 'em get close enough to talk? Or start shootin' as soon as we see 'em?"

"Yell at them and stop them just out of pistol range," Smoke said. "If they try to pass that point after you have warned them, start shooting."

Armed and ready, they stood next to each other, waiting for Garneau's men.

Templeton held up his hand to stop the riders. They were on the rest of a ridgeline, and Logan's house and outbuildings were spread out before them.

"What do you think, Templeton?" Jerry Briggs asked.

"I think we should just ride in and shoot the man. And leave no witnesses."

"He's got a woman and kids," Mathis said.

"Like I said, leave no witnesses."

"Don't you think, maybe, we could have a little fun with the woman first?" Carr asked.

"Have you seen his woman, Carr?" Briggs asked. "She's so ugly she'd make a train take ten miles of dirt road."

The other men laughed.

"Hell, what does that matter?" Carr asked as he grabbed himself. "I just want to have a little fun with her. I don't plan to marry her."

Again, the men laughed.

They continued to advance toward the Logan place until they were within about two hundred yards. Templeton stopped them again.

"What it is?" Mathis asked. "What'd you stop us for?"

"Let's spread out and advance in . . . in . . . what was it Garneau called it during our practices?"

"A frontal line attack," Briggs said.

"Right. Spread out and advance at a trot. When I give the word, we'll continue at a gallop."

"Smoke," Logan said. "I've seen this before. There ain't goin' to be no talkin', no callin' out for them to not come any closer. They're comin' at us in a full blown attack."

"All right. Get down behind the water trough." Smoke used his hands as a megaphone and called, "Pearlie, Cal!"

"Yeah?" a voice called back.

"Start shooting as soon as they're in range."

"Right."

"Malcolm?"

"Yes, sir, I heard," Malcolm said.

Smoke levered a round into the chamber of his rifle, then got behind the cottonwood tree and waited.

The line of trotting horses came within a hundred yards of the barn, which was the closest building to them.

"Now!" Templeton shouted.

The ten riders broke into a gallop, firing pistols as they advanced.

Cal was the first one to fire. Standing in the open window of the hayloft, he fired at the rider closest to him, and that rider went down. Pearlie fired next, then Smoke, Malcolm, and Logan all fired at about the same time. The defenders had not picked out individual targets, so only two more attackers went down, a couple of them hit twice.

"What the hell?" Briggs shouted. "He ain't alone! We've been ambushed!"

"Let's get out of here!" Templeton shouted, and he jerked his horse around, leading the retreat as all seven remaining men galloped away.

"Hah!" Cal shouted from just inside the window in the hayloft. "Did you see them boys run?"

Cal, Pearlie, and Malcolm came down from their perches, and the five men gathered just in front of the watering trough.

Pearlie laughed. "You know what I think? I think them boys got a huge surprise."

"Yeah," Cal said.

"How did you know they were comin'?" Logan asked.

"Believe it or not, one of Garneau's men told us," Smoke said.

"Who was it? Gately or Anderson?"

"Both of them, actually."

Logan nodded. "Yeah, I thought so. They were about the only two men still workin' over there who had any good left in 'em."

CHAPTER TWENTY-EIGHT

From the *Big Rock Journal:*

Gun Battle at Logan's Ranch

On Thursday previous, several mounted gunmen attacked Chris Logan and some of his neighbors at Mr. Logan's ranch. Long time residents of Eagle and Pitkin counties will recognize that Logan's ranch is near Carro de Bancada, which once belonged to the late Mr. Humboldt Puddle. They will also remember that Humboldt Puddle was killed in an occasion similar to the most recent gunfight.

Colonel the Marquis Lucien Garneau, owner of Long Trek Ranch, suggests the assailants were cattle rustlers, with the intention of stealing Chris Logan's entire herd. "This validates the concern I expressed to the Cattlemen's Association recently, when I explained my reason for hiring skilled gunmen who could provide protection, not only for my cattle, but for the cattle of my neighbors, such as Chris Logan."

Lucy Woodward to Visit Atlanta

Lucy Woodward, the winsome lass who is the daughter of local farmer Charles Woodward, will be taking the eastbound train on Monday next. The purpose of the trip is to visit her cousin and to enjoy the sights of Atlanta. Mr. Woodward brought his family from Atlanta six years previous, and this will be the first time any member of the family has returned to the old homeland.

New York City

Inspector Laurent stood in the office of Captain Warren Haggardorn of the New York Police Department. "I am Inspector André Laurent of the Gendarmerie Nationale, the French Police, and I am looking for one of my countryman, a person who identifies himself as Colonel the Marquis Lucien Garneau."

"Inspector, if there is such a person as Colonel the Marquis Lucien Garneau in New York, I know nothing of him," Haggardorn said. "How much money did you say he brought with him to America?"

"Half a million dollars in American money."

Haggardorn let out a low whistle. "That is a lot of money. I don't think anyone would keep that much money on his person. I'll do a very thorough check of all the banks in the city. If he made a deposit anywhere, we'll find him."

"Thank you, Monsieur."

"You want this man pretty bad, do you?"

"*Oui*. He not only stole the money from the French Army, he murdered a soldier who was under his command, then attempted to blame that murdered soldier for the robbery. He is a man who is completely without honor. I want to take him home to face the guillotine."

"I don't blame you," Chief Haggardorn said. "I don't know what I can do to help, but I promise you that we'll do everything we can for you."

"*Merci*, Monsieur Chief Haggardorn."

Big Rock

Charles Woodward was driving a buckboard taking his daughter to the depot in Big Rock. In the back of the buckboard was the train case Lucy would carry on board with her, as well as two suitcases that would be checked through to make the trip in the baggage car.

"Now, you are sure you are taking enough clothes?" her father teased. "I wouldn't want you to get to Atlanta and suddenly find that you didn't have a dress, a hat, a pair of shoes, or the pitcher and basin from your bedroom."

"Father, you know what Atlanta is like," Lucy said. "Why, Cousin Doreen will have all sorts of balls and cotillions for me to attend. You wouldn't want me to embarrass you by not being properly dressed, would you?"

Woodward chuckled. "Oh, heavens no. The last thing I want is to be embarrassed because my daughter, who more often than not can be found wearing men's pants, shirt, hat, and straddling a horse, wouldn't be properly dressed at some fancy ball."

"Then you needn't worry, because I won't embarrass you."

They reached the train station and Woodward parked the buckboard under a tree. He grabbed the suitcases, Lucy carried the train case, and they entered the depot. After securing a ticket and checking the suitcases, they took a seat to wait until it was time to board.

Woodward turned to his daughter. "I see you are wearing your mother's cameo brooch."

"Yes, isn't it beautiful? She said I could wear it while I was in Atlanta."

"You be careful that you don't lose it. Your mother sets quite a store by that."

"I'll make sure I don't lose it. I will wear it pinned to my dress, every day."

"I'm surprised you are going anyway. I thought you and young Malcolm Puddle were sparking one another."

"Why, Father, whatever gave you that idea?" Lucy asked, though her cheeks flamed red as she blushed over the comment.

Woodward chuckled. "Nothing, my dear. Absolutely nothing." He leaned over and kissed his daughter on the forehead. "I was just teasing you a little. I want you to have a wonderful time. Give your cousin my regards."

"I will, Father."

"And I want you to send me a telegram as soon as you arrive in Atlanta. I want to know you got there safely."

Lucy laughed. "I swear, Father, you are a bigger worrywart than Mama. Don't worry about me. I'll be just fine. I'm not a little girl anymore, you know."

"It's just that Atlanta is very large, not like the small towns we have here. You must watch yourself while you are there."

"Father, I will be all right."

"Board!" the conductor called.

"Oh, I must get aboard now," Lucy kissed her father then hurried to the train and stepped up onto the car vestibule.

Woodward went down to the track as well, and as the cars began to move, he walked alongside, keeping pace with the train as it pulled away from the depot. "Remember, as soon as you arrive . . ."

"Send you a telegram. Yes, I promise," Lucy called back through the open window. "And I'll write to you in a few days to tell you what a wonderful time I'm having."

"Bye!" Woodward said, waving and calling to her.

"Bye!"

Woodward remained on the platform as the train pulled out of the station, watching it until, moving quite rapidly, it receded in the distance. Not until the train was a remote whistle and a distant puff of smoke in the clear, blue, sky, did he return to the buckboard. Untying the reins, he snapped then against the back of the team, and started home.

* * *

"Ticket, please, miss," the conductor said.

Lucy showed him the long roll of tickets and he perused them before punching a hole in one.

"All the way to Atlanta, is it?"

"Yes, sir, to see my cousin."

"Well, you'll change trains in Pueblo, Denver, St. Louis, and Nashville. You are certainly going to be seeing a lot of the country."

"Yes, sir, I suppose I will."

"Well, Miss . . ."

"Woodward. Lucy Woodward," she replied with a smile.

"Miss Woodward, if you need anything, just let me know. My name is Murtaugh, and I am the conductor. You make friends with all the conductors from here to Atlanta. It's their job to keep an eye on young, unaccompanied ladies."

"Yes, sir, Mr. Murtaugh, I will. Thank you."

Four hours later, the eastbound train, on which Lucy Woodward was a passenger, made a late night stop for water. Lucy, who was sleeping in the front seat of the car, was only vaguely aware the stop had been made. She was too comfortable and too tired from all the packing and preparation for her visit to Atlanta to pay too much attention to it.

Turning her head away from the window she closed her eyes again and listened to the bumping sounds from outside as the fireman lowered the spout from the trackside water tower and began squirting water down into the tank.

"Whoowee. This is one thirsty train," the fireman called.

"It should be thirsty. We haven't taken on a drop of water in the last sixty miles," the engineer called down.

Lucy could hear the two men talking, and she thought of them working hard to drive the train while she was inside on a comfortable and padded seat.

The train was alive with sound: from the loud puffs of the actuating cylinder relief valves venting steam to the splash of water filling the tank to the snapping and popping of overheated bearings and gearboxes. Lucy, the fireman and engineer, and everyone else on the train were unaware of Briggs and Carr outside the train, slipping through the shadows alongside the railroad track.

They had been in position for nearly an hour, waiting by the tower where the train would have to stop for water. Behind them, tied to a willow tree, were two horses. One of the horses was pulling a travois.

"Which car is she on?" Carr asked.

"Well, according to what we was told, she was goin' to be in the first car," Briggs answered.

Glancing up toward the tender, they saw the fireman standing with his back to them as he directed the gushing water from the spout into the tank. Satisfied that his attention was diverted, the two men stepped up onto the vestibule platform between the mail car and the first car. They remained there for just a moment to make certain they had not been discovered. Satisfied they were safe, they pushed open the door and stepped inside. The car was dimly lit by two low-burning, gimbal-mounted lanterns, one on the front wall and the other on the rear. The aisle stretched out between two rows of seats. Nearly all the passengers were asleep.

"Is that her?" Briggs whispered, indicating a woman who was sleeping in the front seat.

"Yeah, I think so," Carr answered.

Briggs reached out and touched the young woman. She awakened with a start, and looked at the two men with her eyes wide in anxious confusion.

"Are you Lucy Woodward?" Briggs asked.

"Yes, why do you ask?"

"Your mama has had a terrible accident. Your papa sent us to get you and bring you back home."

"Oh! What has happened?"

"Come with us. We have a buckboard and a fast team outside."

Concerned about her mother, Lucy got up to follow the two men outside. They approached two saddled horses, one of them dragging a travois.

"What is this? I don't see a buckboard," Lucy said.

One of the men dropped a looped rope around her to hold her arms close to her side. She screamed, but the scream was drowned out by the sound of the locomotive whistle. Before she could scream a second time, a gag was stuffed in her mouth.

No one on the train had even noticed when she left the car, nor did anyone see them putting her on the travois.

"Let's go," Briggs said.

The two men mounted and rode off, even as the train, its tank full of water, got underway again.

It wasn't until half an hour before the train pulled into Cañon City the next morning that the porter, who had been told by the conductor to keep an eye on the young, unaccompanied woman in the front seat, realized that she was gone. He made a thorough search of the two cars he was in charge of, but didn't see her.

When he checked with Julius, the other porter, a look through his two cars was also fruitless.

"What happened to her?" Julius asked.

"Lord, I wish I knew," the first porter answered. He took his concern to the conductor.

"Well, she has to be on the train somewhere. Let's look through every car."

"Mr. Murtaugh, me and Julius done looked through ever' car on this train, and we ain't found her."

"Conductor, are you looking for the woman who was sitting there?" one of the passengers asked, pointing to the front row of seats.

"Yes. Do you have any idea where she might be?"

"No, sir. But I see a piece of paper on the floor under her seat, and I know it wasn't there before. Maybe it's a clue."

The porter picked up the folded over piece of paper and handed it to the conductor.

Woodward—

We've got your daughter. It's going to cost you $5,000 to get her back. We will tell you where to deliver the money.

"What are we going to do, Mr. Murtaugh?"

The conductor thought a moment. "We'll turn this note over to the sheriff as soon as we reach Cañon City."

From the *Big Rock Journal:*

Mysterious Disappearance of Woman from Train

The fate of Miss Lucy Woodward, daughter of prominent Eagle County farmer, Charles Woodward, is still unknown. The porter on the Pueblo Special noticed she was missing shortly before the train reached the Cañon City station. He reported her disappearance to the conductor, Miles Murtaugh, and a search of the train was conducted, but to no avail.

Subsequently, a note was discovered which leads the sheriff's department to believe the woman was snatched from the train, though nobody remembers seeing the event actually happen.

The local train agent reports the note, which demands a five thousand dollar ransom, has been turned over to the sheriff.

"We've done all we can do," a railroad official reported. "All the stations along the line have been notified and we are asking that anyone who has any information on Miss Woodward's whereabouts to please contact any Denver and Pacific Railroad official."

CHAPTER TWENTY-NINE

Malcolm was sitting in a chair on the front porch of Woodward's house. Charles Woodward sat across from him. Sue Woodward was in the house, taken to bed with worry over her daughter.

"Sheriff Carson said the train only stopped twice between here and Cañon City, once for water, and once at Buena Vista," Woodward said.

"Did anyone notice her at either of those stops?" Malcolm asked.

"They don't know if she was on the train at Buena Vista or not. Nobody noticed that she was missing until shortly before the train reached Cañon City."

"It seems unlikely anyone could have taken her off forcefully without being seen," Malcolm said.

"But I don't think Lucy would have left the train on her own."

"She might have, if she was convinced to."

"How could someone convince her to leave the train in the middle of the night?"

"If she thought something had happened to either you or Mrs. Woodward, perhaps," Malcolm suggested.

"Yes, I see what you mean. That is possible, I suppose. Say, did you see in the paper that the Frenchman is offering a reward for her safe return?"

"I saw it. I don't believe it."

"I don't know. Maybe he realizes he's gotten off on the wrong foot with everyone, and he's trying to make it up. After all, nobody would want all of his neighbors hating him, would they?"

"I'm still mighty suspicious," Malcolm said. "Say, who's that coming up your drive?"

Woodward squinted as he stared at the man approaching in a buggy.

"I don't know. He's too far away to— No, wait, there's only one man I know who takes up the entire seat of a buggy. That has to be Robert Dempster."

"Who?"

"Robert Dempster. He's a lawyer in town. I wonder what he wants?"

"Maybe it has something to do with Lucy," Sue Woodward said, her comment surprising both Woodward and Malcolm, who had not seen her come out onto the porch.

Woodward reached over to take his wife's hand. "Don't get all worked up over it one way or the other. Let's find out what this is about."

They stood as they watched the buggy approach. Malcolm went down the steps, and Dempster halted the horse, then handed the reins to him. Malcolm tied the reins around a hitching post.

The buggy tilted to one side as Dempster, wheezing and puffing, climbed down. He was sweating profusely and held a handkerchief to his face as he climbed the steps to the porch.

"Can I help you, Mr. Dempster?" Woodward asked.

"Actually, Mr. Woodward, I rather hope I can help you," Dempster replied. "It's in regards to your daughter."

"What about Lucy?" Woodward asked anxiously. "Do you know where she is?"

"No, no. I'm sorry if I've given you the wrong impression," Dempster said, waving his hand. "I don't know where she is . . . but . . . I may be in a position to facilitate her safe return."

"What do you mean you can facilitate her safe return?"

"The amount of ransom being asked is five thousand dollars. Do you have five thousand dollars, Mr. Woodward?"

"Mr. Dempster, what does it matter to you whether I have five thousand dollars or not?"

"Because I told you, I may be in a position to help you. You see, Mr. Woodward, my office has been contacted by the person, or persons, who took your daughter. They have asked me to act as the agent in negotiations between you and them."

"Where is Lucy?" Malcolm asked. "You tell me where she is!"

"Easy, young man. I don't know where she is. As I

told you, they contacted me and asked me to be the go between."

"How do you know they have her?" Woodward asked.

"They sent me something to give to you, something they said would prove they have her."

"What is it?" Sue Woodward asked.

"This," Dempster said, taking an ivory cameo brooch from his pocket and showing it to them.

"Oh!" Sue put her hands over her face and began sobbing.

"Give that to me," Woodward said, grabbing the brooch.

"Is that Lucy's brooch?" Malcolm asked.

"Yes. Well, it is her mother's brooch, but she was wearing it for her trip to Atlanta."

Sue reached for the brooch then clasped it in her hands again, bringing her hands to her face as she wept.

Dempster frowned. "So, Mr. Woodward, I ask you again. Do you have five thousand dollars?"

"No, God in heaven, I don't have it."

"That's too bad," Dempster said.

"Too bad? What do you mean, too bad?" Sue asked. "Are you saying that they are going to . . . that they will . . ." She was unable to finish the question.

"No, they want the money. They don't want to hurt the girl," Dempster said. "All you have to do is come up with five thousand dollars, and they'll release her unharmed."

"Where am I going to get that kind of money?"

Dempster stroked his triple chins as he fixed his gaze on Woodward. "I tell you what. I don't want to see this innocent girl hurt, any more than you do. I don't believe it is just by chance that they chose me as the agent between you and them. I can't promise you anything, but it just may be that I will be able to arrange the money for you."

"How?"

"You let me work on that. I'll be back tomorrow with a proposal that just might work."

"Oh, bless you, Mr. Dempster. Bless you," Sue said, reaching her hand out toward him.

"Don't despair, Mrs. Woodward. I'm almost certain I can work something out." Dempster walked back down the steps, climbed into the straining buggy, turned it around, and started back toward the road.

"I wonder what he means by saying he will work something out," Malcolm said.

"I don't know," Woodward said. "But I do know he is a pretty smart lawyer. You ask anyone in town and they'll tell you Dempster is a smart lawyer."

Malcolm grimaced. "Yes, that's what bothers me."

Sugarloaf

"That looks like Malcolm coming up the road," Sally said as she stood looking out the kitchen window.

"Yes, I believe it is," Smoke said, joining her at the window. He went out onto the porch to meet his young friend. "Hello, Malcolm. Climb down and come on in."

Malcolm followed Smoke inside, then accepted a cup of coffee. "I just came from Mr. and Mrs. Woodward's place."

"How are they doing?" Sally asked.

"They're both very frightened. To tell the truth, I'm also frightened."

"Have they heard anything else from whoever took Lucy?" Smoke asked.

"Yes, that's why I've come to see you."

"What have they heard?"

"Well, nothing directly, but they have heard indirectly. By that I mean Mr. Dempster drove out to speak to them. He said the people who took Lucy have gotten in touch with him, and asked him to be an agent between them and the Woodwards."

"Were you there when he came to see them?"

"Yes, I was visiting with Mr. Woodward. Uh, the truth is, Smoke, you may not know it, but I've got me sort of a personal reason for wantin' Lucy back all safe and sound."

Smoke smiled. "Malcolm, I don't think there's a man in the whole county who doesn't know about that personal reason."

"Oh. Well, then you can see why this has me about as anxious as the Woodwards are."

"Did you believe Dempster, when he said that he had been contacted?"

"Oh, yes. He's been contacted all right. There's not the slightest doubt about that."

"Really? Why do you say that?"

"Because he gave Mr. Woodward an ivory brooch Lucy was wearing."

"That sounds like proof enough," Smoke said. "Did he have anything new to add?"

"Well, not about Lucy. I mean, not about where she was or how she was doing. He says they want five thousand dollars, just like the ransom note said."

"And he's supposed to transfer the money?"

"I don't know. He didn't say. But here is something strange that he did say. When Mr. Woodward told him he didn't have five thousand dollars, Mr. Dempster said he would come back tomorrow with a way that Mr. Woodward could get the money."

"Did he?"

"Yes, sir."

"Now, that's interesting," Smoke said. "In fact, that is very interesting. Suppose you and I go over to Woodward's farm and be there when Mr. Dempster returns tomorrow."

Malcolm smiled. "I was hoping you would suggest that."

CHAPTER THIRTY

New York City

Inspector Laurent was standing at the window of his hotel, looking down on Forty-second Street when there was a knock on his door. Opening the door, he saw one of the hotel staff.

"Mr. Laurent?"

"*Oui?*"

"Could you come to the lobby, sir? There is a telephone call for you."

Puzzled as to who would be calling him on the telephone, Laurent rode the elevator down to the lobby, then followed the messenger over to the check-in desk.

"This phone call is for you," the desk clerk said, inviting Laurent around behind the desk. The telephone was mounted on the wall, and the receiver was standing on a shelf just below the instrument.

Laurent picked up the receiver, held it to his ear,

then leaned in to the phone. "*Oui*, this is Monsieur Laurent."

"Mr. Laurent, this is Captain McKenzie of the New York Police. Could you come down to the Fifth Avenue station, please, sir? I think we have something here that you might find interesting."

"*Oui*, right away."

In front of the hotel, Laurent summoned a hansom cab. "The police station on Fifth Avenue, *si vous s'il vous plait.*"

The city was alive with activity. Jangling bells from the harnesses of horses played against the staccato beat of hooves and the ring of iron-rimmed wheels on cobblestone streets. The cab driver maneuvered the two-wheeled vehicle expertly through the heavy traffic—omnibuses, carriages, freight wagons, other cabs, and even chugging locomotives.

It took but a few minutes before the cab came to a stop in front of the police station. Paying him, Inspector Laurent went inside to inquire about Captain McKenzie.

"I am Captain McKenzie," a uniformed man said, coming to greet him.

"You said you had something that I might find interesting, Capitaine?"

"Yes," McKenzie said. "I believe you were searching for one of your countrymen, a man named Garneau?"

"That is the name he has assumed. His real name is Pierre Mouchette."

"Would someone going by the name of Colonel

the Marquis Lucien Garneau be of any interest to you?"

A broad smile spread across Laurent's face. "You have him, Capitaine?

"No, but I know where he is."

"Please, Monsieur, I beg of you. Arrest him."

"I can't do that, Inspector. He isn't in my jurisdiction. In fact, he isn't even in New York. But I can show you where he is, and you can go make your case with the local authorities."

"Where is he?"

"Of course, this may not be your man. It could be another Colonel the Marquis Lucien Garneau."

"There is no Colonel in the French army, nor is there a marquis, by the name of Lucien Garneau. If you have located someone who is using that name, Monsieur, he is my fugitive."

Take a look at this, Inspector," Captain McKenzie said, opening the *New York Times* and laying it before him. "This is an article the *Times* picked up from the Associated Press. It has the name of the man you are looking for."

McKenzie put his finger on a specific article.

Gun Battle at Logan's Ranch

Big Rock, Colorado (AP)—(From *The Big Rock Journal*)—On Thursday previous, several mounted gunmen attacked Chris Logan and some of his neighbors at Mr. Logan's ranch. Long time residents of Eagle and Pitkin counties will recognize that

Logan's ranch is near Carro de Bancada, which once belonged to the late Mr. Humboldt Puddle. They will also remember that Humboldt Puddle was killed in an occasion similar to the most recent gunfight.

Colonel the Marquis Lucien Garneau, owner of Long Trek Ranch, suggests the assailants were cattle rustlers with the intention of stealing Chris Logan's entire herd. "This validates the concern I expressed to the Cattlemen's Association recently, when I explained my reason for hiring skilled gunmen who could provide protection, not only for my cattle, but for the cattle of my neighbors, such as Chris Logan."

"*Oui!* Yes!" Laurent said excitedly. "This must be Mouchette. It can be no other. Where is this place, this"—Laurent looked back at the article—"Big Rock, Colorado?"

"Come over here to the map. I will show you," McKenzie said.

Laurent followed McKenzie to the wall where there was a large map of the United States.

"Here is New York where you are now," McKenzie said. "And way over here"—he reached far across the map with his other hand—"is Colorado."

"Mon Dieu, that is a long way."

"Yes, it is. But we have trains that go there. You can be there in less than a week. You aren't going to let a little thing like a long trip get in your way, are you?"

"*Non, monsieur.* If Mouchette is in a place called Big Rock, Colorado, then that is where I shall go."

"I thought you might."

"May I take this newspaper, Capitaine?" Laurent asked.

"Certainly, be my guest."

"*Merci.*"

With the newspaper under his arm, Laurent returned to the hotel where he packed his bag, checked out, then took a cab to Grand Central depot where he bought a ticket to Big Rock, Colorado. Before boarding the train, however, he sent a cablegram to General Moreau.

HAVE DETERMINED LOCATION OF MOUCHETTE
STOP AM PROCEEDING THERE NOW STOP
INSPECTOR LAURENT

Ajax Mountain Range, Pitkin County, Colorado

Lucy had been in the small cabin for two days, tied up for the entire time. Her back and legs were cramped and her wrists were raw from the rubbing of the ropes. "How long are you going to keep me here?"

"We're going to keep you here until your papa pays us five thousand dollars," Briggs said.

"My father is not a wealthy man. There is no way he can raise that much money."

"If he wants to get you back in one piece, he'll raise the money," Carr said.

"Are you hungry? Do you want something to eat?" Briggs asked.

"No, thank you," she replied.

"Here, take a piece," Briggs said, offering her a piece of jerky.

Lucy shook her head. "I don't want it. I would like a drink of water, though."

"You got to eat something. It's been two days and you ain't et nothin'. All you've done is drink water. Maybe you'd like somethin' to drink other than water. You want some whiskey?"

"No."

"Come on. It'll make you feel better." Briggs held the bottle out toward her.

"Please, no," she said.

"Leave her alone if she don't want it," Carr said harshly. "It don't make no sense tryin' to give whiskey to someone who don't want it. You'll just be wastin' good whiskey."

"Why won't you eat somethin'?" Briggs asked.

Lucy didn't answer.

"Miss, we're just tryin' to be nice to you. I don't really care whether you drink or not, and that's the truth of it."

"Nice to me? You haul me off the train by telling me a lie about my mother, then you bring me here and tie me up, but you say you are being nice to me?"

"Miss, maybe you don't know what sometimes happens to women when they get took," Briggs replied.

Lucy gasped in quick fear as she realized what he was saying to her.

"Don't be threatenin' her with that," Carr said. "The colonel was just real particular about that."

"The colonel? Who is the colonel?" Lucy asked.

"You got a big mouth, Carr," Briggs said.

"She don't know what I'm talkin' about. Hell, you heard her. She don't have no idea who he is."

"Just don't say nothin' about him no more."

CHAPTER THIRTY-ONE

Smoke, Pearlie, and Cal were waiting on a road about a mile east of the farm of Charles Woodward. They were expecting Dempster to call on Woodward, and when he left the farm, Smoke wanted to know where he planned to go.

"Don't stop him," Smoke said. "And don't let him see you follow him. I just want to know where he goes after he leaves Woodward's farm."

"All right," Pearlie said.

"What if he leads us to the girl?" Cal asked. "Can we rescue her?"

"I don't think he'll be going to the girl, but if he does, and you see the opportunity to rescue her without getting her hurt, of course you can do it."

"I'll bet she would give me a dance at the next dance if I did that," Cal said with a broad smile.

"If she did, it would only be the one dance to thank you," Pearlie replied with a chuckle. "Ever'body knows she has her cap set for Malcolm."

"Yeah, well, all I'd want is one dance anyway."

"You two get over there, on the other side of that ridgeline," Smoke said. "When he leaves, this is the way he will go. And if I have this figured correctly, when he gets to the T in the road, he'll turn left."

"Left? Town is to the right," Cal said.

"Uh-huh."

"The Long Trek is to the left," Pearlie said. "You're thinkin' the Frenchman is behind this, aren't you?"

"That's exactly what I'm thinking," Smoke said. "And today, we're going to call his bluff."

"Smoke, you don't really think the Frenchman is that evil, do you?"

"I don't think it's a coincidence that someone has tried twice to kill me, and someone has tried to kill you two. I think the Frenchman believes that if he can get us out of the way, he'll have a clear track to owning the entire valley."

"Yeah? Well, he don't know Miss Sally, does he?" Cal said. "He might kill you, but he would still have Miss Sally to contend with."

Smoke chuckled. "Well now, Cal, that's just real comforting."

"Yeah, well, that's what I'm saying."

Pearlie laughed as well. "Cal, quit while you're ahead."

"What'd I say?"

"I see dust way up the road," Pearlie said. "I'll bet that's him."

Smoke nodded. "I'm sure it is. I'm going on up to

the house. You boys get out of sight." He sat his horse until he saw that Pearlie and Cal were well out of sight, then he rode on the rest of the way to Woodward's farm.

Woodward and Malcolm were sitting in chairs on the front porch. Because they were expecting Smoke, there was a third chair on the porch, empty and waiting for him. At Woodward's invitation, Smoke took it.

"Is he coming?" Malcolm asked.

"I saw someone coming up the road. I didn't wait around long enough to see who it was, but I'm sure it's Dempster."

"I'm sure it is, too," Woodward said.

"Have you got the money with you?" Smoke asked Woodward.

"Yes, sir," Woodward answered. "And I can't thank you enough. But I have to be honest with you, Smoke, I don't know how, when, or even if I can ever pay you back."

"I'll pay him back, Mr. Woodward," Malcolm said. "I can borrow enough money against my ranch to do that."

"Neither one of you will have to pay me back," Smoke said. "I'm pretty sure I'll be able to get it back on my own."

"I think that's our man coming, now," Malcolm said.

Looking up the road they could see dust roiling up, though as yet, they couldn't see the buggy. Then a moment later, the buggy came into view, and they watched as Dempster drove all the way up to the porch. He sat there for a moment as the dust cloud rolled over him, but didn't bother to climb down from the buggy. "I've got good news for you, Mr. Woodward. Very good news."

"Mr. Dempster, the only good news you can have for me is that my daughter has been found and is safe."

"Well, unfortunately, it hasn't advanced that far yet. But I'm reasonably certain we aren't far from a successful end to this terrible ordeal. I think you will be happy to know that I've arranged to get the five thousand dollars for you."

"Have you, now?" Woodward asked.

"Yes, sir, I have. It wasn't easy, mind you. It took a lot of talking before I could convince Mr. Montgomery to go along with it. But, I have the five thousand dollars."

"Do you have the money with you?" Woodward asked.

"What? Oh, heavens no. It's still in the bank. You'll have to come to the bank with me and sign some papers before the money can be released. But not to worry," he added with a big smile. "The money is there for you, and Joel Montgomery has agreed to make the loan."

"I'm not signing any papers," Woodward said.

"What?"

"You heard me. I'm not going to the bank to sign any loan papers," Woodward repeated.

"But you must! Mr. Woodward, I don't know if you understand the seriousness of the situation here. The ransom demand is for five thousand dollars. This is your daughter's life you are dealing with. Surely you aren't going to balk at signing a few loan papers, are you?"

"I'm not going to sign any loan papers, because it isn't necessary. I have the money." Woodward reached around behind his chair, and brought forth a small cloth bag. He held the bag out toward Dempster. "It's all here. Five thousand dollars. You can count it."

"What?" Dempster asked, his voice weak with shock and disbelief. "But I thought, that is, you told me you didn't have the money."

"I lied," Woodward said. "I wasn't going to let the outlaws know I had the money until it was absolutely necessary. But, it's like you said, Mr. Dempster. This is my daughter's life I'm dealing with, so I'm not going to let five thousand dollars get in the way of her safety."

Dempster made no effort to take the money, so Malcolm took the cloth bag from Woodward, then stepped down to Dempster's buggy. He held the sack up, but the lawyer still made no effort to take it.

"What's the matter, Dempster?" Smoke asked. "Why aren't you taking the money? Aren't you the agent for this?"

"Oh . . . uh . . . yes. Yes, of course. I'll . . . uh . . . I'll take the money."

"Count it," Woodward said.

"No need to. I'm sure if you say it is all there, then it is all there," Dempster replied.

"Count it in front of these witnesses," Malcolm said. "Mr. Woodward wants it well understood that the ransom money for his daughter's release has been given to his"—Malcolm paused for a long second—"agent."

"All right." Dempster opened the sack, took out a stack of one hundred dollar bills and began counting them.

"Count them out loud," Smoke ordered.

"One hundred," Dempster started, and he enumerated each bill until he reached five thousand dollars.

"What will you do with that money now?" Smoke asked.

"I don't know. Uh, I wasn't told about this."

"What do you mean? You were told to collect five thousand dollars, weren't you?" Smoke said.

"Well, yes."

"They must have told you what to do with the money when you received it. Well, you've collected the five thousand dollars. Seems to me, your next step is to put that money into motion, so Mr. Woodward's daughter is returned to him."

"Y-yes," Dempster stammered. "Yes, that's what I will do." He put the money on the floor beside him, clicked at his horse, turned the buggy, and drove away.

"Where do you think he's going now?" Woodward asked.

Smoke grinned. "I believe he is going to see Garneau to see what he's supposed to do next."

"Pearlie, looks like he's comin' back from the Woodward place," Cal said.

"Get back down behind the crest so's there no chance of him seein' you," Pearlie said.

Cal turned his horse and guided him back down. The two men waited until they heard the buggy pass on the road below the ridge, then they rode back to the top and watched. They waited until the buggy was at least quarter of a mile down the road before they followed.

"You think we're far enough back?" Cal said. "What if he looks behind him?"

"That buggy's kickin' up so much dust, there's no way he can see us."

The two men continued to follow, then saw him turn left when he reached the T in the road.

"Smoke was right," Cal said. "He's goin' straight to the Frenchman's place."

Pearlie nodded his agreement. "You ride back and tell Smoke. I'll keep on Dempster's tail."

Long Trek

"How did it go?" Garneau asked. "Did Woodward take out the loan?"

Dempster was sweating profusely, and he wiped his face with a handkerchief. "I wonder if I might have a drink of water."

"Yes, of course. Mr. Reeves, get Mr. Dempster a glass of water," Garneau ordered. Then he glanced back at Dempster. "Would you care for a little brandy?"

"Just water is fine, thank you."

Reeves poured a glass of water from a pitcher that sat on a side table, then brought it over to Dempster.

Dempster gulped it down, then handed the empty glass back. "Thank you."

"Now, how did it go?"

"He gave me the money," Dempster said.

"Good, good," Garneau said, smiling as he rubbed his hands together. "Then he took out the loan. Did you explain to Montgomery that it was to be a forty-eight-hour loan? I want to be able to redeem it and—"

"There was no loan," Dempster said.

"What?"

"There was no loan," Dempster said. "Woodward had the five thousand dollars in cash. I have the money with me."

"I don't understand. Where did he get the money?"

"I don't know for sure," Dempster said. "But Smoke Jensen was there with him. As was Malcolm Puddle. It is my belief that one of them gave him the money."

Garneau swore, hitting his fist into his hand.

"What should I do with the money?" Dempster asked.

"I don't care what you do with the money," Garneau replied. He shook his head, then went over and poured himself a glass of brandy, swallowing it down before he spoke again.

"This isn't working out the way I planned."

CHAPTER THIRTY-TWO

"You was right, Smoke," Cal said. "Dempster went straight to the Frenchman's place."

"Is he still there?"

"Far as I know he is. I left so I could come back and tell you about it. Pearlie is still there, watchin' out."

"Well, that confirms it," Smoke said. "Garneau is the one who took your daughter. That whole loan business was just to set up a situation where you would have to pledge your ranch in order to get the money."

"Who's this comin' up the road now?" Cal asked.

"Well, I'll be," Malcolm said.

"What is it, Malcolm?"

"That is Curly Roper. I had a brief . . . uh . . . meeting with him the day I arrived in Big Rock."

"Yes," Woodward said. "I heard about that meeting."

"I know Roper. He works for Garneau," Cal said.

"I wonder what he wants," Smoke said.

"Probably bringing some offer from Garneau—my farm for my daughter," Woodward said.

"No, I don't think so. Roper isn't someone he would send for that," Smoke said.

Roper rode all the way up to the porch, then stopped. His horse began cropping some grass and he patted him on the neck.

"What do you want, Roper?" Woodward asked.

"I think I know where your daughter is."

"What? Where? Is she all right?"

"Look, I'm not sure of any of this, but I have a pretty good idea."

"What did Garneau tell you to say?" Malcolm asked.

Roper looked over at Malcolm. "Mr. Puddle, I know me 'n you didn't get off on the right foot, and that's all my fault. I'm sorry 'bout that. As for Garneau, that damnable excuse for a man didn't tell me nothin' to say. I can't work for him no more, not after all he's done.

"Like I said, I don't know for sure, but I got me an idea that your daughter might be in a cabin up on Ajax Mountain. The reason I say this is 'cause I know there's a cabin up there. Some of us have used it now and then. Well, the other day a couple of us was talkin' 'bout maybe goin' up there to do some huntin', but we was told we couldn't use it no more. Then Briggs and Carr left with some provisions like they was goin' to be gone for a long time. It turns out they left right after there was that article in the paper 'bout your daughter goin' to Atlanta.

"That didn't mean all that much to me until today,

when that lawyer come to see Garneau. Reeves—he's the English feller that works as a valet—he overheard Garneau and the lawyer talkin'. Turns out Garneau was all upset that you had come up with the money, Mr. Woodward. Seems he had set up a loan for you, that if you didn't pay it back in forty-eight hours, he would be able to pay it off and take over your farm.

"When Reeves told me that—Reeves, he says he can't work for Garneau no more neither—well, sir, it got me to thinkin'. I wouldn't be none at all surprised if Garneau didn't send them two, Briggs and Carr, out to snatch that girl, just so's you'd have to borrow that money. I can't be sure, but if I was layin' a bet on it, I would bet that Briggs and Carr are holdin' her, more 'n likely in that cabin up on Ajax."

"Mr. Roper, I appreciate you telling us this," Woodward said.

"Yes, sir, well, I just hope I'm right and that you can find the girl and get her back safe 'n all." With a nod, Roper turned, then rode away.

"Can we believe him?" Cal asked.

"I think so," Malcolm said. "It took a lot of guts for him to come over here to tell us that. The question isn't whether or not he is telling us the truth. The question is whether or not he is right."

"It's easy enough to find out," Smoke said. "I'm going to the cabin."

"I'm going with you," Malcolm said.

"You'd better let me go alone, Malcolm," Smoke said. "This is more my kind of game than yours."

"I'm going, Smoke, whether I go with you or by

myself," Malcolm said. "I've got a personal interest in this."

Smoke looked at the intense young man for a moment, then he nodded. "All right. I see how it might be something pretty important to you. You're welcome to come along with me."

"What about Pearlie and me?" Cal asked.

"I think maybe the two of you should stay here with Mr. and Mrs. Woodward. If Garneau went so far as to take Lucy off the train, there's no telling what he might do next."

"All right," Cal agreed.

Ajax Mountain

"Who's that comin' this way?" Briggs asked, looking through the cabin window to the right of the door.

Carr went to the window on the other side to have a look. "It's Templeton."

"Huh. I wonder what he wants."

The two men stepped out in front of the cabin to watch as Templeton rode up, then dismounted.

"Did you bring us any whiskey?" Briggs asked. "We're near 'bout out."

"You don't need any more. You won't be staying here much longer," Templeton said.

"Why not?"

"Because it didn't work out the way Garneau wanted. Woodward got the money for the ransom somewhere else."

"You mean the ransom's been paid?" Carr asked.

"Yes."

"So what are we goin' to do now? We can't just let her go. Hell, she's seen us. She even knows our names," Carr said.

"Who said anything about letting her go?"

"So, what are you saying? We're supposed to kill her?"

"You got a problem with killing women?" Templeton asked.

"The only problem I got is, ever'body in the state of Colorado will be lookin' for us," Briggs said.

Templeton opened his saddlebag and pulled out two packets of money. "Here's twenty-five hundred dollars for each of you. That ought to be enough money for you to leave the state."

"Yeah!" Carr said, taking the money. "That'll do it."

"I got a question," Briggs said. "Since we're goin' to kill her anyway, is there any objection to us . . . uh . . . havin' a little fun with her?"

Templeton smirked. "Not as long as I'm first."

It had been a three-hour ride from Woodward's farm to Ajax Mountain. Smoke saw the cabin at the base of the mountain. "There it is."

"What do we do now? Just ride up to it?" Malcolm asked.

"No. We'll tie our horses off here in the trees, then go up through that arroyo until we get to the other side of the cabin." Smoke pointed to a steep-sided dry gulch that led up the mountain.

The two men worked their way up until they were

even with the cabin, then Smoke climbed up a little farther to take a look. The cabin was small, no more than ten feet by ten feet, with a single window in the back. There were no windows on the side.

"Somebody's coming to the cabin," Smoke said.

"Maybe we've made a mistake. Maybe Lucy isn't there."

"Wait a minute. No, she's there, all right. That's Templeton."

Smoke watched as two men came out of the cabin and began talking to Templeton. They talked to him for a moment, then all three went inside.

"What do we do now? Wait until nightfall?" Malcolm asked.

"No. I don't know what Templeton is doing here, but I don't like the looks of it. If we wait until nightfall it might be too late. We're going to have to go in now."

"Have you got any ideas?"

"I can approach the cabin from the side, but before I go in, I'm going to need something that will divert their attention from the front door."

"What if I break the back window?" Malcolm suggested.

"No," Smoke said. "I can approach the cabin from the side because there's no window. But if you come from the back, there's no cover, and they might see you."

"I can get as far as that big rock without being seen," Malcolm said, pointing to a boulder about twenty yards behind the cabin.

"That won't do you any good. You can't break it from there."

"Sure I can," Malcolm said with a smile. "I not only boxed when I lived in New York, I also played baseball. If I can find the right sized rock, I can throw it through the window from there."

"All right," Smoke said. "You get in position behind the cabin, I'll approach the side. When I give you the signal, you count to five, then throw it. That'll give me the opportunity to get around front at the same time you break the window."

"Wait. Let me find the right rock," Malcolm said, looking at the scattering of pebbles on the floor of the arroyo. "Ah, this one will do." He picked up one about half the size of a baseball.

The two men left to go to their chosen positions. Smoke got to the side of the cabin before Malcolm reached the boulder, so he waited as the young rancher worked his way up the gulley toward the big rock. As Smoke waited, he tried to hear what was going on inside the cabin, but the logs were so thick they blocked out any sound from inside.

Lucy looked up as the three men came back into the cabin. Seeing a third man gave her some hope.

"Has the ransom been paid? Have you come to get me?" she asked anxiously.

"Ha! Yeah, it's been paid, all right," Carr said. "Five thousand dollars. I got twenty five hundred and Briggs, he got the other twenty five hundred."

"Then you're going to let me go?"

"Yeah," Briggs said. "After," he added, grabbing his crotch.

When Malcolm nodded that he was in position, Smoke gave him the signal to begin counting, then moved quickly to the front of the cabin, counting softly. A moment after he reached the number five, he heard the sound of crashing glass, then someone called out, "What the hell?"

Pulling his pistol, Smoke kicked open the door then fell to the floor inside, rolling away from the door with his gun at the ready. Because they had been startled by the breaking window, all three men had their pistols in their hands.

"It's Jensen!" Briggs shouted as he fired.

The bullet sped by Smoke's ear and plunged into the plank floor beside him. Even as Briggs shot at Smoke, Templeton rushed by him, fleeing the cabin. For the moment, Smoke had to let Templeton go. He was busy with the two men trying to kill him.

Four more shots were fired inside the little cabin, and Smoke fired two of them. Briggs went down with a hole in his forehead and Carr went down with a bullet in his heart.

Malcolm was running around to the front of the building just as Templeton came running out.

"Hold it!" Malcolm shouted.

Templeton turned and shot at him, but Malcolm dived to the ground and rolled, avoiding the bullet.

Not until then did Malcolm pull the pistol he was carrying. "Shoot kinesthetically," he told himself.

He pointed the gun and fired, then saw Templeton get a surprised expression on his face, slap his hand over a bleeding hole in his chest, and go down

Getting up, Malcolm ran over to him and kicked the pistol away from the fallen man, but that wasn't necessary. Templeton was already dead.

Malcolm looked toward the cabin, and with gun in hand, started toward it.

Inside the cabin, Smoke regained his feet and approached each of the downed men to make certain neither of them offered any more danger.

None did.

He looked up as Malcolm entered the cabin with a smoking gun in his hand. "Templeton?" Smoke asked.

"Dead."

They looked around for Lucy. She was sitting on the edge of the bed, a pair of wide-open, frightened blue eyes staring back at them. She was bound, head and foot, by ropes.

"Malcolm! Mr. Jensen!" Lucy said. "I have never been happier to see anyone in my life!"

Malcolm rushed over to her and began untying her. As soon as her hands were untied, she threw her arms around Malcolm and began smothering him with kisses.

Smoke chuckled. "If you folks don't mind the interference, I'll untie her feet."

"Did they do anything to you?" Malcolm asked. "What I mean is . . . uh . . . did they?"

"No," Lucy said. "But they were about to, just before you got here."

Malcolm smiled in relief that she had not been harmed, and also at the idea of playing a role in saving her.

"Well, there's no sense in being a hero, unless you can be a hero who arrives just in the nick of time," Malcolm said.

"Oh, the money!" Lucy said.

"What money?"

Lucy pointed to the bodies of Briggs and Carr. "The ransom money. They have it. But even though the ransom was paid, they weren't going to let me go."

"You don't even have to think about that," Malcolm said. "You're safe now, and I'm not going to let anything else happen to you."

CHAPTER THIRTY-THREE

Big Rock

Curly Roper was standing at the bar in the Brown Dirt Cowboy, staring into a mug of beer as he tried to decide what he should do next. He no longer had a job, and was pretty sure none of the local ranchers would hire him, not after having worked for Garneau. If he was honest with himself, it wasn't just that he had worked with Garneau.

Roper had been pretty much a troublemaker all along, often getting into fights, sometimes getting drunk and destroying private property. There was nothing left for him around Big Rock.

"Roper!" a loud high-pitched voice called.

He knew at once who it was.

"Roper, I'm talking to you."

Roper turned toward Jeremiah Priest.

"The colonel's not very pleased with you, Roper."

"I don't care whether he's pleased or not," Roper said. "I don't work for the colonel no more."

"It ain't you quittin' that's got him upset. It's how you done it. Word is, you went to see Smoke Jensen, and you told him about a huntin' cabin. A cabin that the colonel wanted to keep private, just for his own men."

"What if I did?"

"Well, then that means that me 'n you are goin' to have to come to some sort of a settlement."

"I got nothing to say to you, or do with you."

"Yeah, you do. I'm callin' you out, Roper."

"You can call me out all you want. I ain't drawin' on you." Roper doubled up his fists. "But if you'd like to settle this with your fists, why, I'd be glad to oblige you."

"I said, draw," Priest repeated in a cold, flat, voice.

The others in the saloon knew there was about to be gunplay and quietly, but deliberately, moved to get out of the way of any flying lead.

Roper held his hand out in front of him. "Look here. I'm takin' off my gun belt, and I'm layin' it on the bar." He held both hands up in the air. "Now, as you can see, I ain't wearin' no gun. So whatever you got in mind, you can just forget about it."

"Go ahead and pull your gun from the holster," Priest offered. "I won't draw till you got it in your hand."

"I told you, I ain't goin' to get into no gunfight with you."

Roper picked up his drink, hoping by that action to show his defiance. What he showed instead was his fear, for his hand was shaking so badly he had to put the mug back down before all the beer splashed out.

"Pull that gun, Roper."

Roper reached out toward his gun and holster. Instead of pulling the gun, he pushed the belt across the bar, and it fell with a loud thump to the floor on the other side of the bar.

"What gun?" Roper asked with a nervous smile.

"Somebody give him one," Priest said coldly. He pulled his lips into a sinister smile. "Mr. Roper seems to have dropped his."

"I don't want a gun," Roper said.

When no one offered Roper a gun, Priest pointed to the cowboy standing at the far end of the bar. "Give him your gun," Priest ordered. "You aren't going to be using it, are you?"

"He don't want a gun," the man said.

"Oh, I think he does."

"Listen, Priest, we can all see that Roper don't want to fight. Why don't you just leave it be?"

"I said, give him your gun."

"I ain't goin' to do that. If I give him a gun, you'll kill him."

"That's right."

"Well, I don't want no part of it."

"You got no choice, friend. You'll either give him your gun so I can kill him, or you can keep the gun, and I'll kill you. Now, which one is it goin' to be?"

"Now, just wait a minute here! I don't know what kinda beef you got with Roper there, but I got none with you, and you got none with me!" the cowboy said, holding out his hands to stop Priest from doing anything.

"Give him the gun, or use it yourself," Priest said again.

The cowboy paused for just a moment longer, then he looked over at Roper.

"This ain't my doin', Roper. I want you an' ever'one in here to know this ain't none of my doin'." The cowboy took his gun out of the holster, put it on the bar, then gave the gun a shove. It slid down the bar, smashing through a few of the glasses that had been abandoned by drinkers who, when the trouble started, had stepped away from the bar.

The pistol stopped just in front of Roper.

"Pick it up," Priest said to Roper.

Roper looked at the pistol. He chewed his bottom lip, while sweat broke out on his forehead. "I . . . I ain't goin' to do it. You ain't goin' to have no excuse to shoot me."

"Do it," Priest said again.

"No, I ain't goin' to, and there ain't nothin' you can do that will make me fight you."

Priest jerked his pistol from his holster and pulled the trigger. There was a flash of light, then a roar of exploding gunpowder, followed by a billowing cloud of acrid blue smoke.

Shouts of disapproval came from everyone in the saloon who thought Priest had shot Roper. But when the smoke drifted away, they were able to see what had actually happened. Roper was holding his hand to the left side of his head with blood spilling through his fingers. Priest's bullet had clipped off a piece of his earlobe.

"Are you goin' to fight or not?"

"I told you, I ain't goin' to fight you!" Roper yelled angrily.

A second shot sounded and flesh flew from his right earlobe.

"Pick up the gun!"

"No!" Roper shouted back, covering both ears. Blood streamed through the fingers of both hands. "You people! Do something! Stop him! Can't you see he's goin' to kill me?"

"What's goin' on in here?" a new voice said and, looking toward the swinging doors, everyone saw Deputy Worley standing just inside the door with a gun in his hand.

"This ain't none o' your business, Deputy," Priest said.

"Deputy, this man is trying to force me into a gun-fight," Roper said.

"Is that right?" Worley asked.

"Hell, Deputy, I'm just tryin' to give him a little backbone is all," Priest said.

"All right, Priest, take your gun out. Do it real slow. Then drop it on the floor."

"Deputy, if I take my gun out, it ain't goin' to be slow. Now, why don't you just back on out of here and leave the two of us to settle our difference of opinion?"

"No, Deputy, don't go!" Roper said.

"Do what I told you, Priest. Take your gun out and drop it on the floor!"

"I warned you, Deputy. There can't nobody say I started this here fight between me 'n you."

"There ain't goin' to be no fight. You are going to pull your pistol out and drop it like I told you, then me 'n you are goin' to jail till whatever is goin' on here is all settled," Worley said.

Priest drew, fired, and replaced his gun in his holster so quickly that some in the room, who were looking at Worley, trying to gauge his reaction to what was going on, didn't even see what happened.

There was the sound of a gunshot, a look of shock and pain on Worley's face, then his pistol clattered to the floor. With his hand over his wound, he took a couple steps forward, then collapsed.

There were gasps and shouts of surprise from the others in the saloon.

Priest turned his attention back to Roper. "All right. Now it's just me 'n you again. Pick up that gun."

Roper made no move toward the gun, so Priest fired again, sending a bullet crashing into Roper's kneecap. Roper shouted out in pain, then bent over to grab it. "You're crazy!"

"Pick up the gun," Priest said calmly.

Roper stared at Priest through fear-crazed, hate-filled eyes. Suddenly, the fear left his eyes. They became flat and void, as if he had already accepted the fact that he was a dead man. He had one emotion left, and one emotion only, and that was absolute, blind fury. He let out a bellow of rage that could be heard all up and down Center Street, from the undertaker's establishment all the way down to the stagecoach depot.

"You pig-faced, scum-sucking—" Roper made a mad, desperate, and clumsy grab for the gun.

Priest watched, smiling broadly. He waited, not only until Roper had the gun in his hand but actually brought it to bear.

For just an instant, but an instant only, Roper thought he might have a chance, and he raised his thumb to cock the pistol. His thumb didn't even reach the hammer before Priest fired.

Unlike the other bullets that had been used to tantalize, enrage, and torture Roper, the bullet was energized to kill, hitting him in the neck. Surprised by the suddenness of it, he dropped his gun, unfired, and clutched his throat. He fell back against the bar, then slid down, dead before he reached the floor.

Priest looked around the saloon, a broad smile on his face. "Is there anyone in here who feels that I didn't give these two men a fair chance?"

When nobody responded, Priest walked over to the bar and picked up Roper's beer. "I may as well drink this." He laughed. "Roper sure as hell ain't goin' to be finishin' it."

CHAPTER THIRTY-FOUR

Carro de Bancada

The aroma of cooking meat wafted over the ground as Cal and Pearlie turned a quarter of a steer on a spit over a fire. The meat had been salted, peppered, and basted with a spicy sauce, and the forty men, women, and children gathered in Malcolm's front yard visited, laughed, and made comments as to how good everything smelled. A piano had been brought over from Sugarloaf, and Johnny McVey had been invited to the party to provide the music.

There was a dual reason for the gathering. All the neighbors had come to celebrate Lucy's safe return, as well as the announcement that Malcolm and Lucy were soon to be married.

"I reckon we don't have to worry none about you goin' back to New York now, do we, Malcolm?" Tom Keefer asked.

Malcolm put his arm around Lucy and drew her to

him. "Now, if I've come two thousand miles to find someone like this, why in the world would I want to go back to New York?"

The others laughed.

"No reason at all, Malcolm," Logan said.

"Hey!" Pearlie called. "This meat's done if you folks are ready to eat."

"Ready to eat?" Keefer said. "I been smellin' that meat cookin' so long I'm near 'bout ready to come over there and start gnawin' on it while it's still on the spit."

"Come on, Johnny. You're the only one who's been working," Malcolm said. "So you get to go first."

"Hey, what if I start playing my Jew's harp?" Logan asked. "Could I go next?"

"I've heard you with that thing," Otto Speer said. "I think if you promise *not* to play it, you should go first."

Again there was laughter, but the laughter was interrupted when Keefer called out, "There's riders comin'! A lot of 'em!"

"At least four of them," Logan said. "Maybe we'd better get our guns, and get the women and kids out of here."

"No, wait," Smoke said. "I know those men. That's Taylor, Gately, Anderson, and Calloway. They're working for Garneau, but I don't think they mean trouble."

"They sure ain't ridin' in a way that would make you think they're lookin' for trouble," Keefer said.

The four riders came up to the yard, then stopped.

"Hello, Gately," Smoke said. "What brings you boys over here?"

"We've all left the Frenchman." Gately looked over at Woodward. "Mr. Woodward, it was the Frenchman what took your daughter. There didn't any of us know about it for a while. Then, Curly Roper, he found out, an' he quit. Then, this mornin', the Frenchman sent Priest into town."

"And Priest killed Roper and the sheriff," Anderson said.

"What? Monte has been killed?" Smoke asked in shock.

"It wasn't the sheriff," Taylor said. "It was one of his deputies. Worley."

"Smoke!" Sally said, grabbing Smoke's arm.

"Was Worley a friend of yours, Mr. Jensen?" Taylor asked.

"Yes, he was."

"I'm sorry to be the one to tell you about the deputy," Taylor said. "But, I reckon you already know that Curly Roper was a friend of mine."

"Mr. Jensen," Calloway said. "We didn't just happen to come this way. Colonel Garneau wanted me to give you a message. After the others and I found out what happened to Curly, we decided to quit Garneau. At first, I wasn't even goin' to bring you the message, but we talked it over and figured you probably should be told."

"What is that?"

"Priest is in town waitin' for you. It is Colonel Garneau's intention to have Priest kill you. With you out of the way, he intends to take over the whole valley. Sugarloaf, too."

"He's not going to be able to do that if I kill Priest, is he?" Smoke asked.

"Have you ever seen Priest in action?" Taylor asked.

"No."

"Well, I have. I've seen some awful fast gunmen in my day. I know you're fast, 'cause I've seen you. But I feel I ought to tell you, Mr. Jensen, that I think Priest is a mite faster."

"There's always that possibility," Smoke agreed.

"You also should know that Priest is settin' himself up an edge," Gately added.

"What kind of edge?" Malcolm asked.

"Merlin Mathis. He's goin' to be somewhere that'll give him a chance to take a shot at you."

"Plus, Garneau is in town his ownself," Anderson added. "So, really, you got three of 'em to worry about."

"What about the others?" Woodward asked. "What about the army he's put together? Will they be in town as well?"

"There ain't that much left of the army." Taylor said. "If Garneau gets his way, and Smoke Jensen is kilt, what's left of the army—them that ain't already been kilt—will more 'n likely stay with him. But if it winds up that Priest and Mathis was to happen to get kilt, I doubt the others will stay with Garneau. Since we left this mornin', I can tell you that Garneau ain't got no cowboys left at all."

"And you say Priest is in town now?"

"Yes, sir, he is."

"Smoke," Sally said anxiously.

Smoke reached over to put his hand on hers. "Listen, where are our manners?" He smiled broadly. "You men go tie your horses off somewhere and sit down to eat with us. As you can see, we have plenty of food."

"And it's good, too," Cal said. "I've done been sampling it."

Taylor looked quickly toward the others as if determining whether or not the invitation was from all of them.

"Yes," Woodward said, nodding his head and smiling at the Long Trek riders. "Smoke is right. You boys get down off your horses and come join us."

"We'll eat first, then I'll go into town," Smoke said. "I don't like to work on an empty stomach."

The men dismounted, secured their horses, and joined those who were celebrating Lucy's safe return and the engagement announcement of Lucy and Malcolm.

Big Rock

By midafternoon, nearly everyone in town was aware of the possibility of an upcoming gunfight between Smoke and Priest. To a person, they wanted to see Smoke triumph, and not just figuratively. They actually wanted to see the gunfight go down. To that end, nearly three hundred people were out on the streets when Smoke, Sally, Cal, Pearlie, and Malcolm rode into town.

"You folks wait here at Longmont's," Smoke suggested to the others.

"Where is Priest?" Cal asked.

"I expect he'll be here soon enough," Smoke said. "As soon as he gets word I'm in town."

Priest was waiting in the Brown Dirt with Garneau when one of the citizens of the town came into the saloon.

"You was waitin' on Smoke Jensen?"

"Yes."

"Well, he just come into town. He's over on Front Street, standin' out in front of Longmont's.

Priest smiled, then glanced over at Garneau. "Here's where I earn my money."

"Let me go first," Garneau said. "I want to be in position to watch this."

"All right." Priest smiled. "I don't mind performing before an audience."

"Well, you've got a good one today," the man who brought the message of Smoke's arrival said. "Looks to me like damn near the whole town is linin' both sides of Front Street."

Priest waited until Garneau left, then looked over at Mathis. "Get in position."

Mathis nodded, then stepped out front and pulled a rifle from his saddle sheath. He hurried down Center, cut in between the post office and the McCoy building, then stepped in between Kathy's Dress Shop, and Earl's Barbershop. He pressed up against the wall of the barbershop and looked across the street. He saw Smoke in the road in front of Longmont's. Garneau was standing on the boardwalk in front of the newspaper office. Looking to his right and down the street, he saw Priest approaching Jensen.

Most of the crowd got out of the street then, going into the buildings that fronted the street in order to see what was going on. A few of the braver ones stayed outside, though they did step back. One of those who remained outside was Lucien Garneau.

Priest stopped a few yards away from Longmont's and smiled. "Well, now, you're here. I have to tell you, Jensen, I wasn't sure you had the guts to face me. I admire you for that." The smile left his face. "But this is where it all ends for you."

"It may. But whatever happens between you and me, it will definitely end for your boss."

"Ha! Are you saying you are going to kill Garneau?"

"That is exactly what I'm saying."

"Go ahead."

"Priest!" Garneau shouted. "What are you saying? What are you doing? He means it. Can't you see that?"

"Oh, yes, I see that. But Jensen knows that I mean it too. Go ahead, Jensen. Kill Garneau."

"If he's dead, who pays you?" Smoke asked.

"Oh hell, I'm not worried about that," Priest replied. "I've already got half the money I was going to get. But this here thing between me 'n you ain't about money anymore. I can't leave town without killing you. You understand that, don't you?"

"That's probably true," Smoke said. "But that's your problem."

"Not just my problem," Priest said. "We're going to

have to deal with it, both of us, right here, right now. You can see for yourself, Jensen, ever'one wants to see us shoot it out. Well, what they really want to see is you kill me." He chuckled, then took in the crowd with a wave of his hand. "I almost feel bad about disappointin' them."

"Well, I'll try not to disappoint them. I'll kill you, right after I kill Garneau."

"Look, either kill him or quit talkin' about it. I really don't care which. Then, let's you and me settle this thing, once and for all."

"Malcolm?" Smoke called.

"Yes, Smoke?"

"Keep an eye on Garneau while I take care of Priest."

"I'll be happy to do that," Malcolm said, pulling his pistol and pointing it at Garneau.

Smoke turned toward Priest. The crowd backed away even farther to give the two men more room."

"Ever since I first heard of you, I've been wonderin' which one of us was the fastest," Priest said. "I reckon we're about to find out."

"Smoke, across the street!" Malcolm shouted.

Smoke looked around to see that Mathis was raising a rifle to his shoulder. Smoke drew and fired, and Mathis dropped the rifle, then tumbled forward.

Smoke knew, without having to look, that Priest was taking advantage of the distraction to draw. Smoke fell to his stomach an instant before Priest fired, feeling the concussion of the bullet as it passed less than an inch over the top of his head.

Smoke returned fire from his position on the

ground, and Priest caught the ball high in his chest. The gunman fired a second time, but it was more a convulsive than an aimed shot, and the bullet went into the dirt.

Priest took a couple of staggering steps toward Smoke and tried to raise his pistol, but it fell from his hands. He smiled, then coughed, and flecks of blood came from his mouth. He breathed hard a couple times. "I was sure I was faster than you."

"Looks like you were wrong," Smoke said easily as Priest fell to the ground.

Someone leaned down and put his hand to Priest's neck. He looked up at the others. "He's dead."

Sherriff Carson, who had watched the whole thing, walked over to Garneau. "You are under arrest."

"For what?"

"For conspiracy to murder."

CHAPTER THIRTY-FIVE

One month later

Robert Dempster was tried and found guilty of fraud and grand larceny. He was currently in jail, awaiting transportation to the state prison in Cañon City.

Lucien Garneau was tried and found guilty of conspiracy to murder. He was sentenced to hang. A gallows had been constructed at the east end of Front Street, right in front of the blacksmith shop. It was visible from the window of Garneau's jail cell.

On the day he was to be hanged, Inspector Laurent presented himself before Sheriff Carson. "Sheriff, I am Inspector André Laurent of the French Military Police. I have tried, without success, to extradite your prisoner back to France."

"Oh. Well, I have to tell you, Mr. Laurent, if you were to take the Frenchman away from us now, there would be a lot of very upset folks. You see, he has been responsible for quite a few people getting killed since he came to Colorado."

"I do not doubt that, Sheriff. Before he left France, he committed murder, and he stole two and one half million francs from the French Army."

Carson let out a low whistle. "Damn! How much money is that in American?"

"One half million dollars."

"That's how he was able to buy so much land," Carson said. "Yes, I can see why your government would want him. But, if it's any consolation to you, he has been sentenced to hang, and he will hang this very afternoon. You can watch him, if you like. We can furnish an affidavit signed by the judge that the sentence was carried out. That should satisfy your government."

"Yes, I'm sure it will. May I see him?"

"Sure, I don't see why not. He is in back. I'll take you to him."

Laurent followed the sheriff into the back of the jail. When they reached the back corner, the prisoner was staring out the window toward the gallows.

"Garneau, you have a visitor," Sheriff Carson said.

"When you address me, Sheriff, you will address me as Colonel the Marquis Garneau," the prisoner said. "You may hang me, Monsieur, but you will not rob me of my honor."

"*Vous ne pouvez pas être dépouillé de l'honneur, Mouchette, parce que vous êtes dépourvu de tout honneur!*" Laurent said. To Sheriff Carson he added, "I will translate for you, Sheriff. I told him he cannot be robbed of honor, because he is devoid of honor. He is neither colonel nor marquis. And his name isn't Garneau. It is Mouchette, Pierre Mouchette."

"*Qui êtes-vous?* Who are you?" Garneau asked.

"I am Inspector André Laurent of the Gendarmerie Nationale. I have come to see justice done for the murder of Sergeant Dubois and for the theft of two and a half million francs. Did you really think you would get away with it, Mouchette?"

"Ha! I did get away with it. There will be no guillotine for me."

"The guillotine is quick and painless. Hanging is a much slower, and more agonizing, way to die."

Involuntarily, Garneau-Mouchette lifted his hand to his neck.

Laurent turned to Sheriff Carson. "Will there be some sort of reading of the pronouncement from the gallows?"

"Yes, the judge's order and authorization must be read."

"Please, Monsieur Sheriff, when you read the orders, do not dishonor France by calling this imposter a colonel and a marquis. And could you add that he is also being executed for murdering an innocent soldier who was under his command?"

Sheriff Carson nodded. "I don't know how the judge is going to like that, but I'll do it for you."

He was no longer thinking of himself as Garneau. It was as Mouchette he was born, and it would be as Mouchette that he would die. As he stood on the gallows floor, his arms tied to his sides, his legs tied together, he looked out at the faces of the people drawn to the event. Some of them reflected a sense of fear and horror, others morbid fascination, and still others, an obvious show of satisfaction that he was paying for his crimes.

Near the back of the crowd he saw Amy, the whore from the Brown Dirt Cowboy, and recalled the night he spent with her. He smiled and nodded. Amy looked away.

He had seen his coffin when he climbed the steps, but it was beneath the gallows floor and he couldn't see it any longer.

A camera had been set up on a tripod. The photographer was taking pictures. He had just taken one, because he was removing the plate and replacing it with another.

"Hey, Garneau, when you hit the bottom of the rope, are you going to dance for us?" someone shouted.

Mouchette didn't answer. He had already vowed to himself that he would not perform for them. He would exhibit no emotion whatsoever.

A priest approached him. "Mr. Garneau, I am—"

"My name is Mouchette. Pierre Mouchette."

The priest looked toward Sheriff Carson, who was also standing on the gallows floor. "I don't understand. I thought the man I was to minister to was named Garneau."

"Garneau was his assumed name, Father. His real name is Mouchette."

The priest nodded, then turned back to the prisoner. "I am Father Sharkey, an Episcopal priest. May I minister to you?"

"I am Catholic, *Père* Sharkey. Or I was when I was a boy and actually went to church."

"It's the same God."

"Yes, well, it's a little late for all that, isn't it?"

"With God time is both instantaneous and eternal."

"Go ahead."

Father Sharkey began reading from the Book of Common Prayer. "O Father of mercies, and God of all comfort; we fly unto thee for succor in behalf of this thy servant who is now under sentence of condemnation. The day of his calamity is at hand, and he is accounted as one of those who go down into the pit."

Sharkey made the sign of the cross. "Unto God's gracious mercy and protection we commit thee. The Lord bless thee, and keep thee. The Lord make his face to shine upon thee, and be gracious unto thee. The Lord lift up his countenance upon thee, and give thee peace, both now and evermore. Amen."

Sharkey looked over at Sheriff Carson and nodded. Carson walked with him to the thirteen steps that led down to the ground. The priest continued down the steps.

The sheriff looked at the crowd. "I am instructed to read the death warrant issued by the court of Eagle County, Colorado."

He began reading the judge's warrant of execution. "For the crime of accessory to the murder of Humboldt Puddle and others, and for the murder of Sergeant Antoine Dubois, Pierre Mouchette, also known as Lucien Garneau, is to be hanged by the neck until pronounced dead by the attending physician in pursuance to the instructions contained in this warrant. Let no one present question this warrant."

A moment later, the sheriff went over to Mouchette, holding a black hood in his hand. "Are you ready?"

Mouchette chuckled. "Suppose I told you that I needed about forty more years before I was ready. Would you wait?"

"I'm afraid not."

"Wait, before you put it on, let me find Laurent in the crowd. I know he is here. Where is he?"

"He is standing just to the right of the foot of the steps," Sheriff Carson said.

"Laurent, tell those with whom I served that I died like a soldier," Mouchette shouted.

"I shall," Laurent answered.

Mouchette watched as the hood came down over his face, realizing that, as of that very second, he had seen the world for the very last time. He could see some light coming through the hood, but nothing else.

With the outside world gone, he saw—as real and present as it had been in his youth—a small boat upon the Seine. A man was rowing the boat, and a pretty woman, holding a red parasol against the sun, was sitting in the bow.

"Look, Mama, the woman in the small boat is holding a red parasol," he had said then, and, quietly, he mouthed those same words again. "*Rechercher, Maman, la femme dans le petit bâteau est la tenue d'une ombrelle rouge.*"

He held on to that peaceful and innocent scene as

he felt the rough texture of the rope when the noose was fitted over his head, and the knot pushed up against the back of his neck.

"May God have mercy on your soul," Sheriff Carson said, speaking so quietly only Mouchette could hear him.

Mouchette heard Sheriff Carson's footsteps as he walked back across the gallows floor.

He heard the pealing of church bells.

He heard the whistle of an approaching train.

He heard the sound of the trapdoor opening, then felt his stomach leap up into his . . .

EPILOGUE

Smoke and Sally were in a spring wagon, driving back to Sugarloaf after having attended the wedding and reception of Mr. and Mrs. Malcolm Puddle.

"It was nice of Laurent to sign a quit claim on behalf of the French government for Garneau's land," Sally said. "Now it belongs to the state of Colorado, but I'm wondering what is going to happen to it?"

"The ranchers and farmers who have land adjacent to his are going to buy as much of it as they can afford to enlarge their own holdings. I expect I'll buy the rest. That way, we aren't likely to ever run into any more Mouchettes. Or Garneaus, for that matter."

"What about Frying Pan Creek? What will become of it?"

"It will remain property of the state. That way nobody can ever dam it up again or use it as a weapon against other landholders."

"Good idea." Sally moved closer to Smoke, took his

upper right arm in both her hands, then leaned her head against his shoulder. "Wasn't the wedding beautiful?"

Smoke chuckled. "You say that about every wedding you've ever attended."

"Well, every wedding I've ever attended has been beautiful. Ours was the most beautiful of all."

"Yeah," Smoke said. "It's almost a shame it wasn't a real preacher, and we aren't really married."

"What?" Sally shouted.

Smoke began to laugh, and Sally started hitting him on the arm. "You are impossible. Why would you say such a thing?"

"I don't know. Maybe to put a little excitement in your life?"

Sally laughed as well, then kissed him on the cheek. "Kirby Jensen, being married to you is all the excitement I will ever need . . . or ever want."

JOHNSTONE ON JOHNSTONE

William W. Johnstone was born in southern Missouri, the youngest of four children. He was raised with strong moral and family values by his minister father, and tutored by his schoolteacher mother. Despite this, he quit school at age fifteen.

"I have the highest respect for education," he says, "but such is the folly of youth, and wanting to see the world beyond the four walls and the blackboard."

True to this vow, Bill attempted to enlist in the French Foreign Legion ("I saw Gary Cooper in *Beau Geste* when I was a kid and I thought the French Foreign Legion would be fun") but was rejected, thankfully, for being underage. Instead, he joined a traveling carnival and did all kinds of odd jobs. It was listening to the veteran carny folk, some of whom had been on the circuit since the late 1800s, telling amazing tales about their experiences that planted the storytelling seed in Bill's imagination.

"They were mostly honest people, despite the bad reputation traveling carny shows had back then," Bill remembers. "There was one guy named Picky, who got that name because he was a master pickpocket.

He could steal a man's socks right off his feet without him knowing. Believe me, Picky got us chased out of more than a few towns."

After a few months of this grueling existence, Bill returned home and finished high school. Next came stints as a deputy sheriff in the Tallulah, Louisiana, sheriff's department, followed by a hitch in the U.S. Army. Then he began a career in radio broadcasting at KTLD in Tallulah that would last sixteen years. It was here that he honed his storytelling skills, creating oddball characters and unusual situations to put them into, for his radio program. Bill played all the parts as well as writing them. "My favorite was a flimflam man named Skip Towne, a con artist who operated one step ahead of the law and was always trying to sell you stuff like left-handed screwdrivers and Norwegian smoke snifters. And then there was Newton Chickenheart, the most cowardly man in the West.

Bill turned to writing in 1970 but it wouldn't be until 1979 that his first novel, *The Devil's Kiss*, was published. Thus began the full-time writing career of William W. Johnstone. He wrote horror (*The Uninvited*), thrillers (*The Last of the Dog Team*), even a romance novel or two. Then, in February 1983, *Out of the Ashes* was published. Searching for his missing family in the aftermath of a post-apocalyptic America, rebel mercenary and patriot Ben Raines is united with the civilians of the Resistance forces and moves to the forefront of a revolution for the nation's future.

Out of the Ashes was a smash. The series would continue for the next twenty years, winning Bill three generations of fans all over the world. The series was often imitated but never duplicated. "We all tried to copy *The Ashes* series," said one publishing executive, "but Bill's uncanny ability, both then and now, is to predict in which direction the political winds were blowing." (The Ashes series also, Bill notes with a touch of pride, got him on the FBI's Watch List for its less than flattering portrayal of big government.)

In late 1985, Bill's first western, *The Last Mountain Man*, was published and it was here that Bill has found his greatest success. In fact, western fans couldn't get enough of Smoke Jensen, so Bill created *Preacher*. Next came *Blood Bond*, the western adventures of blood brothers Matt Bodine and Sam Two Wolves.

Today, Bill's western series, co-authored by J.A. Johnstone, include *The Mountain Man, Matt Jensen the Last Mountain Man, Preacher, The Family Jensen, Luke Jensen Bounty Hunter, Eagles, MacCallister* (an Eagles spin-off), *Sidewinders, The Brothers O'Brien, Sixkiller, The Last Gunfighter,* and the upcoming new series *Flintlock* and *The Trail West,* most of which have propelled him onto both the *USA Today* and *New York Times* bestseller lists. Coming in May 2013 is the hardcover western *Butch Cassidy: The Lost Years.*

"The western," Bill says, "is one of the few true art forms that is one hundred percent American. I liken the western as America's version of England's

Arthurian legends like Robin Hood or the Knights of the Round Table. Starting with the 1902 publication of *The Virginian* by Owen Wister and followed by authors like Zane Grey, Max Brand, Ernest Haycox, and of course Louis L'Amour, the western has helped define the cultural landscape of American entertainment.

"I'm no goggle-eyed college academic, so when my fans ask me why the western is as popular now as it was a century ago, I don't offer a 200-page thesis. Instead, I can only offer this: the western is honest—we can't change the way real events turned out. Sure, we can embellish, exaggerate, and yes, I admit it, occasionally play a little fast and loose with the facts, but only to enhance the enjoyment of readers.

"Put another way, there's a line in one of my favorite Westerns of all time, *The Man Who Shot Liberty Valance,* where the newspaper editor tells the young reporter, 'When the truth becomes legend, print the legend.'

"These are the words I live by."

THE MOUNTAIN MAN SERIES BY
WILLIAM W. JOHNSTONE

Available Wherever Books Are Sold!

Visit our website at **www.kensingtonbooks.com**

THE LAST GUNFIGHTER SERIES BY
WILLIAM W. JOHNSTONE